THE WATERS OF TALADORO

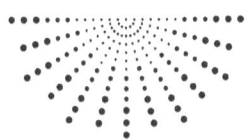

THE WATERS OF TALADORO

BOOK TWO OF THE RIDNIGHT MYSTERIES

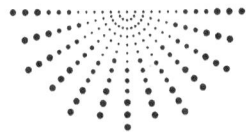

STUART JAFFE

Charlotte, NC
FALSTAFF
BOOKS
WWW.FALSTAFFBOOKS.COM

For Gabe
I'm blaming you for this one, too

PART I
THE PARTY

CHAPTER ONE

Zev Asterling clenched his eyes tight. The steady pounding headache, the rank vomit stench, and the cold stone floor against his cheek told him enough—he didn't need to see it, too. Besides, this wasn't the first time he had drunk to the point of losing an entire evening. The past year had been filled with them.

The pointed tip of a shoe nudged his shoulder. "Wake up," Bellemont said. She had been the one shining part of his life lately, the one part his sodden mind could count on, his assistant and friend—and she was a Dacci witch no less. Yet he could hear the exasperation in her voice. She wouldn't put up with much more of this.

A harder kick and his eyes snapped open. The bright morning shot a blade through his skull. He winced.

"I'm not cleaning that up," she said as she settled on the chair near his office desk.

"I wouldn't ask you to." Rising to his elbows, Zev added, "Sorry you had to even see me like this."

Though she had given up the traditional Dacci garb of black cloth strips and instead dazzled in a peach sundress with a wide-brimmed hat, she still wore the veil that hid her mouth. Since witches had to sacrifice their own teeth as part of any spell, they did not like to advertise how accomplished they were when they opened their mouths. But that was in the West. Here in the Frontier, Zev suspected Bellemont simply wanted to avoid the horrified looks from their neighbors.

With a huff, she stepped close to him and offered a hand. "What set you off this time?"

Zev shrugged as he clasped her fingers and stood.

"It's not the bills. I'm the one keeping the paperwork for this agency organized, and we had our latest discussion of lack of funds over a week ago. It's not a woman. You broke it off with Harlell more than a month before that."

"Do I need a reason?"

"You always have one. Plus, you taught me to search for the motivations behind behaviors."

"That's in the detection of crimes. Not personal stupidity."

Zev walked toward the back wall where a sink had been recently installed. By pumping a handle at the side, water flowed directly into the office via pipes. Another new invention from the East making its way across the world. Mayor Adler fell in love with the idea of piping the entire town, and most of Fernbund agreed. Splashing cool water onto his face, Zev had to admit it had been a good call.

The office had quite a few additions suggested by Mayor Adler. He had been the one to urge Zev into purchasing a beautiful desk with the corners sculpted to look like vines twining up the sides. He also convinced Zev to place several chairs on the empty side of the office to make a waiting area—not that there were ever so many clients to fill it. Mayor Adler even dropped off a few paintings by his wife—landscapes of Fernbund—to brighten the place.

At first, Zev wondered why Mayor Adler cared so much. But after a few conversations, it became clear that the Mayor banked on Zev's newfound fame to bring in money.

As Zev wet a rag in the sink, preparing to wash his vomit from the floor, he said, "I am sorry. It's been hard lately. Right after we came back from Ridnight City, we had the money King Robion rewarded us, this agency attracted regular work—I thought it could only get better. But two years and it's all gone. The work, the respect, the money. Let's face it, I was a terrible farmer before all of this, and now it's clear that I'm a terrible businessman, too."

"I see." Bellemont returned to the desk and crossed her legs. "You were indulging in a night of self-loathing." Her eyes fell upon an opened letter. Snatching it up, the crackle of the paper reverberating in Zev's hungover brain, she said, "Ah! Here's the real answer. A letter from your brother."

Part of Zev wanted to rush across the room and snatch that letter away. But the thought of moving so fast, of spanning such a wide gulf, set his stomach churning. Besides, Bellemont would find out eventually.

Snapping the paper in her hands as if about to read one of the King's proclamations, she straightened in her chair. Though he could never prove it, he felt certain she smirked behind her veil.

She read:

Dear Zev,

I write to you with my heart breaking. While I am, of course, completely aware that we've not been close over the years, and I certainly understand that you and Father were even less so, I still feel duty bound to inform you that our father is ailing. What troubles his body is not clear. His symptoms mimic many common diseases. High fever, aching bones, congestion. These sorts of maladies. At first, we both thought he had simply come down with a regular, minor issue and would soon be well. However, his condition has only worsened.

I have taken the liberty of placing him at the hospital in Palon Mechanical Institute. He is under the care of Doctor Everett. There is none finer in the world and the school has many promising inventions in the medical field. You can trust that I would only give our father the best care.

In light of the situation, I write you, I implore you, to set aside your animosity for me and him. I ask that you come to the East at once, so that you might have a chance to say goodbye, should that be required. This is not meant to sound an alarm. Father has always been a strong man, and I believe he will fight back to being healthy. Still, no son and no father should part of this world with such unresolved matters between them. If ever there was an opportunity for you, now is it.

I won't insult you by suggesting that I care whether or not you spent the rest of your life regretting not seeing him, but I do care about him. If this is indeed the beginning of his end, which I refuse to accept, then I wish it to be as gentle and peaceful as possible. Though you might doubt me, the truth is I can sense within him a desire to reconcile with you. Please, come home. Please, see him.

Always your dearest brother,
Marcel

Bellemont looked over at Zev, all sense of humor drained away. "I'm so sorry."

Zev trembled between a grin and a sneer. "I guess I'm not handling it very well."

Getting drunk had been stupid—it certainly did not solve anything —but no solution that came to mind seemed any better. Despite Marcel's letter proposing otherwise, Zev had tried to reconcile with his father on several occasions. Most recently, he wrote a lengthy letter describing all that had happened on his journey into the Feral Lands of the West. The monsters he fought, the spells he witnessed, everything that led to him being praised by King Robion. Not a word came in reply.

Zev's eyes drifted up to the rifle mounted on the wall above his desk. An old gift from Marcel—another grand invention from the East. It had proved a useful tool, but it gave those in the East a false sense of security. Both Marcel and Zev's father seemed to think the East could invent its way out of any problem. Though Zev did not hold beliefs in any of the religions—certainly not the Frontier's devotion to the Cassun nine deities—he had seen firsthand the power of the Western deity, Nualla. Of course, that thing was no god. Rather it was a creature that lived underground and had formed a near symbiotic relationship with the Dacci, a creature that showed immense power, a creature that demanded respect.

To Zev's father, such forces were only a trick that could never withstand the power of an Eastern mind. Marcel merely laughed in that patronizing tone that grated up Zev's spine.

Scratching the stubble on his jaw, Zev eased into the seat behind his desk. He put out his hand and silently waited until Bellemont handed over the letter. As he folded it and tucked it away in his desk drawer, he felt his senses awakening and his mind clearing. At least, a little.

"How bad is business?" he asked.

"It's not too encouraging. The problem is that Fernbund is filled with fairly law-abiding folks. They mostly don't kill each other or steal from each other or do anything that would require the services of somebody like us. And when we do on occasion have a job, you won't charge enough to cover our costs for the lean times."

"How can I charge a high fee when I'm supposed to be this hero who helped save the Frontier from the West? Heroes don't gouge their customers."

"Heroes don't have customers. They're not in business. You are."

Zev glared at Bellemont. They had argued these points before, and it appeared neither one would give any ground. They would have spent the rest of the morning glowering at each other until one would finally suggest having lunch, at which point they would let the matter get buried and move on. However, the soft whine of an autocart—a horseless vehicle that continued to grow in popularity—announced the arrival of somebody. Somebody with money.

Bellemont jolted to her feet and peeked out the window. "Well, Hero, I hope you're ready to finally ask for some financial compensation because we have a big job coming our way."

"Just tell me who it is."

Bellemont glanced back, her eyes crinkling with joy. "There are Royal markings on the autocart. The King is sending for you."

Zev had not heard from King Robion in two years, and he had hoped the trend would continue. A messenger from the King could only mean trouble. Despite his reservations, though, Zev could not hold back a smile at Bellemont's enthusiasm.

She had become a fan of royalty over the last year. A fan, really, of anybody wealthy and notable. The King and his court, of course, but also the giant leaders looming over their vast industrial empires in the East. As for the Feral Lands, she preferred to keep her distance. Though born there, her experiences with the Dacci had left her empty and hurt. She was one of the Stolen—a group of Dacci taken as children and raised in the East. Foolish idea of Easterners who thought they knew better than a child's own parents.

It felt good to see Bellemont giddy.

She opened the door, her eyes glimmering. A young woman with a serious expression entered the office, approached Zev's desk, and snapped to attention. Her hand darted out as she presented a sealed envelope.

"May I?" Bellemont hurried over.

Zev leaned back in his chair and waved her on. As she accepted the envelope, he could not help but notice the messenger's troubled glance. Probably the first time the poor child had ever seen a Dacci witch—especially one wearing a peach sundress.

Bellemont broke the wax seal and pulled out a piece of paper. Holding it firm and reading with a respectful tone, she said, *"Mr. Zev Asterling, your immediate presence is requested at Ridnight Castle for the celebration of Axon Coponiv's successful return from her grand quest for an object of such renown and value, of such beauty and power, that the world will be forever changed."* Bellemont peeked over the letter. "This is a big honor."

Zev snorted. "The only reason they're asking is because we went with Axon previously. But at least we know where Axon has been. I was beginning to think she was angry with me when she no longer returned my messages. Pilot, too. He was probably with her."

"You see? Your friends have not abandoned you."

"I never said they did." But he had thought it. And Bellemont knew.

To the King's messenger, Bellemont said, "Are we to reply to you?"

With an uncomfortable shift of her body, the messenger looked over Bellemont before facing Zev once more. "I am to be your driver, sir. I will take you to the castle at once. And only you. The invitation did not mention another."

Zev stood, shaking his head. "Get your horseless autocart thing ready. Prepare for two passengers. You will take us both or you will take neither of us. I don't think you want to explain to King Robion why two of the people responsible for saving the Frontier from the Beast of the West could not attend."

Swallowing hard, the messenger bowed. "Yes, sir. At once."

After she rushed out of the office, Bellemont lifted an eyebrow toward Zev. "Feel better?"

"Actually, I do. I can't say I really want to go to this thing, but I wouldn't dream of denying you the chance to attend a royal party."

"Huh. You've actually got a soft heart."

"Don't you dare start talking like that. Let's go before you want to give me a hug or something."

Bellemont chuckled as she headed out. Zev paused to glance back at the rifle mounted on the wall. His father would have to wait. Marcel said the man was strong and would probably pull through. Good enough. Zev had been summoned by a King, and that simply could not be denied.

CHAPTER TWO

As the autocart rumbled along the uneven dirt road, Zev marveled at how much the contraption had changed in two short years. Where the original design had focused on the practicality of moving without a horse, this newer model took a greater interest in the comfort of passengers. The seats were soft and spacious. A canvas roof had been put in place to protect against the weather, and Zev swore that the ride itself felt smoother despite the greater speed with which the vehicle could now achieve.

The forest flew by. The ride to Ridnight City would have taken several days by horseback. Zev guessed they would be there before nightfall.

"What's wrong?" Bellemont said.

"Nothing," he said. "Just noticing how quickly things change."

Bellemont gestured to the passing forest. "Doesn't change as much as you think. Those trees have been there for centuries."

"Trees don't pay our bills. Trees don't point to you and say *You did something great for us and we appreciate it.* People forget quickly."

"Don't be ridiculous. The King himself has invited you to this party out of respect for who you are."

"Maybe. Maybe Axon simply asked for us to be there." He clenched his jaw. "I just want to be back at the office and left alone."

Bellemont opened her mouth, and Zev braced for a witty retort. But her eyes narrowed and her mouth stayed locked open. Or Zev assumed—he couldn't be sure with her veil covering her mouth. To avoid staring, he glanced ahead. An old farmer limped along the side of the road, his arm around the shoulder of a younger man, both bleeding from small abrasions.

"Stop this thing," Zev said.

The messenger, now the driver, shook her head. "My job is to get you to Ridnight Castle."

"Stop this autocart, or I'll jump out and you can explain to King Robion why I have a broken leg."

With a huff, the driver brought the autocart to a gentle stop. Zev leaped over the side and hurried toward the two men.

The younger stepped in front of the older and raised his fists. "We've got nothing left. Get on your way or I'll break your nose."

Zev raised his hands as if approaching a rabid animal. "Easy, there. I'm not trying to fight. You looked like you could use some help. Nothing more."

The old man nudged the young one's elbow. "I think it's okay." Stepping forward and offering his hand in friendship, the old man said, "Forgive us."

Zev shook the man's hand. "What happened to you?"

"Bandits."

"Bandits? Here?"

"We were as surprised as you. My son and I were heading toward Fernbund in our haycart. Two men launched out of the woods and attacked us. They roughed us up and stole the cart."

"A haycart? That's it?"

"They were strange. They never asked us to empty our pockets, never tied us up to detain us in any way. They punched us a few times, took the haycart, and they were off."

The oddity of this attack piqued Zev's interest. *Or perhaps, I'm simply looking for an excuse to avoid getting back in that autocart.* "Well, we can't let you walk all the way back to your farm like this. Allow us to drive you."

Fumbling her way out of the autocart, the driver said, "No, no. I'm sorry, but I cannot allow that. This is a Royal autocart and can only be used on business sanctioned by the King."

Zev glanced over his shoulder. "Do I really need to go through all of the threats again?"

"Mr. Asterling, this is not the same thing. I have no fear of standing behind the rules I've agreed to follow. The King will not side with you on this."

"Really? This farmer and his son are the King's subjects. Don't you think he would want us to take care of his subjects?"

The driver hesitated. "Stop trying to confuse the matter. We can give them some money, but we must be on our way."

Zev turned toward Bellemont. "Will you help me?"

As she stepped out of the autocart, as she tilted her head to Zev, the farmer noticed the witch's veil. He exchanged a look with his son before pointing at Bellemont. "You? I've heard about you."

"Oh?" Zev said.

"You're the Dacci witch who helped a group of the King's best fighters against the Beast of the West. Isn't that right? Is that you?"

Bellemont offered one gentle nod.

"We're sorry to trouble you," the farmer said, backing away from the autocart. "We appreciate all you did for us, and we do not mean to offend, but I do my best to stay away from spells and such. In the name of Qareck, Lord of All Existence, please accept my humble apologies. We'll be on our way."

The farmer's son dutifully shouldered the old man, and they struggled down the road.

Before Zev could go after them, Bellemont put out her hand to stop him. "You'll only make it worse. Let them be. We should get back on our journey."

Zev pulled away from her touch and followed the farmer for a few steps. But he could feel Bellemont and the driver staring into his back. He did not move for quite some time. Not out of indecision or stubbornness, but rather, he did not want either woman to see the redness on his face. He hated to admit it, but part of him cringed at the fact that the farmers recognized Bellemont yet had no clue that Zev Asterling stood right before them.

Lowering his head, he sauntered back to the autocart. He remained silent most of the drive to the castle.

CHAPTER THREE

Ridnight City and Ridnight Castle had always been impressive, but for this celebration, the King had his small section of the world transformed into a dazzling, boisterous display. Not even the grand balls that Zev had been forced to attend as a child came close to touching this grandeur. For a breath or two, Zev stopped thinking about the haycart, the farmer, and his own father and focused entirely on the party. Thankfully, the hours of travel had availed him of his hangover.

Their driver brought the autocart up a curved path filled with autocarts delivering guests. When their turn arrived, well-appointed attendants helped them out and guided them up the marble stairs leading into the castle. Guards armed with pikes stood at attention at every corner and most doors. Nearby, a quartet of musicians played a pleasant song while other music drifted throughout the halls as Zev and Bellemont worked their way toward the main ballroom.

Leaning closer to Bellemont, Zev said, "You know, the previous times we were here, I didn't realize we hadn't gone through the main entrance. I had no idea any of this was part of the castle. Didn't even know it existed."

"It is rather breathtaking."

"It's a bit over-the-top, don't you think?"

Cocking her head toward a gathering off to the right, she said, "Those are Easterners, right?"

There was no mistaking the slim fitting, well-tailored styles of the East. Particularly, the latest men's fashion—pieces of cut cloth tied around the neck and hung down the front. It served no purpose that Zev could discern, but the men appeared to be fascinated by each other's choices in color and design.

Gesturing toward the left, Bellemont said, "Now look over there."

Three women stood firm and straight. Each wore black strips of cloth and dark veils that denoted them as Dacci witches. Westerners.

"What are they doing here?" Zev said. "After everything we've been through fighting the Beast, I would've thought no Dacci would dare show her face in the Frontier. Present company excepted, of course."

Bellemont chuckled. "You really don't pay attention to what's going on."

"About what?"

"Following royalty isn't all about glamour and opulence. It's also about politics. This quest that Axon went on—she did not go alone. The big news was that her team from the Frontier only achieved success with the help of teams from both the East and the West. That's why they are here. This celebration honors all three groups and unveils whatever treasure they've brought back."

Zev pulled Bellemont out of the main traffic path. "Are you saying this is a big political party? Some kind of peace talks?"

"All parties, all marriages, all celebrations and mournings—when it comes to royalty, every one of those events is a political event. I thought you knew all this."

"I knew it in the broad sense, of course. But it never affected my daily life, so I didn't pay that much attention."

"Perhaps you better pay attention now."

Returning to the embroidered carpet leading to the main ballroom, Bellemont put out her arm and waited. Though he had more questions, Zev decided that following her lead might prove the wisest choice. He linked their arms and escorted her onward.

Before they could enter the party, however, they were stopped by another guard. This one had a serious expression that brooked no argument. "Any projectile weapons must be stored outside the ballroom," he said.

Zev glanced around the entrance to see several members of the East removing their rifles and pistols. Oddly, the witches were walking in unmolested. "Shouldn't you be taking away the casting bags of those women?"

"Not my orders. Do you have any weapons or am I going to have to search you?"

"I've got nothing but curiosity."

That answer did not satisfy the guard. He patted Zev's legs and waist, checked his coat, and finished with a snarling toss of the head. "Enjoy the party."

Bellemont snickered as they walked through the main doors.

The overwhelming opulence of the event slammed into Zev like a massive storm emerging out of nowhere. The walls and ceiling glittered with light that shifted colors when seen at different angles. As he tried to determine if the effect came from a spell or unique glass, Bellemont nudged his side pointing to the twelve-piece band on a circular stage in the middle of the room. Though they played traditional instruments like stringed ortars and the double-horned vopet, they managed to produce a full and lively sound. The stage spun slowly as the band performed one song after another—some popular in the Frontier, some from the East, and even one Dacci tune. The rich aroma of slow-cooked meats filled the air, combating the sickly sweet desserts that had been piled on tables running the perimeter.

Most impressive of all, the nine deities of the Cassunites stood watch over the evening via statues that reached floor to ceiling. The six deities of the cycle of life bracketed two sides—three statues to a wall. Tiq, Ovlar, and Bieck—birth, childhood, and adolescence respectively—watched from one side while Sazieck, Orlar, and Wiq—adulthood, the gray years, and death—watched from the other. Standing guard on either side of the entranceway, everyone could see Tortu, God of Woman, and Pralma, Goddess of Man. But the most magnificent statue stood alone at the far end—Qareck, Lord of All Existence. Zev did not subscribe to any religion, but he had to admit the display inspired both awe and confidence.

"Look there," Bellemont said, pointing to a grouping of Easterners. "That's Lavin Metter."

"That name sounds familiar."

"I should think so. He's one of the wealthiest men in the world. He invented the autocart. Oh, and he's talking to Lady Darwith. Her family runs metalwork factories for just about everything. The two of them together would make quite a match."

Zev tittered. "This is a paradise for you, isn't it?"

"It's certainly entertaining. But it's no paradise. Look around—it doesn't take a careful eye to see how tense things are."

Obliging, Zev checked over the entire ballroom, and he was not surprised to find that Bellemont was right. The Easterners stood stiff and tall. The women with their hair piled high and in curls, the men with their colorful neckwear, yet their faces showed no joy. Zev noticed an odd-shaped table deep within the Eastern circles. Shifting his feet, he managed a better angle. Not a table—a coffin.

"Why would they bring that to a party?"

"I don't know," Bellemont said. "They're your people."

Zev noticed her eyes had drifted toward the other side of the room —the Western side. The Dacci witches made no effort to feign a party-like atmosphere. They stood like a wall of black-clad statues. The smell of blood and bile drifted through the air. Only the strength of the cooked foods kept their stench from spoiling everybody's appetite.

Like the Easterners, these witches had brought an unusual object with them. Not a coffin, but a palanquin. The Dacci kept their distance from this litter, except for two who stood directly in front, their arms locked behind and their heads bowed. Zev assumed these were the bearers assigned to carry the occupant around. The palanquin had an ornate design that reminded Zev of the prayer statues he had seen in honor of Nualla. "You may not understand the coffin, but you certainly know what's going on there. Right?"

Bellemont closed her eyes as if offering a short prayer. Then she looked directly at Zev. "The witches in front of that litter are not Dacci witches. They were once, but they broke away. The Dacci call them the Lost. I don't know what the Lost call themselves. They roam like a nomadic cult, wandering the land in search of some unknowable answers toward life. Or something like that. I'm not one of them, and I want nothing to do with them."

"I'm guessing that their leader rides inside that."

"Stories I've read suggest that there is a piece of Nualla in there. That it gives them the ability to perform spells wherever they go. The fact that they are here only means the political aspect of this gathering is far more serious, far more complicated than we realized."

At the end of the ballroom, sitting upon a raised stage, King Robion gazed out at the crowd. He wore a subdued outfit, respectful but not flashy, yet he also wore his crown with its nine jewels to honor the deities. Sharing this stage of honor with him were Axon, Pilot, a member of the East, and one of the West.

Zev said, "That man is Philune, Captain of the Eastern Guard."

"Follow a little royalty, then, after all?"

"I wouldn't call him royalty."

Philune certainly did not dress the part—either royalty or soldier. He wore a fine enough suit, but he looked uncomfortable on that stage. His eyes, however, proved another matter. Philune sat stiff and let his view roam across the ballroom like a strategist surveying a battlefield. Those eyes held a frosty calm with a simmering vindictiveness underneath. Zev had seen that look before—mostly from politicians.

Bellemont said, "Rumor is that Philune's father is being groomed as the next president of the East."

Zev snorted, garnering a displeased eyebrow from one lady. "Groomed? I thought the East had adopted a voting system. Don't the people decide who run things?"

Bellemont chuckled. "That's what we're told."

"And the witch sitting next to him—do you know who she is?"

"Of course. Her name is Thalia. She's the leader of the Lost."

She sat stiffer than Philune and wore traditional Dacci garb, including the black veil to cover her mouth. But whereas Philune watched the crowd with calculating eyes, Thalia appeared more impatient than anything else. She clearly did not like being a focus of attention. Zev caught the tension in her hands as she gripped the arms of her chair and the way her focus continually returned to the witches standing near the palanquin.

Mulling at the foot of the stage, the wealthiest of the Frontier smiled and nodded at each other. They were a strange synthesis of combating cultures. Dressed with all the elegance of the Easterners, those of the Frontier maintained a harsher look as if they wanted all to remember that they shared the border with the West. They bore the hardship.

Bellemont indicated one particular couple—a large man resting his elbow on the stage as he beamed toward Axon and a prim woman wearing the finest gown who watched the crowd with all the eagerness of a starving catrat willing to munch on carrion if it would keep her alive another day. "Lord and Lady Coponiv," Bellemont said.

"Axon's parents?"

"A few years back, they were a failing family trying to marry off their daughters, but thanks to Axon's success with us and now this, things are better than ever for the Coponivs."

Taking in one more scan of the various groups at the party, Zev's nerves rattled. Leaning closer to Bellemont, he whispered, "We should offer our congratulations to Axon and the King, and then we should get out of here. Whatever King Robion plans to make of this evening, I don't see how he'll succeed. Unless he wants to assassinate everybody here. Whatever the case, I don't want to be here when it happens."

Bellemont turned a sharp look at him. "Thank goodness you only solve mysteries about who stole a cake and where the farmer's horse ran off to. You know nothing about this world. Of course it's tense, but these people don't kill each other. They have armies to do that. These are the ones who profit from war, who benefit from the conflicts, and capitalize on their solutions. If King Robion brought them all here for a reason, then you can bet that whatever his plan, he intends for the Frontier to profit the most." She backed away. "Or perhaps it's just a celebration of Axon's victory. I suggest you mingle and try to find out what the answer is before we make any rash decisions."

Before he could object further, she allowed the crowds to absorb her in their forced revelry. Zev wanted to run after her, but fighting the throngs of people did not seem wise—he had no desire to draw attention his way. After all, he had been to many upscale parties in his youth. His father had him going to all the balls designed to marry off daughters, and his brother had forced Zev to attend rich gatherings designed to forge business relationships. While Bellemont was right—he did not know the depth of this world—he did understand these kinds of parties.

Or at least, he intended to before the night was over.

CHAPTER FOUR

W hile he had been to many parties with the rich, Zev never felt comfortable in those surroundings. He never knew the right thing to say, never laughed at the right volume, and the looks sent his way were filled with disdain. As he meandered through the crowded Eastern section of the ballroom, his nerves flooded with that familiar sensation of unease. A dark thought popped in his head—it was a good thing his father had fallen ill; otherwise, Marcel would have been sure to attend this gala.

"Pardon me," a five foot woman with a one foot hairdo said as she approached him. "Am I mistaken or are you Zev Asterling?"

A grin snapped out of him. "I am. I'm surprised anybody would remember me from when I was young. I haven't been to a party in ages."

"Oh? Are you originally from the East, then?"

Zev paused. "How is it you know who I am?"

"You were quite famous for a short period of time. Correct? You helped Ms. Coponiv fight the Beast of the West a few years back."

The woman licked her lips, and Zev swore her teeth had been sharpened.

"I see. People make that mistake quite often. I'm not that Zev Asterling."

She blushed. "My apologies. You do look much like the sketches I saw in the papers."

"Whoever the artist was did me no favors."

The woman did not laugh. In fact, Zev felt extra tension rise in the air between them. "My friend, Lady Cho, is the artist's mother." Without another word, she turned her back on him and walked away.

Clasping his elbows as if a gust of cold wind had crossed his path, he looked from one gabbing group to another. They all knew each other. And as the insulted woman whispered to one friend, and that friend to another, people started gawking at him.

Well, so much for making friends with the Easterners.

Zev strolled toward the middle of the room, listening to the band and watching the musicians perform with impressive skill. His focus moved beyond them and settled on the Dacci witches. If the point of this party truly was to benefit everybody in some type of peace, then why not make the first good faith gesture?

He would not be foolish enough to stride right into the center of that contingent, though. Rather, he inched along the edge until he stood within talking distance of one of the witches. While he could feel the eyes of the Westerners upon him, he perused a table of delectable sweets which he hoped would help those on the Eastern side ignore him as a fool.

After a moment, it became clear that the witches would not begin the conversation. So, Zev decided to open with a compliment. "The palanquin you brought is exquisite. I've never seen anything like it."

He could hear the witches catch their breath. The one nearest him turned her head slightly, enough that her narrowed eyes burned at him with their intensity. "You should never talk of the Virgin Cart."

The next witch over lifted her chin. "Then again, why don't you go over and open the door? Take a look inside."

Another witch, one wearing a red face veil, stormed over. "Don't talk to him. Don't talk to anyone not Dacci," she said. The way her words sounded malformed suggested a lack of teeth. Zev want nothing to do with that powerful a witch.

Backing away, he said, "My apologies. I meant no offense."

As he headed back, he could hear them complaining. "You won't let us tease the foreigners. You won't even let us talk to Ashturov or Inx."

"They are Lost," Red Veil said with such acid that Zev wouldn't have been surprised if the floor burned away. "We don't need them for anything. Especially for what happens tonight."

More than ever, he simply wanted to enact his initial plan—offer up gratitude to the King and Axon, collect Bellemont, and go home. But as he headed toward the raised stage, he saw a crowd gathering around the front. Everybody wanted the ear of the King or to be seen talking with Axon. If Zev took his place in line, he would have to wait hours for his chance.

"Zev? Zev Asterling?" a pleasant voice said.

He turned to find a lovely woman wearing a formal gown that managed to be both stylish and understated—Lady Jos. Like her friends, Lady Jos had a mound of hair reaching unnatural heights. She had the added touch of sprinkling her locks with small flowers.

He bowed and the petals' distinct fragrance surprised him—Feral Moon, a rare and expensive flower. "Lady Jos. It's a pleasure to see a friendly face."

"You remember me? How wonderful."

"I could never forget the one person who made all those stuffy parties bearable."

"Not bearable enough, I guess. After all, you abandoned me for the Frontier—and, if the stories are true, for fame being a brave warrior in the West."

"I was no warrior."

She pinched his arm. "You have muscles, and you look roughened by your adventures. If you weren't a warrior, you were still something strong out there. After all, your King Robion wouldn't have invited you for no reason at all."

"He's not really my king."

"Oh? I thought you gave up on the East."

"I don't have a country of my own. I guess, if I had to claim allegiance anywhere, it's to the town of Fernbund."

Lady Jos giggled and covered her mouth with a gloved hand. "Fernbund? What kind of name is that?"

"The kind given to a very small town. No big society moves or big money. You'd hate it."

She gave his shoulder a playful shove. "Don't be mean. Just because I was born into money doesn't mean I can't appreciate simpler things. You did, after all. Or did you forget about the Asterling fortune you were born into?"

The band broke into a lively number, and Zev considered grabbing Lady Jos by the hand to dance. He recalled that she liked dancing, and he figured that this conversation would go much better if they stopped talking. But nobody else was dancing. This wasn't that kind of party.

"Come," she said, "let's get you a drink."

"No. No, thank you. I don't want another drink for days."

"Oh, come anyway," she said, yanking Zev toward a small group. "I want you to meet someone."

They stopped in front of a young, fit man who scanned the crowd like a sentry. Lady Jos put out her hand for the young man to bend over and kiss. "Ma'am," he said with a formal yet cold tone.

"Zev, let me introduce you to one of the heroes of this event, my old friend, Vost Wellows. And Vost, this gentleman is a hero as well. He helped fight the Beast of the West."

Vost's attention perked at this revelation, and he put out his hand. He wore a far more subdued outfit than most Easterners. A fine suit, well-tailored, but lacking the flourishes designed to accentuate the display of wealth and power. "Always happy to meet another person who has seen the real world."

Shaking the man's hand, Zev said, "There's a lot to see. If this is your first visit to the Frontier, you probably haven't experienced a castle like this before."

"It is rather expansive."

Zev chuckled. "I prefer less grandeur, personally. I think I would have enjoyed hiking the mountains on an expedition."

"It had much to offer. Far more than one gets at overstuffed parties like this."

"Don't start that again," Lady Jos said, shoving Vost's shoulder much like she had Zev's. "The two of you with your disdain for the great traditions of the East—why, one would think you were brothers."

"I don't disdain the East," Vost said. "I only want it to be better."

"I know what would make this evening better—you tell us what the big surprise is. Come now, you went on the whole expedition. What did you find out there?"

Vost bowed. "Enjoy the evening." He walked away.

Trying to take advantage of the moment, Zev headed off into the opposite direction. Lady Jos hastened to his side. "I'm sorry. Vost is usually not so grumpy. I suppose it's to be understood, though. After all, one of his good friends died on their journey."

Zev said, "Is that who's in the coffin?"

"I imagine so. It's a new honor the government thought up. Bring a coffin to an event as some sign of those who made a sacrifice, or something like that. I do appreciate not having to live under a king—no offense—but the way they make up holidays and traditions and such every few months is getting ridiculous."

A heavyset man with rosy cheeks and a large mustache laughed hard and loud. Zev refused to look—there always seemed to be some-body at these parties intent on getting noticed for having a good time.

Lady Jos glanced back and paused. Her hand rested on Zev's arm as she bit her lip. "I'm sorry, but I have to go over there. I'd invite you, but I don't know how much the Radugos and the Asterlings get along, and well, you get to live out in the Frontier, but I have to return East when this is done."

"Go ahead. I wouldn't want to sully your name with my presence."

"Stop that," she said, with a final shoulder shove. "I certainly hope this is not goodbye for long. I expect to see you the next time you visit your family. Understood?"

"Yes, ma'am," he said and bowed over her hand.

As she walked away, he grimaced at the thought of his father. But King Robion stopped those dark thoughts by stepping to the end of the stage and raising his hands to shush the crowd. The band ceased playing. All eyes turned upon the King.

In a deep baritone that rumbled throughout the ballroom as if the castle's architect had designed the room specifically for the man's voice, King Robion said, "My dear friends from other countries, my new friends from other countries, and my always loyal subjects, I welcome you to Ridnight Castle. We come tonight to celebrate a success that could only have been achieved through the cooperation of us all. I have heard from these three marvelous leaders of their arduous, challenging, and—one might say—enlightening experience. Later this evening, you will all have an opportunity to hear their engrossing story as well, and I promise you it is well worth listening to. It is the kind of truth that could change us all for the better."

As the King continued on with magnanimous platitudes and glorious praise, the vast ballroom shrunk tight around Zev. He felt the press of the crowd as they attempted to get closer and closer to the stage. He felt the tension between the East and West like magnetic forces shoving against each other, unsure whether to repel or cling together. His neck dampened with sweat and his chest tightened.

King Robion segued into a childhood memory, and Zev understood the speech would be a long one. He weaved through the thick, flowery perfumes and strong bite of alcohol hanging in the air until he reached a side exit. Stepping out to a cool, stone hallway, he released a relieved breath.

Bellemont would simply have to understand. He had tried.

CHAPTER FIVE

Walking along the back corners of the castle, Zev chuckled at the lack of guards. Even a king did not have endless resources, and clearly the budget for decorative guards only covered the entranceway and the ballroom. Still, he expected to see a few—if for no other reason than to stop wandering guests from veering into the more private sections of the King's home.

After passing several closed doors, Zev came upon a large window. He gazed out across the city. Candlelight and small fires dotted the streets. A few lamplighters brightened darker sections. Closer to the castle walls, he noticed a group of Eastern soldiers circling a small fire —attendants to the autocarts brought in by all the Easterners. Not far away, but at a cautious distance, Zev spotted another gathering— Dacci witches standing firm as they kept their suspicious eyes on their surroundings. Still, the city appeared quiet and peaceful. He wondered if any of those sleeping tonight knew of the potential changes to the world occurring within the guise of a giant party.

The smell of burning tobacco drifted from ahead. Zev strolled along and when he turned the corner, he spotted a guard leaning against an open window, smoking a swig—another invention from the East. Until the swig came along, people smoked pipes. But a bit of inspiration, or possibly drunken madness, led a young woman in the East to place a small portion of tobacco in some jau leaves. The result was a swig—a small, easy to carry smoking device.

When the guard noticed Zev, he tried to hide the swig. Zev shook his head and waved his hand. "It's okay."

With a sheepish smile, the guard said, "You want one?"

"Thank you, but no."

"Smart man. Me? I can't stop smoking these things."

"I'm surprised they let you smoke on duty."

The guard looked at the swig with worry. "I guess they don't. Probably the smell of the stuff throughout the castle and all."

"Yet here you are."

The guard grinned. "As long as nobody sees me and I'm back on duty before the King finishes his speech, I figure I'll be fine."

"Yet here I am."

A flash of worry crossed his face.

"Relax," Zev said. "I don't want to cause trouble for anybody. In fact, I'd appreciate it if you helped me out. Do you know the quickest way to get out of here without having to go through the front where everybody would see me?"

Taking one final drag, the guard stared at Zev, clearly appraising the man. At length, he nodded and put out his hand. "I'm Kallot. And I can certainly help you. I've known my way all around this castle since I was a kid—my mother worked in the kitchens when I was growing up."

"Zev Asterling." They shook hands. "Lead the way."

Kallot swiped his guard's pike off the wall and headed down the corridor. Zev followed. They took several turns, and he quickly lost his bearings. Little in the way of clear markers made his task difficult.

"Right through that door," Kallot said, pointing to a wooden door with a black metal latch at the end of a narrow alcove.

"I sure appreciate it. Thank you."

Zev opened the door and found two men bound and gagged on the floor of a musty storage room. As he turned back, as his brain thought that he should warn the guard of trouble, he saw the guard's fist swinging towards his head. Instinct took over.

Raising one arm to block the attack, Zev shoved the man's chin with his free hand. The guard had clearly not expected resistance. The chin strike knocked him back. With an unbalanced stance, he stumbled on his heels and smacked his head against the stone wall.

Zev stormed forward and snatched the pike away. His mind raced through possibilities—why were these men bound and gagged? Why was the guard trying to do the same to him? What should he do with the guard? And why didn't the guard attack with the pike? But the flood of questions eased back as his brain kicked into action.

The details didn't matter—not yet. Clearly something bad was happening.

Raising the pike, he said, "Sorry about this, Kallot. I just don't have time to knock you unconscious."

With the swift swing, Zev brought the axe section of the pike down against Kallot's leg. The man screamed out. He rolled to his side clutching the bleeding gash.

Zev turned to one of the bound men and quickly released him. The man ripped off his gag. "That man is no guard," he said.

Zev handed the pike to the freed man. "Then you guard him. I've got to go to the King."

Without waiting for an answer, Zev tore off into the halls of the castle.

Though Kallot had done a good job of throwing off Zev's sense of direction, King Robion's speech could be heard nearly everywhere. Whenever Zev came to an intersection, he merely had to stop and listen. Whatever direction brought him closer in sound brought him closer to the ballroom.

Sweat broke out on his face, and his heart hammered against his chest. He had not farmed land for a couple of years, and the last big bit of fighting he had done was with Axon. Since then, he'd been behind the desk in an office using his brain muscles instead of his physical ones. Panting hard and feeling his legs burn, he saw a large door ahead with two guards on either side. It had to be one of the ballroom entrances.

"Hurry," he shouted. "The King's in danger."

The guards snapped to attention, their faces dropping into concern—this was supposed to be an easy job. They might not even have been fully-trained. One thing was clear to Zev, though—the guards had no clue what to do.

"Open the doors," Zev said from halfway down the hall.

Thankfully, they obliged. As Zev burst into the ballroom—about three quarters of the way back—he saw the King on stage with a large curtained object to his right.

"And so, it is my great honor to present to all the leaders of our world, the fruits of our finest people. From the West, from the East, from the Frontier, our heroes returned with this great gift to us all. A legend—some believed a myth—that they have brought home. A relic of ages long forgotten. A powerful tool which we can all use to bring peace to our times."

Zev scanned the room for any sign that somebody meant ill—an assassin, a group of mercenaries, anything. But he only spotted faces locked in rapt attention to the stage.

King Robion grabbed the curtain. "I give you the Shield of Taladoro." He ripped down the curtain to reveal an empty glass chamber.

Shocked gasps rolled across the audience. Zev shoved aside those in his way. He had to get to the stage. He had to get to people who would listen to him. Because though the King and Axon and all the guests may have realized that the Shield had been stolen, only Zev knew something more important—the robbery was still in progress.

CHAPTER SIX

A handful of the smarter guests headed for the exits while the rest gawked at the stage as repeated gasps rolled across the gathering. King Robion noticed the movement in the back and gestured towards his guards. Closing the doors behind them, the guards blocked anyone from leaving. Even the barely-trained guards grasped the seriousness of their job.

"How dare you!" One heavy voice followed the waving of a fist. "Do you know who I am?"

A sharp female voice said, "Step aside or I'll see to it that you're demoted."

Before more outraged, pompous voices could rise up, King Robion put up his hands to quiet the crowd. "Please, if everybody would stay calm, we can address this problem."

One of the overly coiffed ladies said, "I would say your problem has already been addressed. You're just slow to catch up. You don't have the Shield anymore."

The Dacci witch wearing the red veil said, "How can we be sure the Shield has actually been stolen? Is this just a ruse to commandeer a great tool of Nualla's power from the rest of us? Or perhaps this is a move against us instead of an offer of peace."

Several of the witches scowled across the ballroom at the gentleman of the East.

"Stop it!" Zev pushed further through the crowd. "There's still a chance to stop this."

"The witch is right," an Easterner with a thick mustache said. "How do we know you aren't double-crossing us all? You've already had your guards lock us down. This is an outright attack against our sovereignty."

The ocean of people swallowed Zev's movements. He knew he pushed further and further toward the stage, yet he had no sense of real progress. The heavy grumbling drowned his calls for attention.

King Robion said, "If I had wanted to steal the Shield for myself, I would never have called you all here. And if I had wanted you all dead, I wouldn't bother with a charade like this party. I'd have assassinated you the moment you arrived to see the Shield."

Behind him, the leaders of the expedition sat like stone temple statues. Zev could not see a path to reach the stage in time.

Red Veil spoke quietly to her fellow witches. When she finished, they circled around her and pulled out their bags—the ones with which they carried bones, small dead animals, and other vile substances used in casting spells.

The mustached man stabbed his finger in their direction. "Stop them before they turn us all into muck. Or are you in it together? The Frontier and the West in a plot against the East."

"There is no plot against you," King Robion said, his voice booming through the walls. "There will be no Dacci spells cast. My personal spellcasters, the godwalkers, are at this moment blocking the castle off with their power. The Dacci witches will find their abilities dampened. No other spells can be cast until I order the godwalkers to stop theirs. Now, we must all calm down. No single one of us can have control over that Shield. That was the point of this gathering—that we find a peace between us all, so that none could threaten the other with such a powerful weapon. With the Shield stolen, there is only one possibility I can see to prevent us from destroying each other—no one will leave this building until we find out what happened to the Shield."

An unsettled hush overcame the ballroom, and Zev knew he had an opening. With as much authority as he could muster, he said, "We can still catch the thieves."

King Robion, Axon, and the rest of the stage leaned forward, searching the crowd for who had spoken. Pilot jumped to his feet when he spotted Zev. The strong, dark-skinned fellow pointed and smiled. "Zev? Great to see you, ol' friend."

All eyes turned toward Zev. "Um, good to see you, too."

"Let that man up here. If he's got something to say, I guarantee it's worth listening to."

Shucking off the sudden attention, Zev focused on the King. "Your Highness, I don't have time. Give me Pilot and some of your guards. There's still a chance to stop the thieves."

King Robion's face wrinkled, but as a new commotion of unrest grew through the crowd, he nodded. Pilot jumped off the stage and raced toward Zev.

As he led Zev out of the room—the door guards threatening the rest of the crowd to stand back—Pilot snapped his fingers at several of the King's Guards. Real soldiers with real training. "Where we going?" he asked.

Zev opened his mouth, ready to suggest finding the fake guard he had wounded, but then he remembered the old farmer and his son limping along the road. They had been attacked by bandits who did not take any money or goods. They had only stolen the haycart. "Stables. I know how they're going to escape."

CHAPTER SEVEN

The stables and the newly-built adjoining garage stood in the back of the castle grounds. It was a large complex capable of housing all of the horses for the King's Guard as well as the royal family plus the workhorses. A second floor stored hay but also boasted numerous rooms for the staff needed to keep the castle running. Nearly a hundred horses in all. Plus, they had extra stalls for the animals of visiting guests.

The garage had once been a covered rink for riding but now housed autocarts. Rows upon rows like slumbering, armored soldiers.

When Zev, Pilot, and four guards reached the entrance to the stables, Zev felt a breath of hope surge through his body. Two men wearing ill-fitting uniforms stood in front of the haycart—a shoddy thing that probably looked shoddy the day it was made. The kind used by a poor farmer. Blocking their way, two real guards with pikes stood. By the time Zev and his group approached, several others had surrounded these men. They all recognized that these criminals had stolen their uniforms.

One of these men, the one with stringy black hair, had shot his hands straight in the air. "Go ahead and search the cart. There ain't nothing there. We got nothing on us. None of this is happening the way it's supposed to."

The other man—a big, broad-shouldered, muscular man— smacked Stringy Hair in the back of the head. "Close your mouth."

"We ain't the thieves. We was only hired to haul away an item— and we don't even know what it was. We ain't stole nothing."

As Pilot stepped forward, all the guards stood at attention, even as they kept their pikes pointing at the thieves. One of the guards with bars on his shoulders said, "Sir, we caught these two trying to make a hasty exit."

Pilot nodded. To Zev, he said, "Are these the thieves?"

"*Sir?* Are you Captain of the Royal Guard?" Zev asked.

"Does that really matter now?"

"Of course not. Sorry. Just took me by surprise."

"Me, too. How about these fellows? Are they the thieves or not?"

Zev approached Big Man and Stringy Hair. "You two knocked out some guards in the hall, right? Left your friend, Kallot, behind to keep watch while some others stole the Shield. We got you, and your friend guarding the hall is either on his way to a doctor or is dead. But none of you have the Shield. So, who hired you?"

"We don't know. Honest," Stringy Hair said. "We just ain't nothing but a crew to take it away. Nothing else. Don't know nothing about any shield."

Big Man slapped Stringy Hair's face. "I told you to shut it."

Before Zev could utter another question, Axon and Philune arrived. Axon strode forward, her powerful presence not missed on a single soldier. Zev wished for a different situation, one in which he could embrace her, sit down over a drink, and laugh—well, Axon didn't laugh much, but at least they would languish in a quiet evening and reminisce.

Instead, Stringy Hair said, "We'll give ourselves up to King Robion."

With a forceful swing of his hand in the air, Philune said, "You'll deal with me first."

Despite Big Man's disapproval, Stringy Hair turned to Zev. "Please. I fouled up. Put me in a dungeon. Lock me up for years."

"Make way," Philune said, the power of his tone enough to part the guards in the back.

As Big Man watched Philune approach, Zev spotted a change on the man's face. He seemed to recognize the Captain of the Eastern Guard. Before Zev could fully understand it, it was too late. Big Man leaned his head against Stringy Hair. He whispered.

Stringy Hair had the briefest second to raise his shaking eyes and mouth the word *No*. Big Man lifted his right arm overhead and opened his clenched fist. A handful of dark granules dropped over the two men.

"Stop!" Philune broke into a run. The surrounding guards took an instinctive step back, their armor clanging like warning bells.

And the two thieves burst into flames.

Stringy Hair shrieked. His skin bubbled as it turned raw red. He tried to break free, perhaps wanted to roll in the dirt, but Big Man wrapped his thick arms around in a tight hug.

Everybody watched in silent horror. Nobody ran for water or attempted to put out the fire. Nobody could think, let alone move. Nobody dared to even breathe.

The ripple of flames produced a song of cracks and sputters. Big Man never made a sound, and that proved far more disturbing than Stringy Hair's dying cries. Enough so that Pilot turned away, pressing the back of his hand against his mouth.

The wind shifted, and Zev inhaled the nauseating aroma of cooking flesh. He wondered if he would ever stomach the idea of a steak again.

He could not recall how long he stood there, but after a time, Axon walked over and placed her hand on his back. "This is certainly not the way I thought our reunion would look." She snapped a finger at two guards, and they hurried off to douse the fire. "Would you mind helping us search this area? I've not forgotten how observant you can be."

Zev nodded, afraid to attempt speaking. He could not take his eyes away from the gory sight before him. The tender warmth coming off the flames perverted the idea of a campfire, and Zev wondered if he would ever be able to put this moment safely away.

Adding a little strength to her touch, Axon guided Zev away from the charred men and toward the haycart. "Let's see if we can find that Shield."

The search did not take long. Within a few moments, it became obvious that the haycart contained only hay. Something had gone wrong for the thieves—a betrayal, perhaps.

Clearly, they had not planned on Zev discovering the bound and gagged guards, but by the time Zev made it to the ballroom, the King had already reached the point in his speech where he revealed the Shield of Taladoro. Unless these thieves were highly incompetent—doubtful considering the size of the prize they sought—they must have expected to have escaped the castle with the stolen Shield by that moment.

Zev glanced at the haycart. Perhaps they planned another way to escape?

His stomach churned. If these haycart thieves had anything on them that would help find the Shield, now was the time to grab it. He would have to sift through their ashes. Grimacing at the idea, he headed toward the smoldering corpses. But Philune stepped in the way.

"Nobody is to touch these," he said.

Zev said, "I need to look at them. If we're to find out who stole the Shield—"

"Once trusted members of the East have had a chance to inspect things, then a commoner like you can take a look. Or whatever you Frontier people do. I'm sure King Robion and those representing the West will also want to inspect these remains. The entire stable for that matter." He snapped his fingers at the nearest guard. "Set up a perimeter around the stables. Make sure nobody comes in here to disturb things."

Zev turned to Axon, but she shook her head. "Do as he says," she ordered, and the guards got to work. "Pilot, make sure that—"

"Are you kidding me?" Zev said. "If you let this arrogant idiot shut everything down—"

Philune bounded forward. "You do not talk about me that way. You have no clue the serious nature of what is going on here. This is a matter for those who run businesses, for lords and Kings and those who have influence in the world."

Zev wanted to roll his fingers into a tight fist and pop Philune in the jaw. However, the Captain of the East stood almost a foot taller and had many more soldiers under his command. Actually, he had all the soldiers under his command while Zev had zero. This was not the time.

Stopping Zev from saying something he would regret, one of the King's pages rushed in. Through panting breaths, he said, "King Robion demands the presence of Master Zev Asterling."

Zev grinned at Philune. "I see now that you are quite correct, kind sir. This is a matter for those who have real influence."

Following the page into the castle, he could feel Philune's eyes raging behind. Axon and Pilot's attempts to hide their smiles only sweetened the taste. Sometimes the little victories mattered most.

CHAPTER EIGHT

When Zev reentered the ballroom, the tension had only grown worse. But instead of shouting, bickering, or nasty glares thrown from one side of the immaculate room to the other, dead silence consumed the air. Like the audience at a wedding finally seeing the bride, they all turned to stare at Zev's entrance.

This time, he did not need to muscle through the crowd in order to reach the King. Nobody blocked his way. Those closest to the center had pushed back leaving an aisle for him to pass through. As he walked, each footfall could be heard echoing throughout the cavernous room. The enormous statues of the Cassun nine stared down on him, making his quiet steps even less. The band still sat on the rotating stage in the center, but their instruments had all been packed. They simply had not figured out a polite way to get out of everyone's view.

Zev knew exactly how they felt.

After he walked by the band, King Robion gestured in his direction. "Everybody, this is Zev Asterling. We can all see that he is empty-handed. Mr. Asterling, can we assume you did not recover the Shield?"

Zev stopped, but the King waved him further toward the stage. Swallowing hard, Zev said, "No Shield. But it appears that we stopped the men tasked to escape with it."

As he stepped onto the stage, the King shook his hand. "Then the Shield is still here in the castle?"

"I believe so."

Soft but energetic talking rumbled through the crowd. King Robion nodded. "You all understand now? My people have done their job and stopped this terrible event from becoming a true tragedy."

From the crowd, a witch stepped forward, wisps of gray hair poking out of her black headpiece. With marbled speech, she said, "We know what you want to do next, and we cannot allow it. We will not be subjected to physical searches."

"Nor us," one of the Easterners said.

As the voices rose in panicked protest, King Robion looked over at Zev like a schoolteacher at his wits' end dealing with ignorant students. "Nobody will have to be searched. We are not implementing such a thing. You have my word."

As the shouting settled down, concerned eyes returned to the stage. Zev dreamed of slipping into the wings, finding a horse, and galloping away. He already guessed where King Robion intended to take the matter, and he wanted no part of it. Yet when he managed one small step backward, King Robion laid a heavy hand on the back of his neck and pulled him close with what must have appeared like brotherly warmth from the outside and felt distinctly like an iron shackle clamping down.

"I promised you a solution, and I will deliver. Zev Asterling is one of the finest minds in the world. He is neither an inventor nor businessman nor does he cast spells. But he has perfected the art of deducing solutions from a minimal amount of information. I have witnessed his acumen before, and I can attest that if anybody in this castle is capable of determining who the thief is and where the Shield can be recovered, that person is Zev Asterling."

He faced Zev directly. This would be it. Here would come the request for help. A bold, loud pronouncement that would be embarrassing to deny.

Instead, the King brought his mouth against Zev's ear. With warm breath that still clung to the wine he had been drinking, he said, "I am sorry to do this to you. I know you covet your privacy. But two years ago, you were called upon to serve the Frontier, and you did so greatly. Your King calls upon you once more. You truly are among our greatest minds. Please. Help your country and your King."

When he pulled back, he offered Zev a smile that felt unique—a smile real and personal and only for him. The ballroom with its frustration and privilege disappeared. The small town investigations that lacked notoriety drifted away. His desire to be noticed and left alone swelled like a balloon and popped in his mind. Before he knew what he had done, his head moved up and down.

"Thank you," King Robion said.

Zev almost asked *For what?* but then he understood. He looked out across the crowd. They stared back like children searching for anybody who could promise them safe passage out of this dangerous situation. He would do his best.

"Bellemont?" he called out. A small figure weaved through the crowd until she managed to find the stairs onto the stage. "We have a case to solve."

The King returned to his authoritative boom. "Look before you. Zev Asterling—born in the East and a true Frontiersman. His assistant, Bellemont—a witch of the West and now Frontierswoman. It will be their efforts together that will provide us with the answers we seek. And so, I ask you, Master Solver Zev Asterling, what is your first move?"

Zev gave a moment's thought before doing his best to equal the King's mighty voice. "Take us to where the Shield was held. We'll start there."

PART II
THE INVESTIGATION

CHAPTER ONE

King Robion assigned one of his trusted aides, Mr. Duke, to facilitate any of Zev's and Bellemont's needs. Leading the way to the holding room, Mr. Duke walked with all the grace and stiffness of his position. He wore an outfit of simple browns and tans patterned with Royal appeal yet garnished with flamboyant ruffles around the neck and wrists. He looked like a bird in full plumage.

As they moved down one hall, they walked by a man wearing a floor-length, white cloak with black trim—one of the godwalkers. There were nine godwalkers in all, representing the six Deities of Life, the God and Goddess of the sexes, and of course, the Lord over All Existence. On the sleeve of this particular man, Zev spotted the shining sun design of Ovlar, God of Childhood.

Bellemont could not hold back a scornful glare. "They're nothing but idiots juggling daggers. A cult of mystics who want to learn to do what the Dacci do naturally—arrogance, at best. I wouldn't be surprised if they end up killing a few people by accident tonight."

Zev stayed quiet. To those who followed the Cassun nine, which included Axon among the faithful, the godwalkers signified the possibility of knowing their makers. The way Axon once explained it—the

Dacci had showed the world that spells existed. The godwalkers hoped to harness that power and use it for good, so someday they might speak to the Cassun Nine—to walk with their gods.

Mr. Duke either did not catch on to Zev's silence or he didn't care. Without looking back, he said, "Our godwalkers are highly respected scholars and practitioners of magic. You should be thankful they're here. Without them, the King would have no use for either of you."

"Because the thieves would have escaped," Zev said.

"Well, well. Perhaps the King's faith in you is justified. You figured that one out all by yourself."

Zev gripped Bellemont's hand to keep her from shoving Mr. Duke. They followed the King's Aide further without another word. When they reached a door near the end of the hall, Mr. Duke paused. Holding the handle, his stern mouth twitched before opening the door.

Bellemont whispered, "He's here to watch us as much as help us."

Zev did not move. Even as Bellemont scurried ahead into the room, he stared at the door—just a simple, wooden door. But nothing would ever be so simple. King Robion, and perhaps the Frontier itself, expected his best. Inhaling deeply, Zev tried to clear his mind and become the thing King Robion had described. The Master Solver.

He entered.

The holding room turned out to be a royal study. A layer of dust rested upon numerous scrolls and papers, each piled on waist-high shelves. Marks on the floor denoted where tables had once been placed, but the room had been cleared for the Shield. A small platform had been set up and the outline of where the container had been could easily be seen where it had disrupted the dust. Several steps in, Zev noticed a small pile of animal bones, the severed head of a tiny tree-rat, a dark substance that might have been blood, and a single, human tooth. The foul odor of excrement rose into the air.

To Bellemont, Zev said, "Is it possible to tell what kind of spell was cast with this?"

She shook her head. "Offerings made are not specific. They're not like ingredients in a recipe. Think of them more like promises."

"But this was definitely made by a witch."

"Or somebody wanting us to think there was a witch here."

Mr. Duke cleared his throat. "There was most certainly a witch here. One Dacci representative from the West and a gentleman from the East. They were brought here to witness the placing of the Shield in the display container so that all of us would have equal faith in the handling of the Shield. The witch was then tasked with casting a spell to protect the Shield from being stolen and sound an alarm should such a terrible thing occur."

"I want to speak with these representatives," Zev said.

"The gentleman from the East goes by Vost. He was a member of the Eastern expedition seeking the Shield. I shall be sure to find out who the witch was and see that they are brought to you soon."

"Thank you. Did you, by chance, see the Shield?"

"Of course."

"What does it look like?"

Mr. Duke wrinkled his nose as if the thought of answering detailed questions sullied his dignity. Blurting out information that displayed his intelligence or stature did not bother him, but being questioned sure did. Zev remained silent and patient. He stared at Mr. Duke until the Aide understood that this would be a long, uncomfortable day.

"It's a shield. I don't know what else to tell you. I'm not a warrior. I don't know the terminology."

"How big is it?"

"Large. I suppose from my shoulders to my knees. Not very attractive. No adornments or even a crest. Just a shield."

Zev strolled around the room, looking at the walls carefully. He did not spot a seam to indicate a hidden exit. Which left only the one door. Not even a window provided escape.

On the opposite side of the platform, Zev found another pile of waste used for casting. This one had more bones and less excrement— and, of course, a tooth. He pointed out this second pile, and Bellemont squatted close to inspect it.

"Would a witch need two piles for this spell?" he asked.

"Only if she lacked experience. But this wasn't the same witch."

"You can tell?"

"Every Dacci has their own preferences for casting. Some like small animal bone. Some want a larger pile of waste. Some like the scent of bile while others prefer blood. These two piles are nothing alike."

"They're from different witches."

Mr. Duke said, "I assure you there was only one witch in here when the Shield was secured."

Before Zev could utter his next question, Bellemont said, "Where exactly is this room in relation to the ballroom?"

Mr. Duke's mouth rolled in tight as if he had bitten a sour and vile thing. Lifting his head at an angle that sharpened the impression of his nose, he turned to Zev. "Do you have any requirements for me at the moment?"

Even here. He understood the farmer being afraid of a witch. He understood people from the East fearing them. But here, with an Aide to King Robion—Zev expected them to be more understanding. Especially considering Bellemont's contribution to the survival of the Frontier.

Speaking soft and slow so as not to bark out his words, Zev said, "You will treat Bellemont with all the respect you treat me. More than me. Now, answer her question."

Mr. Duke did not falter. Instead, he gazed down at Zev without adjusting his head. "King Robion wants you to solve this matter, and we need you to do so quickly before problems arise. So, in that light, and only in that light, I will do as you request." He stepped away from Zev and narrowed his focus on Bellemont. "We are underneath the ballroom. That is why there are no windows. The story I was told suggested that back in the time of King Overax, there was a need for a prison cell separated from those found far beneath the castle. One that could handle a criminal with the powers of a witch. So, they created this room. The legend suggested that it had been imbued with certain properties in the walls that prevented a witch from casting spells of escape. It is based on those legends that we chose this room to hold the Shield. Clearly, those stories were more myth than legend."

Bellemont held Mr. Duke's gaze for a short time. Zev wanted to pat her on the back for standing up to Mr. Duke, even with a simple glare. But before he could move his arm or even speak a word, her attention whipped behind her. She sniffed the air.

"You smell that?" she asked.

Mr. Duke said, "There is only one distinct odor here. We can all smell it. If you want more, there is an outhouse I can take you to."

Bellemont crouched, bringing her face close to the stone floor near the doorway. She pointed to a dark splotch. "That's blood."

Zev rushed over. Squatting next to her, he stared at the glistening droplets. His gaze lifted slightly, and he noticed two more just outside the door. He pointed, and Bellemont stepped over to sniff them. She nodded back before gesturing to more droplets further down.

Stepping into the hallway, Zev said, "Looks like we have a trail to follow."

CHAPTER TWO

With Mr. Duke in tow, Zev and Bellemont walked through the hall following the blood trail. Thankfully, the flooring lacked runners down the middle that would have absorbed blood or disguised it within the cloth's colored patterns. The gray stone that their feet clacked upon, even under the flicker of torchlight, made it easy to find the next blood droplet and the next like a dotted line on a treasure map.

Still, Zev felt stuck between two hands pulling upon him. The blood trail pulled him forward, promising the opportunity for a solution while Mr. Duke yanked back, promising an unspoken retaliation should he fail in his duties. Part of his brain promised that he exaggerated the pressures, part of him could not be dissuaded.

"It's possible," Bellemont said, "that a contingent of guards waited until the Shield was put in place. They got rid of the two guards they could not trust and then stole the Shield. They expected to move fast when the alarm went off, but the witch failed her spell."

Mr. Duke said, "So, we're looking for a guard? I'll have them all detained and questioned immediately."

"Hold on," Zev said. "We have no proof that any guards were involved. In fact, what we do know is that two guards were assaulted and dumped in the storage room so that the thieves could have easy access through this hall. The man we've detained only claimed to be a guard. We don't know yet."

"You're saying we should interrogate him?"

"I will want to talk with him, but not until I have more information. Right now, I won't be able to know whether he's lying to me or not."

"Then who stole the Shield?"

"I know you want an answer for King Robion, but it's going to take time." Returning to Bellemont, Zev said, "One thing that I find curious is the pile of refuse used to cast the spell."

"Oh?" Bellemont said as she pointed out another droplet of blood to follow.

"Well, if you're asked to perform this extremely important spell, one that will create an alarm against any unsuspecting criminal, then you would remove the leftovers of the casting when you're finished so as not to point out the spell's existence. Especially on the floor of the King's Castle. If for no other reason, then out of respect."

Mr. Duke snorted. "The Dacci witches do not show the Frontier much respect at all."

"Perhaps. But they're here for the same reason that we all are—to broker peace. Seems rather foolish to begin the process by insulting the host."

Bellemont wagged her fingers as she thought. "You are suggesting that the piles left behind came from the thieves."

"Exactly. Is it possible to figure out whose pile that would be? You said some witches prefer certain animal bones and parts than others."

"It would be very difficult. Maybe impossible. However, we do have the teeth."

Mr. Duke snapped his fingers. "Of course, the teeth. You all can only use your own teeth to cast a spell. If we take those teeth and force the witches to open their mouths, we can see whose mouth fits and problem solved."

Both Zev and Bellemont halted. Zev turned to Mr. Duke. "You can't do that. First of all, King Robion would never allow it. That's the kind of thing that people die over. And even if he agreed, the witches would refuse. Besides being a personal invasion, one they've already rejected in terms of being searched, it would require them to remove their face veils. They'll never agree to that."

"You might as well ask them to strip naked," Bellemont said.

"We don't even know if those teeth belong to the thieves. Just because I suspect that the witch who cast the alarm spell cleaned up, that does not necessarily make it so. After all, why would a Dacci have to perform two separate spells with two teeth to get to the Shield? If the protections around the Shield were that strong, you would have mentioned the original witch had gone through more than usual."

Mr. Duke stiffened. "I don't know what *usual* is with these people."

"Luckily, we do. And I'm telling you that if a witch wants to cast a stronger or more difficult spell, she might use more than one tooth, but it would be on the same casting pile."

Bellemont said, "That's true. Which tells us that one pile was for the original protection spell and one was used by the thieves."

"Most likely. It's a good assumption to go on."

Mr. Duke thrust his fists against his hips, flopping his wrist ruffles with comic effect. "Then we know that they didn't clean up after themselves. How does that help? What are we to do?"

"We continue following this blood trail, for now. Once you find the name of the witch that cast the alarm spell, we can question her, and then we'll know more."

Bellemont rushed ahead to a flight of stairs heading downward. From the clatter and aroma drifting through the air, Zev gathered the stairs led to the main kitchen. By the time he reached Bellemont, she had already traveled down to the bottom and back up to meet him.

Her gentle eyes scrunched forward. "It's gone. The blood trail ends here at the top of the stairs."

"Crap. I expected at some point the injured person would figure out they were bleeding and then get a bandage, but I had hoped it would take a little longer."

Mr. Duke stared at the last splotch of blood as if he understood its significance. "Don't we know now that the thief came through here?

No reason to stop at the steps unless you're going down. They obviously went into the kitchen."

Zev clasped his hands behind his back. "Unless King Robion is a complete slob who doesn't care about his guests, I would assume he has the best kitchen staff in the entire Frontier."

"Of course."

"So, not only are they talented at creating delicious confections and unforgettable meals but they also run a tight and spotless kitchen. Any blood would have been wiped away long ago."

Bellemont said, "I'll go ask around. Somebody must have seen a person who didn't belong in there rushing through. Maybe they can give us a hint as to where the thieves went after they reached the kitchen."

Mr. Duke straightened, placing one hand in a pocket as his head looked up. Zev thought he might be posing for a portrait, but under the circumstances, he decided to play along. "You have something to say?" he asked.

"It is a good thing King Robion ordered me along with you two. You would never find a solution without me." Mr. Duke snapped his finger at Bellemont before she could move toward the kitchen. "There'll be no need for that. I know exactly where they went."

After a moment, Zev understood that the King's Aide would not be forthcoming with any information until given the proper respect—at least, the respect he thought he deserved. "Clearly, you know far more about the way this castle works than we do. It is part of the great responsibilities you are entrusted with. What is it that we're missing? What is it in your wise opinion that we need to know?"

With several forceful motions, Mr. Duke walked a short circle as if he needed to gather himself before speaking. The theatrics reminded Zev of the business meetings in the East that he had been bullied into attending. There, he often listened to various managers blather on as if they controlled more power than they ever actually would—all to make a simple point that could have been explained in a single sentence. Zev braced himself for just such an onslaught of words.

"There are many paths to the kitchen," Mr. Duke began, and Zev held back an audible sigh. "Each one is a path to either a dining hall, the ballroom, or the servants' quarters. No thief would dare go down any of those. Too many chances that someone from the kitchen staff would be rushing along to a storeroom, to serve food, or to return with dirty dishes. But there is one other door. One that leads outside. After all, the raw materials need to be brought in somehow."

Lacking Zev's patience, Bellemont blurted out, "And where does that door lead?"

"It does not surprise me that you are the one who lacks manners." To Zev, he said, "If you take the time to travel directly through the kitchen, you'll see the door at the far end near the larder. That door opens to the stables and garage area."

Zev leaned back against the cool stone wall. With a sigh, he said, "Naturally. Let's go back to the stables."

CHAPTER THREE

As they dashed through the kitchen, a few members of the staff attempted to stop them. Once Mr. Duke appeared—he ran a several steps behind—the staff saw the ever-recognizable ruffles and backed away. Zev weaved around the chaotic kitchen and pushed through the back door. When they reached the stables, a relieved rush overcame him—the haycart remained. Philune had not ordered his men to remove it or dismantle it or tamper with it.

Axon, Philune, and the rest had left the area, but three guards remained. Mr. Duke waved them off, and they did not trouble Zev or Bellemont from examining the haycart.

"I do not quite understand the value of looking over this again," Mr. Duke said. "We know the thieves never brought the Shield to the cart. Besides, the two men that were waiting here are now—" Mr. Duke snapped his mouth shut. He had strolled to the other side of a cart and noticed the two charred spots where the men had burned. "Excuse me," he said, clapping a hand over his mouth and running for one of the empty horse stalls.

Bellemont snickered while Mr. Duke's lavish ballroom meal spewed out. Zev made a quick inspection of the haycart and the surrounding area. He'd seen it all before, and though he had more time to take in the situation, he did not feel any closer to a solution.

He kicked one of the wooden wheels. None of this made sense. The idea that a witch would sneak into the holding room, cast a spell to undo the alarm, pick up this large Shield, race through the hallways, into the kitchen, and out to this haycart, all during an enormous celebration in which the Shield was the centerpiece—it defied logic. Not that criminals had to be logical, but this plan did not even seem feasible.

"Which means I have it wrong."

Bellemont looked up from the back of the haycart. "What did you say?"

"If you're trying to steal a Shield as big as a man, why would you take it through the kitchen? There are too many people bustling about in that place. There are too many obstacles to slow you down from escaping."

"You are assuming that they had the brainpower and the time to organize a well-thought-out plan."

As Mr. Duke returned, Zev pointed at Bellemont. "You're right. All the evidence we have found so far suggests a desperate, ill-conceived attempt at the theft. Mr. Duke, when did Axon return with the Shield?"

Wiping his mouth with a pristine handkerchief, Mr. Duke said, "About a week ago. Ever since then, well, the castle has been in the rush of organizing this celebration."

"And where was the Shield kept until it was brought to the holding room for tonight's debut?"

"King Robion wisely kept it with him. Few people knew about it, and it remained in his private bedchamber—one of the most difficult places to gain access to in the castle. It's located near the center, well beyond the reach of most people. One would have to pass numerous guards, navigate the twists and turns of the castle halls, and in the end, would be faced with a heavy-banded door and an iron lock."

Bellemont said, "A spell could take care of all of that."

"Not without leaving behind evidence of its use. Or perhaps lack of evidence. Either way, it was deemed the most secure place to hold the Shield until tonight."

Zev thumped his foot against the side of the haycart and grinned. "This cart was stolen earlier today, the guards that I found in the storage room had been attacked today, and the Shield itself was not in an accessible location until today. Bellemont, you're right. Whether or not the culprits are intelligent, they were certainly one thing—desperate. They had a narrow timeframe in which to steal the Shield and limited time to make a plan."

Mr. Duke threw up his hands. "Then why attempt it at all? It's just a big shield."

Both Zev and Bellemont whipped around to face Mr. Duke. Zev said, "You've never heard the stories of the Shield of Taladoro?"

"Of course, I have heard the stories. But that is all they are. Stories. Myths. You're not stupid enough to believe any of the Cassun Nine would use their power to make such a thing. Not even Tiq, a goddess who loves to create, would be foolish enough to put such a powerful weapon in the hands of people. I suppose a Dacci could have sacrificed a mouthful of teeth to attempt making the Shield, but that idea requires assuming far too many factors to be reasonable. If I had a say, I would never have sent Axon on that expedition."

"But it's just a story. A myth."

"One that apparently had a seed of truth to it. And far more aggravation that it is worth."

Zev rolled his head, letting the tension in his neck crinkle with some satisfaction. As a breeze picked up, the smell of manure mixed with the thick and pleasant aroma of horses. Zev closed his eyes. If he had gone to visit his father, he would have been half-asleep in the back of an autocart, watching the countryside roll away, instead of standing in the King's stables wondering if a valuable mythic artifact had been stolen by idiots or geniuses.

Bellemont said, "Isn't it strange that these two men who self-immolated never even knew what they were hired to take away?"

"Clearly," Mr. Duke said, "if they knew, they would have either refused such a risky job or they might have stolen the Shield for themselves. Best to keep them ignorant."

Zev said, "You're right."

"There. You see?"

"Not you. Bellemont." He moved closer to the witch. "The fact that they committed suicide suggests that they knew the risks of what they were doing."

"And that they were very loyal," Bellemont said.

"To a cause, perhaps."

"Or a person."

Zev pictured the two men right before they killed themselves. They had spotted Philune, and they grew scared. Did they spot him, or did Philune make himself known? Could the presence of a single man induce others to commit suicide?

"Mr. Duke, I think it's time to visit our prisoner."

CHAPTER FOUR

M r. Duke led the way once again. Zev struggled to keep the twisting labyrinth of the castle clear in his mind. Once they were two floors down, he gave up. He would need a map.

They entered a dank area—low ceiling, dirt walls, roots poking out —and approached a large guard sitting on a small chair next to a candle. When the guard recognized Mr. Duke, he jumped to his feet and pulled off a sloppy salute.

"We must speak with the new prisoner," Mr. Duke said.

The guard rifled off a few words that sounded like groveling as he jangled a ring of keys. He grabbed a torch and headed off. Zev and Bellemont followed them down a hall with cells on either side. It reminded Zev of a wine cellar, only this one had too much cruel suffering and metal bars.

After opening one cell, the guard hustled back to his post, his keys making a ruckus all the way. Mr. Duke's contempt read clear, even in the dim conditions.

Zev pushed forward, motioning for Bellemont and Mr. Duke to wait outside the cell. "Hi, Kallot," Zev said as he entered.

Kallot sat in the corner on a mound of moldy hay. Angry bruises puffed the left side of his face. He squinted at Zev before breaking into a wide smile. "This is a surprise. Pretty brave of you to come in here. Aren't you afraid I'll break your neck?"

"Not at all."

"Why's that?"

"No profit in it. You're a hired hand in all of this. Did you even know what they were stealing?"

"Didn't know. Didn't care. Still don't know. Still don't care."

Zev strolled to the opposite corner and leaned against the damp wall. "That's why I'm not afraid of you attacking me. That and I broke your leg."

"But you think you're going to get me to tell you who hired me?"

"I wouldn't insult you that way. I won't even ask for their names."

Kallot perked up. "Really? Then what do you want?"

"I'd like to know how you planned to get to the stables. That was your job, right? Clear the hall of the real guards so the two thieves could escape in the haycart."

"My job was more important than that. Getting rid of the guards was easy. I should have taken you out, too, but I underestimated you. Those are some good fighting moves you have."

Zev thought of Axon. "I had a good teacher."

"That's for certain. Still, I should've had you. Then everything would've gone smoothly."

"If clearing the hall wasn't your only job, what else did you have to do?"

"Everything. I was the key to it all. What? You don't believe me? I'm telling you the truth. Without me, their whole plan fell apart. I mean, isn't that why you're here? If the thieves got away, you'd be out there chasing after them across the Frontier. That says to me the castle has been shut tight and you're trying to figure out who is the wolf hiding amongst the sheep." Kallot tried to grin, but his injuries morphed his features into a hideous scowl.

Zev however could grin. And he did. "Thank you. I appreciate your time."

"That's it?"

"That's all I needed." Zev pushed off the wall and exited the cell.

Though he could feel Mr. Duke's questions mounting, nobody spoke while he closed the cell door and walked back toward the stairs. Once they returned to the fresh air of the night, Zev halted and faced his team. He waited.

Mr. Duke said, "Are you going to explain that? You barely said anything to him."

"And yet, he gave us plenty."

"He did? What are you talking about?"

"Bellemont?"

His partner's eyes crinkled as she said, "You got him to admit there were only two thieves."

"When?" Mr. Duke blurted out. "What are you talking about?"

Zev said, "I specified that there were two thieves, and Kallot did not deny or correct me. He didn't hesitate, either—which would have been a sign that he considered those actions but chose to lie instead. No, he simply accepted the fact and, in doing so, confirmed it for us. He also made it clear that his part in this theft was greater than just clearing the guards."

"He's a braggart. You can't trust that."

"True, he does boast a lot, but if the only thing he was responsible for was the guards, he would have focused his bragging on how he orchestrated their capture. Notice that when I gave him the opportunity to tell us all the marvelous things he did, he pulled back. He wanted to say, but he realized that he should keep quiet. That suggests he was supposed to be more involved. In fact, I would guess that his failure to subdue me, and then getting left to the real guards, has destroyed the thieves' plans. They needed Kallot, and he wasn't there."

"Fine, fine," Mr. Duke said. "That's all quite fascinating, except it doesn't tell us who the thieves are or where to find the Shield."

"No, but it does tell me one more thing—the thieves knew they would need an extra hand."

A wood door squeaked open, and the hustling steps of a King's messenger tapped out on the stone hallway. Zev decided he hated that sound. The messenger rushed up to Mr. Duke, whispered his charge, and zipped off once Mr. Duke gave him a nod.

"Well?" Zev asked.

Mr. Duke fluffed his neck ruffle and stood taller. "His Majesty demands our immediate return to the ballroom. There's trouble."

CHAPTER FIVE

M r. Duke led the way to a back entrance which deposited them on the stage in the ballroom. The Easterner with the ostentatious mustache stood firm at the edge of the East side. With his legs wide apart and his belly pushed forward, he gesticulated wildly as he spoke.

"Your Virgin Cart is about as untouched as a whore's bed. And it's certainly large enough to hide more than one Shield."

With a disgusted shudder, Mr. Duke approached King Robion and whispered in the man's ear. The King leaned back and gazed over at Zev.

On the floor, the witch wearing the red veil paced several feet away with an arc of witches curving behind her. Though she did not speak in such a boisterous manner, her voice filled the ballroom and echoed longer than that of the mustached man. "My word is irreproachable, and I have already given it to you. The Virgin Cart does not hold the Shield of Taladoro. It is a religious vessel to us, and therefore, it shall remain closed."

"Hiding behind religion. Typical."

"And you hide behind the dead. Those coffins you cry over are much more suitable to carry away stolen shields than properly handling the dead."

"We know all about how you *honor* the dead. Chew up the corpses, crap them out, and use the droppings to cast your witchy spells. You won't desecrate our boys with your filthy hands."

Bellemont tugged on Zev's sleeve. "The one with the mustache is Lord Radugo. Prominent in both politics and business. He also is looking for a wife, and it should tell you a lot that a man of such wealth and power still has trouble finding a wife."

"And the witch?" Zev asked.

"Difficult to say for sure. After all the deaths and damage we caused in the West, Nualla had to rebuild. It's possible she's somebody new."

As they waited for the King, Zev considered walking over to Axon. She sat with Philune and Thalia—all three silent and stoic as they watched the bickering below. Zev wanted to hear her thoughts as well as ask Thalia several questions. He knew nothing about the witch, but before he could take a step, King Robion motioned toward one of his men. That gentleman stepped forward, raised a trumpet to his lips, and blew several loud notes which caused the commotion to die down enough for the King to speak.

"My honored guests, please, I have asked for your patience, and while I know it is difficult, you must trust that we're not sitting here doing nothing. An investigation is occurring." King Robion reached back and waited for Zev to approach. "I told you before that this man was my Master Solver. He has now returned to give us his first report on the progress of his inquiry. Mr. Asterling, please inform us how things look."

Zev's steps echoed loud against the hollow stage. His mouth went dry. Looking out at the crowd, he knew what they all wanted—a name. Somebody to point their fingers at. Somebody to behead or hang or punish in half-a-dozen tortuous ways. But he had nothing.

Clearing his throat, he began to outline each step he and Belle-mont had taken. The words tumbled out and he barely noticed.

Instead, his mind played through their discoveries, once again searching for a way to make it add up to something useful.

"The real problem I'm having is understanding *why*." He heard his voice cease, and an awkward silence trickled through the air. Had he spoken that last thought aloud? Glancing at the King, Zev had his answer.

Uttering a low grumble like the first cracks of a falling tree, Lord Radugo said, "I should think the *why* is obvious. It's a priceless, one-of-a-kind Shield. A person could be rich for the rest of their lives off of that. Especially a witch."

"How?" As a few scoffing laughs followed from the audience, Zev continued, "You said it yourself—this Shield is priceless. That can be a wonderful thing but not when you've stolen an object and need money. Who in this world would pay for that stolen Shield? Nobody. Nobody would want to have it because whoever gets caught holding onto the Shield is going to be executed. No amount of money would be worth this risk."

"Well then, man with the brain that King Robion thinks is so wonderful, you tell us. Why steal the Shield?"

Zev glanced back at Axon, Philune, and Thalia. His eyes then drifted to Mr. Duke, the man raised as a religious devotee—one whose only feelings toward the Shield were seen through that filter.

"Since nobody would steal the Shield for money because it would be nearly unattainable, that leaves two possibilities. First, it could be stolen for power. If the legends are to be believed, the Shield is capable of stopping entire wars. Is that not why we are all here? Isn't this a glorified peace talk? But then, if the purpose of the Shield is to create peace, why steal it when it's doing its job?"

Lord Radugo laughed. "A lot of money to be made in war."

"True. But there are less risky and less sloppy ways to go about starting conflict. For that matter, we're already on our way there without anybody's help. Proof of that is the fact that you are all here trying to avoid the very thing. Though one would find that difficult to believe based on the way you talk to each other."

"Careful," Red Veil said. "We are all here on behalf of our countries. You should not be trying to insult us."

King Robion pushed Zev aside. "There is no offense intended. Master Asterling merely pointed out the fact that we all came here to discuss peace, and that should remain our objective."

Lord Radugo said, "He also mentioned a second alternative."

Red Veil said, "I'd like to hear about that, too."

The King gestured for Zev to continue, but Zev did not want to speak. He stood at a precipice, and the drop fell into murky clouds. If he spoke what he thought—but then, he had a duty to the King and the Frontier. They counted on him to work out this problem, to help save the mere possibility of discussing peace, so who was he to hold back?

In a louder voice, he said, "The expedition. Perhaps one of the surviving members, or perhaps somebody close to one of those who did not survive—well, as terrible a thought as it may be, perhaps one of them has more involvement in this matter."

A roar of concern rushed through the crowd.

Zev did not want to look back at Axon. He could feel her hard eyes upon him. More than anything at that moment, he wanted to take her aside and ask her for the truth, but if she had a truth to tell, she would have already told him. The thieves could not be known to her—unless he greatly misjudged their bond. He hoped she understood the position he had been placed in and that he had to go where the investigation took him. Even if it meant uncovering deceit within her ranks.

With a nod from the King, the trumpeter blew several more notes to regain composure in the ballroom. Zev turned toward King Robion. "If everyone here will remain patient and calm, I believe I can get to the answer you all seek. I only need to interview those who went on the expedition." He looked out to the crowd. "Everybody who was on the expedition. Those of the East, those from the West, and those of the Frontier. Otherwise, no answer will be found."

King Robion did not hesitate. "You have the full cooperation of the Frontier. We have nothing to hide. Tell us what you need and we will make it happen."

Not wanting to be outdone, Lord Radugo said, "The East is not afraid for we are not thieves. Interview anyone of us from the expedition or not from the expedition. It doesn't matter."

With less enthusiasm, Red Veil said, "None of the true Westerners embarked on this expedition. But if you want to interview these Lost witches, so be it."

"And what if they want to talk to you?" Lord Radugo jabbed a finger in her direction. "I suppose you'll hide behind some other so-called religious belief."

"We have no reason to trust any of you, but since the alternative is most likely to be forced into searches, then we would accept this request. For now."

As the last acceptance echoed, Mr. Duke escorted Zev and Belle-mont out of the ballroom. Zev wished he had not eaten even the small nibbles from the earlier party—turmoil in his stomach only added to his growing discomfort. It did not help when Mr. Duke said, "You better know what you're doing."

PART III
THE INTERVIEWS

CHAPTER ONE

With Bellemont's help, Zev removed a wide mirror from an oversized vanity and brought the large table to the center of the guest bedroom. Mr. Duke had several men pull the bed and two dressers out of the room. Only the one large table and several chairs remained. Though the wall paintings of flowers spiraling around old statues lacked the intimidation Zev hoped to create, the room looked better than he had expected.

"Will there be anything else before we begin?" Mr. Duke said.

Zev checked over the sparse room. Moonlight shot through the windows, and he considered closing them. Using only candlelight might add to the atmosphere, but he rejected the idea—intimidation would only go so far with these people. They weren't the pampered rich and royalty that argued on the ballroom floor. These were men and women willing to forego comfort in order to travel harsh lands, searching for a mythic shield. What did they care about moody lighting or an empty room? Besides, whatever intimidation he managed to create, one look at Mr. Duke would undermine all efforts.

"A pitcher of water and some mugs, please." Zev kept his eyes off Mr. Duke but waited until he heard the man saunter off.

Bellemont rested her fists on the table. "You think there's any way we could get rid of him during the questioning?"

"Don't plan on it. He's here for the King. We must respect that."

"Must we?"

Zev chuckled. The longer Bellemont spent with him in the Frontier, the less like a Dacci witch she sounded. Part of him wondered if he would ever chance to see the smile on her face beneath the veil. Part of him wondered if he ever really wanted to.

Rolling her knuckles along the wood table, she said, "I think it would be useful if I cast a spell that would allow me to detect lies."

"Thank you, but I couldn't ask that. I don't know how many teeth you have left, but this is hardly worth the sacrifice."

"You are not asking, I am offering. It would only be one tooth. If I wanted to create a spell to force the truth out of our subjects, that would cost too many teeth. But one tooth would help guide us to the truth."

"I appreciate that. I truly do. But I am capable of figuring this out on my own. I want to make sure that if ever the time comes when I must ask you to lose a tooth on my behalf, it will be worth it. Plus, if we discover the culprit due to your spell, the Easterners would reject the truth as a fabrication of a witch, and the Dacci would reject it because you were raised by non-witches. Even the King might suspect manipulation on our part, if Mr. Duke is unconvinced. Best you let me work this out."

It sounded good to Zev, and he hoped Bellemont accepted his words at face value. To some extent, she could—he meant all of it. However, he did not fool himself. He had also refused her offer simply because he wanted the challenge. He wanted to prove that he truly deserved the title Master Solver.

The sparkle in Bellemont's eyes suggested she understood all the angles to what he said. Then she surprised him by pointing out another he had not considered. "Your father will understand."

Zev uttered a few noises before saying, "I'm not so sure."

With a final knock on the table, she said, "If I can't cast a spell for you, how can I help?"

"I'd like you to go back to the ballroom. The Lords, Ladies, royalty, and the witches will be uneasy while I perform the interviews. This process will take time. I'd like you to be paying attention and let me know what's going on there. Your knowledge of who these people are and the connections they share with each other is wasted in this room. But out in the ballroom, you may be able to detect more truth and lies than any spell cast here could ever do."

Bellemont glanced at the door. Mr. Duke's footsteps echoed down the hall. "I'll be happy to do it. Especially because I don't trust Mr. Duke. Or any of them. Having one of us in each of the key rooms is a good idea."

"Thank you."

Mr. Duke entered carrying a tray with a pitcher of water and four mugs. As he set it on the table, he said, "The kitchen staff is a bit busy at the moment, so I graciously offered to carry this in myself. But do not think I'll be serving you on a regular basis."

"I wouldn't even wish it."

Pouring himself a mug of water, Mr. Duke said, "You have your water now and your room. Is there anything else or may we get started?"

Zev said, "I think we're ready."

"Excellent. Who shall we begin with?"

The answer was clear. Zev turned to Bellemont. "When you get to the ballroom, please send Axon up here."

After Bellemont made a short bow and left, Zev set a single chair in front of the table, adjusting its distance to produce the optimal effect. He then walked around and sat. "I would like you seated when she arrives."

Mr. Duke rolled back his shoulders, lifted his chin, but did not voice his protest. He tramped around the table and sat next to Zev as if floating to the cushion required extreme care.

Zev said, "It's vital that I am the only one asking questions. How the person responds is every bit as important as what they say. If you go barging in with your own questions, you could easily disrupt what I'm looking for."

"And what are you looking for?"

"The truth, of course."

"I must be allowed to ask my questions. After all, I am a representative of the King. You are merely his servant."

Zev poured a mug full of water as he thought. "If you have any questions, write them down and hand me the paper. I will do my best to see that they get asked."

"How am I to do that without paper or a writing implement?"

"I suggest you go find some quickly. Because once Axon is in that seat, you are not to get up from the table. Whoever we are talking to must feel the intensity of our inquiry. You understand?"

Mr. Duke tapped one finger against the table rapidly. Zev wondered if the man was going to put his own vanity above orders from the King. At length, Mr. Duke made the smart choice—he left the room in search of paper.

Without warning, Zev found himself alone. He closed his eyes and tried to sort out the mash of thoughts layered in his head. He could still see the letter from his brother. He could still feel the pressure from the King for answers. Above all else, he felt a disorienting blend of pride and discomfort. He would be lying if he denied that the King's trust in him filled his heart. However, a strong part of him wanted nothing more than to be back at his office in Fernbund. Solving cases about stolen livestock and missing desserts did not have a lot of sparkle, but those were the kinds of cases he knew he could find an answer to before the end of the day. And if by chance he failed, the fate of three countries and countless lives did not fall at his feet.

The door opened and Mr. Duke ushered in Axon. He carried a paper and an old quill as if these were the implements he had desired all along. Making a show of arranging his papers on the table, he gestured towards the open seat.

Axon settled in with her back straight and her head held firm like a well-bred lady always cognizant of her manners. Here was the woman raised to be a Lady of the Court. With her dark cheeks reflecting the candlelight like a perfect portrait, Zev wondered where the fierce warrior hid. Her posture appeared to have the desired effect upon Mr. Duke, though. He grinned and eased in his chair.

"Would you like some water?" Zev asked.

She shook her head. "No, thank you, sir."

"Please, there's no need to be so formal. You and I have been through a lot together. I simply need to understand what happened during your journey that may have brought us to this point."

Axon snorted, letting a glimpse of the woman Zev knew slip through. Leaning forward, one hand on her knee, she said, "You and I do not have a long history. We were thrown together out of necessity. I respect you and all you did to help the Frontier, but our time together does not mean that I can trust your interests in this matter."

Mr. Duke bristled, and Zev put up his hand to stop the pompous fool from speaking. Zev sat back and crossed his arms, deliberately sending mixed signals. Adding a touch of weakness to his voice, a bit of deference to a lady, he said, "You are right. In fact, I feel rather foolish asking you any questions. But, unfortunately, the King has required me to do so. Perhaps if you tell us in your own words, this will be easier. And I will do my best not to interfere."

Axon hesitated. She licked her lips and her brow furrowed as she glanced about the room. Finally, she pointed to the pitcher of water. "I'll have a drink before I begin."

"Help yourself."

WITNESS ACCOUNT OF
AXON COPONIV

In order to understand everything that happened and the choices that were made, you must understand that I am not who you think I am. Like so many others in the court, Mr. Duke, you assume that all of my actions are in support of King Robion. I respect King Robion. It has been my experience that the decisions he makes are for the well-being of not only his people, but for all people—even those in the East and the West and those lands yet to be discovered. It is admirable but perhaps a bit unrealistic.

The truth is that my loyalty is not to any king but to the Frontier itself. I love my country. It has given me great opportunities, an amazing and fulfilling life, and I ask you to keep my perspective in mind as you hear about our journey.

Axon adjusted in her seat, sitting taller as she leveled her attention forward.

The whole thing started when a messenger arrived with word that the King had called upon us—myself and Pilot. I had been observing Pilot give the daily orders to the Royal Guard. King Robion had assigned him the position of Captain of the Guard for many reasons. I suppose it was partly due to our success in the West, but also because Pilot had grown tired of life in the castle. He was a born wanderer. He needed a reason to stay, and the King wisely provided him with one.

I remember thinking how beautiful the day was—sunny, warm, perfect training weather. I even remember that as we headed into the castle, I offered a quick prayer to Qareck for gracing us with such a day. Little did I know.

Pilot and I were taken to the King's favorite meeting room—you know the one—plain, unadorned room with a simple wooden table and chairs. Nothing special. Always the gracious host, he had a small tray of meat and cheese set out for us though nobody touched the food. I stared at that tray. I had skipped breakfast that morning for some reason, and I felt the pangs of hunger. But I'm glad I did not eat. What he told us would've turned my stomach.

Zev could feel Mr. Duke's rising agitation. The man wanted to get to the point fast. Hopefully, his urgency would not pressure Axon. Zev still remembered this woman well. She was a warrior, through and through. Any attempt to rush her would only cause a defensive, cold wall to appear. She would stop talking and only answer direct questions. Like a good fighter— holding position and letting the enemy commit to an action so that she could counter with control.

You see, the King jumped right into what he had to say, beginning with the admission that the Frontier had financed numerous spies to infiltrate the East. No matter how distasteful, the need for spies is, of course, understandable in times of war. We must learn all we can about our enemies. But the East are not our enemies. At least, I did not think so.

"The East have long been—" Mr. Duke started, and Zev flashed up his hand. He did not speak a word, but Mr. Duke went silent.

Axon paused, watching between the men, until Zev gestured her way.

I offered a quick prayer to Sazieck and asked the King to continue. These spies had noticed a lot of strange activity in the largest Eastern city, Balica. Supplies were amassed, large sums of money transferred hands, and strong, able-bodied men were being gathered. I expected for King Robion to tell me that the East planned an invasion and that we needed to prepare. In fact, as he spoke, I started to put together ideas to address possible supply issues depending on how much of the border we had to fight over. You can't begin to imagine how I felt when I learned that the spies were convinced the East had formed an expedition to head north for the Shield of Taladoro.

Pilot laughed. He snorted and giggled and outright laughed. I remember him saying that the Shield was nothing but a myth and that if the East wanted to waste its money and resources on foolish whims, all the better for us. King Robion sat at the head of the table with his fingers laced and an amused grin on his face.

He said he agreed. The whole thing sounded ridiculous. Just a waste of time and money. Possibly lives, too.

"But we are all sitting here," I said, and I can tell you that my stomach twisted up again at that moment. "We are sitting here because you summoned us."

And then the King's grin dropped. His spies told him that members in the expedition had uncovered clues to finding the Shield. Old books long forgotten or maps tucked away someplace meant to be safe—things lost for ages. Yet now, the East had these clues in their possession, and they were actively preparing to find it.

He tasked us to form a competing expedition, one with a different purpose. We would head north and attempt to intercept the Eastern group. Our mission was twofold—first, and most important, we were to stop the Eastern group from progressing. We were to steal their maps or books or however they discovered where to search. We were to hinder their party and force an end to their journey. If we were lucky, if we managed to get hold of their information and could use it, then as a second part of our mission, we were to find the Shield ourselves.

I agreed to the mission right away. Not because I believed in the Shield's great power but because the Easterners did. If there was a Shield—even just a regular hunk of metal that became revered over the centuries—then we had to stop the East from gaining it. There's a lot of power in a symbol, and the Shield of Taladoro could have become a great symbol. So, I understood why King Robion and the Frontier required our help.

However, Pilot hesitated.

Zev said, "I'll get Pilot's story in just a moment. He can pick up where you leave off. But tell me, why did you really accept? It doesn't seem like an honorable mission, more of an assassin's mission. And unless you've changed significantly, you would not have accepted this request, even from a king."

No... I guess I wouldn't. I suppose I didn't see much choice in the matter. Because I saw the other side of it, too. The legends of the Shield of Taladoro told of its unbridled power. It was supposedly a weapon of peace, of defense. The way it created that peace, however, oftentimes proved violent. Very violent.

The East are not our enemies, yet I learned at that moment that we have spies in their lands. I thought it safe to assume that they had spies in our lands, as well. With that being true, the East's inevitable attack upon the Frontier would happen sooner than I ever thought realistic.

If they succeeded in finding this Shield, and if it actually had its mythic powers, they would be far more deadly to our people. They wouldn't just have a rallying symbol. They'd have a real weapon. Something that I doubt even the godwalkers could defeat. I recognized all of that, all the possibilities, so the decision was easy. I had no desire to steal anything from the Eastern group or kill any of them, but I had no fear of doing so, either. To protect the Frontier, no fear at all.

"That's quite an analysis."

I've learned a lot watching your brain at work.

Zev grinned. "We'll be getting a lot of details from the others, but I imagine you had some tough times during your journey. After all, no expedition into unknown lands goes smoothly all the time."

We had our share of dangers.

"Were you ever injured? Any cuts or wounds on your arms?"

Sure. I had bruises and some cuts. They're all pretty much healed by now.

"Of course. Thank you," Zev said. "We may ask you some more questions later, but for now, please return to the ballroom and have Pilot sent in."

Pilot? But there's so much more to tell you—the entire journey.

"We'll get to all of that. But I think there's more to be gained from listening to many views on these moments. Thank you, Ms. Coponiv."

Then, I have a request.

She watched Mr. Duke and Zev for any sign of weakness or, at least, intention. But they were both good at presenting a blank slate—though for different reasons.

I would like to remain in the room—at least, for specific interviews. Sitting around doing nothing will only drive me crazy. I need to be out here helping. I need to find the thief who has ruined the hard work of so many. And I need to make sure that those of the East and the West testify honestly to you.

"That's a very odd request."

This is an odd situation.

"I'm sorry, but your presence will influence the others."

Isn't that a good thing? When they see me, they'll know they can't lie because I'll catch them. Having me in the room is like casting a spell that forces the truth.

Mr. Duke said, "Unless you are one of the thieves. Then you'll be protecting the lies."

Honestly, Mr. Duke, do you believe that? I've been working for the King for years now. I should think after all this time that you would have a good understanding of whether you can trust me or not. And Zev knows me well, too. We faced our own deaths together. Doesn't get any closer.

"But what will the other leaders say when they see you? Philune and Thalia will want a seat in the room, too."

Nobody's objected to you being here—the sole individual aside from Zev allowed to see these interviews is also from the Frontier. Shouldn't you have a Dacci witch in here and one of the Easterners?

But they haven't insisted on that. King Robion's reputation means that they'll trust the Frontier. At least, for the moment.

Zev bounced the idea around, causing his head to wobble as he considered the possibilities. He didn't really agree with most of her argument; however, he was under a lot of pressure to solve this matter as fast as possible. Perhaps having her in the room would create reactions that he would otherwise miss. And though it would an unorthodox step, he was the one writing the book on how to do all of this anyway. Who could say? Maybe it would work out in his favor and he could write a few pages on the value of keeping interviews more open. At length, he said, "Okay. We'll try it out for the next interview."

Mr. Duke bristled. "I don't think that's—"

"Perhaps, with one of the main leaders of the expedition on hand, it'll save us a lot of research and questions in the wrong direction. If it turns out to be a bad idea, then Ms. Coponiv will leave without protest."

Mr. Duke clamped his mouth as his skin reddened around his ruffles.

Agreed. And I promise, I'll only observe. I won't interfere. Thank you.

WITNESS ACCOUNT OF
PILOT

Bounding into the room with a bright smile and a nod for every member of the table, Pilot sat, cracked his knuckles, and leaned back. Zev understood. Pilot had complete respect for the process and the seriousness of the crime they investigated, yet he often covered his fear with overexuberance. At least, that was the man Zev remembered.

"I'd like you to tell us about the events from after you were assigned the mission. In your own words, how did you and Axon find the Eastern group, and what did you do after that?" Zev said.

Pilot pushed his chair back on two legs and gave a moment of thought before he spoke.

Well now, you told me to pick two of my best men for the job.

"Please, don't address Axon directly. Tell your story to me."

Sure. Right. Well, Axon said I should pick two of my best men for this. She didn't think we should have a large group since we needed to move quickly and not being seen was part of the deal. I agreed. I chose Kapa and Feddi. They were good men, followed orders well, and devoted to King and country.

"Were?" Zev asked.

They didn't make it. Expect a lot of that. The Easterners didn't bring coffins here for nothing.

Anyway, by the time we were prepared to leave, it was already late-midday. We headed out on horseback. Considering the terrain we were hitting, autocarts would never have endured. Probably would have gotten stuck on the rocky cliffs. And that's only the start of it. The known lands to the north are inhospitable, at best. Brutal, cold temperatures; harsh, difficult terrain; little to eat except for tree nuts and, if you're very lucky, small game. But once you get beyond the Darkened Ridges, that's where things really get hard because nobody knows what's up there. The few brave fools who tried to explore that area in the past—they never returned. Mostly, we had only old fables and local stories of ghosts and such. Nothing one could believe. We really had no idea what we were going into.

As for tracking down the Easterners—those fellows who'd been spying for us, they gave us the initial direction north and a few spots that the Easterners planned to camp. So, we went off that. I knew the spies might have been working from rumors, or if we were unlucky, they had been discovered and the Easterners were feeding our men lies. I suppose we could have been riding into a trap. But I trusted Axon—I still trust her—and that was all the worry I would have.

Took us a few days to get out to the first location that the spies told us about. Boring days really. Just riding a horse. Even if I didn't have such a superior sense of direction, I'd certainly know I was going north. It got awful cold, awful fast. Anyway, this marker

—Lake Romi—we reached it and let the horses rest while we checked around. Kapa found signs that the Easterners had come through.

Not to take anything away from the man, may Pralma watch over his soul, but finding signs was not going to be difficult. These Easterners were not trying to hide their path. My guess is they thought they were the only ones around and had nothing to fear. That made me happy.

For one thing, it all meant the spies were right. No traps. No ambush. The Easterners had no idea we tracked them.

It also meant I could ease a little. I can enjoy travel. I can enjoy a good bit of adventure. But I don't have a death wish. Wiq can wait his godly turn to take me. And as far as I could see, those Easterners were going to be easy to swipe a map from when they couldn't even be bothered to cover their tracks.

So, we started following them.

Turned out they were a couple days ahead of us. But we were only four on horseback. They were a much bigger group, carrying a lot more equipment. We made up the distance fast. We had traveled far north and reached the side of Mount Sputra—too steep to climb, but you can get around it fairly easily, if you don't mind cold drizzle and the occasional heavy snow.

The trail we followed kept weaving between the old forest and the rocky, snowy edges of the mountain. You understand? They had already reached a point where they didn't know the land. That's why they were going back and forth. They wanted to stay in the forest for safety, but they had to keep popping out to see when they could climb over the mountain. So, they didn't know they were never climbing that mountain.

Anyway, a day later, we finally got close enough that we were able to sneak upon the edge of the camp. Night had fallen and a cool breeze had picked up.

Pilot cocked his head to check that the door was closed.

Between all of us, these Easterners were complete idiots. Axon can vouch for that. I'm shocked that they had survived at all.

Their tents were these garish, oversized, miniature homes. Very colorful. With frilly lacy things around the edges that served no purpose but decoration. They had three different campfires going which lit up their location as far as one could see. From my count, there were at least ten people, not including servants that kept scurrying between the tents like little gezzits pecking for a nibble here or there. And to top off all this nonsense, they had three men with instruments making music.

You understand?

They brought entertainment. I guess to pass the time until they had to get up the next morning. About the only thing that made sense was that I could see Philune, Vost, and Wrest cleaning their rifles. Of course, I didn't know who they were at the time, but that's who they were. I'll tell you this—if not for the East's weapons, I don't think they would be much of a threat to us at all.

Anyway, one of these tents was a touch bigger than the others and a little bit more elaborate. Everything about it said this is where the important person is—eventually, we would know it belonged to Philune. At that moment, though, all we knew is that's where the items we needed to steal would be. Now, if you're going to have a big tent that's screaming *this is where the important stuff is,* and you have a big loud camp like this, the sensible thing to do is stick that tent in the middle and surround it by the other tents. But, as I think I've made clear, these Easterners are not sensible people. This tent was right up against the edge of the woods.

So, Axon decided we would wait for everybody to go to sleep and the fires to die down, and then we'd sneak right up to the backside of the tent, cut open a hole, walk in, and take what we needed. I offered to do that job while Axon, Kapa, and Feddi staked out positions on the other side of the camp. If they heard a commotion like I was in trouble or saw I might get caught, they would start attacking which would bring everybody to the opposite side of me. I would be able to escape, provided I could deal with whatever situation I was in.

"But that didn't happen, did it?" Zev asked.

No, it didn't. How did you know?

"If you had succeeded in any of that plan, you wouldn't have been sitting up on stage with Philune this evening."

You're right about that. That guy would not forgive his buttons if one of them accidentally fell off. He can be a bit of a prissy coward, but when he gets mad, duck your head. That man has a vicious mean streak.

I probably would've found that out hard if we had gone through with the plan. But see, right about the time I was getting ready to head for that tent and steal that map, Axon stopped me. She listened closely to the trees and peered into the darkness. I knew the look on her face —seen it many times. She sensed trouble.

She heard a couple creatures walking around in the woods. Said they were large. Dangerous. I assumed she meant dangerous to us. That they were stalking us. But that wasn't the case.

Shouldn't have surprised me. We weren't the ones throwing up a big sign saying *hey, if you're hungry, here's the easy pickings.*

I'll admit to this next thing freely—I suggested to Axon that we sit back and let whatever was in the woods attack the camp. If we were lucky, the creatures would kill everybody there and we could walk in and take the map and books and stuff in the morning. No trouble at all for us and no risk, either. Worst case, they all start fighting, and we have to slip in during the battle. But Axon is wiser than me and more compassionate.

I remember her exact words. She said, "These Easterners are clearly just a bunch of rich boys who don't understand the wild at all. We can't let idiots die like that."

I said that the Easterners wouldn't hesitate to let us die that way.

She looked right into my eyes and said, "We have to be better."

She was right. Not only because of all the obvious moral arguments, but because we needed them. Without Axon making that decision at that moment, we would never have found the Shield. I didn't know that at the time. So, while I sat there digesting everything she had said, she snapped her fingers at Kapa and Feddi. They jumped into action, and as she charged toward the camp, they followed. Me—I had to hustle to catch up.

CHAPTER TWO

Z ev rose from the table, walked to the door, and opened it. "Thank you for your time, Pilot. We'll probably call upon you again before the evening is out."

Pilot and Axon shared a confused look. Axon made a slight shrug, one that perhaps Zev had not been meant to see.

"Okay," Pilot said, slapping his knees as he stood. "But I can tell you the rest of the story."

"That won't be necessary. Just yet." Zev smiled. As Pilot reached the door, Zev added, "Oh, one last question—how badly were you injured on this expedition?"

"You mean in the animal attack I was about to tell you about?"

"Overall. Including everything, even the things you didn't get a chance to tell me about."

"I took my share."

"No broken bones?"

"Nothing like that. I had a nasty cut on my arm."

"May I see it?"

Pilot rolled back his sleeve to reveal a lengthy scar along his forearm. The scab had yet to peel off. "Itches all the time."

Zev stepped aside. "If you would please let Philune know that we need to see him next, thank you."

After Pilot left, Axon jumped to her feet. "I don't understand anything you're doing. If you want to know what happened, let me tell you. Or let Pilot. Why are you having us tell you only a small portion?"

Mr. Duke chuckled and tapped the side of his head. "He's not so crazy. I see through you, Mr. Asterling. Very clever." Placing a hand on Axon's elbow, Mr. Duke said, "You see, he is trying to keep all of you off balance. Trying to provoke reactions. When you're sitting in that chair, you don't know how much of the story you're going to get to tell which means you can't fabricate too much—after all, you don't know who's coming in next and what they'll say. And for those outside waiting, all they have is more confusion. They have the worry of not knowing if or when they'll be called, what they'll be asked, and now that Pilot is going back to the ballroom, they'll ask him what happened. His answer will only worry them more."

"Or," Zev said, "perhaps I just needed a break." He stretched his arms and stepped into the hall.

Axon came up beside him. They leaned against the wall and stared forward at a portrait of a beautiful black and white stallion. Zev thought back to when they rode through the Feral Lands on horseback. With Axon at his side, and Pilot and Bellemont in the group—as terrifying as the whole experience had been, now that it lay years in the past, he remembered it with both fondness and fright as if those two emotions could lace together like fingers.

"You're right, you know. This entire process would be far easier if I could have you tell me the whole story," he said. "There's nobody I want to trust more."

"Then why not let me?"

"Because you're holding something back. I'm sure you have a good reason, or at least, a reason you think is good, but that doesn't make my job easier. And until that stops, I can't discern truth from fiction with you."

"Why would you think I'm lying? What have I done?"

"I didn't say you were lying. I hope you aren't." Zev considered several approaches, but if he wanted her to tell the truth, then he figured he should do the same. "What you did was nothing. But I've been watching you—you and Philune and Thalia. During all the arguing and fear and concern over this stolen Shield, the three of you sat on that stage and simply watched."

"That's not true. Philune and I hurried to the stables. You were there, you saw us."

"But I also saw you not reacting to the stolen Shield." He put up his hand to stop her from objecting. "I understand that when it comes to the political dance I don't know enough. Perhaps the King ordered you to stay emotionless. Perhaps it was important for the three of you to show a united front as a way to calm the panic. I don't know the details. What I do know is that even if everything you have done so far is innocent of suspicion, you are still holding something back from me. Until I know what that is, I can't rely solely on your version of the story. I'm sorry."

Axon patted his shoulder as she turned back toward the room. "I understand."

Any other response would have pleased him. She should have been angry, offended, objecting. Her sense of right always guided her, and he wanted to see that flash of fire that would say he should never dare question her honesty. But calm acceptance—that simply confirmed his suspicions. She knew more than she would willingly tell.

Zev heard a scuffing from the end of the hall. Somebody stood just around the corner. He expected his pulse to race—somebody watched him—but instead, he felt tired of such ineptness. Mr. Duke already spied on him in a direct, overt manner, and he worked for the Frontier. With the East and West stuck in the ballroom, there surely would be others watching.

Still, controlling the flow of information was vital. Mr. Duke had been correct when he said that part of Zev's approach involved keeping the interviewees off-balance. If somebody at the end of the hall reported back to those in the ballroom, Zev might lose his advantage.

Pushing off the wall, he headed down the hall, but Bellemont's careful steps approached from behind.

"What's wrong?" he asked as he turned toward her.

Though she still looked prim, proper, and beautiful in her peach sundress, her brow revealed growing tension. "The groups have segregated within the ballroom."

"They were like that when we arrived, and everybody was happy enough."

"Before, they were separated but willing to share the same room. They were willing to listen to the King. They were all there to reach across to the other side. Now, a thin chasm runs straight down the middle of the ballroom, and the Frontier people keep pushing closer and closer to the stage. Instead of a mass of uncomfortable people unsure of how to deal with each other, they have broken off into three separate camps, each eyeing the other."

"They were always like that. This is nothing more than an excuse to be blatant about it."

"You don't understand. In politics, as long as everybody is willing to pretend that they get along, progress can be made. But when they are openly hostile, that's when things can turn ugly."

Zev glanced down the hall, then turned back to the interview room. "I suppose you're trying to tell me that I better move faster with these interviews."

"That's the other thing. Philune is not coming."

"He doesn't have a choice. Unless he's trying to blow everything up?"

"He said he's willing to come later, but right now he's trying to stop his group from getting more aggressive. Lord Radugo—the one with the mustache—he's a political opportunist, and this moment is rife with opportunity."

"Fine. But please make sure Philune understands that he is coming in here at some point."

"I will tell him, but I think he already knows. And he is sending in one of the other Easterners from the expedition. A man named Vost."

"Thank you," Zev said and returned to the interview room.

It did not take long before the door opened and Vost entered. Outside of the crowded party, Zev took the time to observe the man. He had sharp features, and the way his eyes evaluated each person sitting behind the table, he clearly had a sharp mind, too.

As he sat, his focus tapered on Axon. "Why are you here?"

Axon stiffened, but Zev said, "I've asked her to sit in on these interviews. She brings a unique perspective and is someone I've fought side-by-side with. Unless you have evidence that suggests she stole the Shield?"

"Her? No. Axon is many things I do not like, but a thief is not one."

Axon squirmed in her chair. Zev wondered if Vost knew the truth —that Axon had come to steal their map, to thwart their expedition.

"Well, I suppose I must accept this," Vost said, clearing his throat. "On behalf of Philune and all representatives of the East, I apologize that I am a humble replacement for the time. I trust you understand that this is a highly unusual situation, and we must all be a bit flexible as we navigate through it."

"Well spoken," Mr. Duke said. "It's good to see that some members of the East still understand true diplomacy."

Zev could feel Axon stiffen, and he imagined her fingers clawed into her knees to prevent attacking Mr. Duke. He smirked.

"My name is Igrasiuslomata Vost, but that's quite a mouthful. Most people call me Vost. And before we begin, I have to say, Zev, that it is charming to see how things turned out for you."

Zev's muscles tensed. "Have we met before—that is, before Lady Jos introduced us earlier?"

"I would be surprised if you recalled—I didn't, at first—but then, Lady Jos only introduced you by your first name. When the King put our attention on you and revealed you were an Asterling, it all snapped together in my head. We actually attended school together for a short period. First Form, I was nine years old, you were ten. A year later, you left for a private academy, I believe."

"First Form—there must have been nearly a thousand students in that school. How could you know who I was?"

Vost crossed his legs and grinned. "The rumor is you don't like to admit it, but let's be honest—the Asterling name has always been well-regarded. Everybody in that school knew who you were. As well as your esteemed brother, Marcel. But you developed quite a reputation —rebellious and rule-breaking. A naughty child, they would say. When you left the East to go farm in the Frontier—well, that made a bigger stir. Everybody talked about it. As a result, it is a bit of an honor to meet you. Again." Vost glanced around the room. "Though I would have preferred other circumstances."

Mr. Duke said, "So would we. Do you need anything to drink or shall we begin?"

Placing his hands in his lap, Vost said, "I am ready whenever you are."

Zev noticed a bit of white flash beneath the man's cuff. "Would you mind pulling back your sleeve?"

"Oh, this?" Vost slid his sleeve up to reveal a bandage.

"How did that happen?"

With casual confusion, he said, "Isn't that why I'm here? I'm supposed to tell you about my experiences on the expedition—which would include how I got this injury. It's mostly healed, but a bit unsightly for such an auspicious occasion, so I wrapped it up. Wouldn't want to offend the delicate sensibilities of the Ladies and even some Lords."

"Please, then," Zev said." Continue."

WITNESS ACCOUNT OF
VOST WELLOWS

Not quite sure where to begin. There is a lot of material to cover. I suppose I shall start with where it began for me, if that is okay.

You see, Philune and his backers had already begun preparing for the expedition long before I was contacted. After you and I parted ways from First Form, I went through the usual routes of education culminating in a rather bland graduation with few prospects. Not that I was not desired by any, but I was not of the fortunate ones who seemed to have job offers lining up as well as political ones. I did, however, chance upon an internship with the Baxtery Corporation.

Zev leaned toward Axon and Mr. Duke and whispered, "An internship is much like an apprenticeship here in the Frontier—though not as long and they don't give you a place to live."

Mr. Duke snorted as he turned his head away. "Of course, I know that."

"Please, continue," Zev said. "You took an internship with the Baxtery Corporation?"

I did. They are a prestigious firm that represents both public and private interests. The promise of good pay and plenty of opportunity for greater achievements is what we all seek.

Again, Mr. Duke snorted and made little effort to hide his words. "Not everyone."

Philune—you probably only know him by his first name for that is how he prefers to be known. He's like you in that regard, though I believe his reasons had nothing to do with rejecting his family and everything to do with making a name for himself first. You may not be aware of it, but he is Philune Baxtery. His family helped found the Corporation. And that is how it came to be that I was asked to partake in the expedition.

"Why you specifically?" Zev asked.

Not me, specifically. No. Rather, Philune posted an opportunity to join him and a select few on an unnamed expedition that promised pay of triple what I was currently receiving as well as the possibilities of great promotion in the future. I have no wife, no children, nothing to hold me back and plenty of desire for the things Philune had promised. So, I applied for the position, and I received it. Along with a dozen others, including Wrest.

I must admit that once we learned of the goal of our expedition, the whole thing seemed rather ridiculous. The idea that we were going to travel north, beyond Mount Sputra, beyond the Darkened Ridges, and into lands none had ever explored—well, it seemed ludicrous. And to do it all for an object that might not even exist? The whole thing looked mad. Especially when we learned what drove Philune to follow this path. An old book, a fragment of map, and a visit from a Seer.

Oh, I see on your face that you did not know that little bit. Not even you, Axon? Philune never told you that part?

Zev said, "A Seer? Have things changed so much since I left the East? Because I was raised to believe that there were no gods or goddesses, no people who could peer into the will of the universe."

Just because the government wants you to believe something, does not prevent your parents teaching you otherwise. The Baxtery family was raised in the Cassunite tradition. It goes back very far—long before the Frontier existed. And while the influence of the Nine on the East has diminished significantly, it has not disappeared. You call them Shul, but the Baxterys subscribe to the older term of Seer.

At the initial meeting where Philune explained the journey we were going to partake in, he also presented a rather truthful discussion on the more mystical aspects of his discovery. He did not want any of us taking on such risks without knowing the whats and whys.

As Philune relates the tale, this particular Seer sought him out. Actually came right to Philune's door and presented himself as having received a vision that he had to act upon. Under most normal circumstances, Philune would have disregarded the man. This time, however, the Seer provided details as to where Philune could find the book that contained a key to translating certain maps held by scholars at the University.

Philune told us that he did not believe any of this at the time. That is, until the Seer related a story that occurred in Philune's youth, a story only Philune knew, one that he had never shared with anyone and did not involve anyone but himself. Before you ask, I do not know the story. He refused to tell us. But this Seer knew the details, and you could see on Philune's face—even just as he recalled the moment—that it unsteadied him. It changed everything.

He followed the Seer's instructions, found the book, translated the maps, and well, here we are. I suddenly found myself in a long line of individuals hauling equipment toward the Darkened Ridges. My friend, Wrest, also managed to secure a spot on the expedition.

All of it went pretty smoothly, at first. Not very exciting, just trekking through the woods. The air grew colder. The ground rockier. We knew eventually we would have to cross quite difficult terrain, but those first days were pleasant enough.

I think I first recognized Philune's shortcomings when we neared the base of Mount Sputra. The maps became vague at this point, or the translations were poorly done, but whatever the case, Philune clearly did not have a strong grasp of where to go. We would spend hours hiking along the tree line only to stop for hours more while he attempted to climb up part of the mountain. When that inevitably failed, he would return to us and we would continue on in search of a way over. Of course, I realized that no matter what, we would eventually come around the side but that would take days. At least.

"How long were you continuing this pattern before you met Axon and her people?"

That very night. We had set up camp like usual, and it looked to be another serene evening with which to regain our strength for the coming day. I had no interest in drinking or chattering all night long as some of the men seemed to enjoy. Instead, I slipped into my tent and curled up for the night. Rest was all I required. That and a good glass of wine.

I must admit that while I have no fondness for formal gatherings like this evening—all the pomp and fake smiles and pointless banter of people unwilling to take any risk—I do love some of the comforts that come with it all. Never underestimate the power of a quality wine.

Anyway, I can't tell you when the attack had begun because I had fallen asleep. But when the growls and cries reached my ears, I jolted awake. Grabbing my rifle, I burst out of the tent, and I will never forget that sight. Four burly beasts with tusks growing from the bottom jaw and equally thick horns poking out from the top of their snouts. Rock-like muscles that rippled and a thin brown-haired hide. They stood like men, but they had far more numerous arms. Their main pair operated like yours and mine, but they had smaller arms below. Some had thick curved claws, perhaps good for digging. And then there were the smallest two arms which ended not in hands but in knife-sharp nails. Those were the most deadly. This creature could run up to you, grab you by the shoulders with its manlike hands, and the lower small arms jabbed in and out of your gut, spilling your innards all over the ground.

In the seconds that I stood there I saw four men die. I lifted my weapon and pulled off a shot. The bullet struck one of these creatures in the back shoulder. It cried out, and I have never heard such a horrendous sound. Despite this creature's obvious pain, it continued its assaults. In seconds, I saw myself, Philune, Wrest, Tagge, and Sekat standing. And that was it. Everywhere else I saw bleeding men. Dead men.

It happened so fast. One shot was all I managed. Two of the creatures pressed closer on us. The other two creatures had begun to feast on the dead. As I struggled to reload my weapon, I heard the thunder of horse hooves approaching.

Vost stared at Axon, a shimmer in his eyes.

If only you had come sooner. No, don't say anything. I know you came as fast as possible. And I know I have you to thank for saving my life.

You see, Mr. Astlering, Axon and her three men roared in. She wielded an amazing blade of water that dripped glowing energy as she sliced through these creatures.

Where Pilot or any man had to attack and parry, Axon's blade simply dismembered those creatures with a touch.

Their arrival created such a distraction that my dear friend, Wrest, thought he had an opportunity. In a moment of courage, bravery, and quite honestly, stupidity, he rushed the nearest creature. He should never have moved. He'd still be alive. Attuned to its surroundings in ways we could never achieve, the creature swiftly lowered its head and skewered Wrest on its horns.

And as fast as I have said all that, it was over even faster. Only four of us from the East had survived that assault. Even the servants had perished. I remember staring at Axon and her group, and none of us could understand what had happened.

Not sure how long we continued to stare at Axon with dumb-founded, gaping jaws, but she quickly took control of the situation. She ordered us to douse two of the three campfires and get tools together so that we could bury the dead. At first, I thought this was a great show of respect. However, I fast realized it was all practical measures. You see, Axon explained to us that the creatures were called bowbacks, and that they were preparing to hibernate for the next several months. In preparation, they gorged on as much meat as they could find. We were simply an irresistible target.

We started digging the graves—for us, a way to bury our friends; for the rest, a way to prevent more of these bowbacks from coming upon us. Axon said they would be able to smell the fresh kills several mountains over.

While we worked, we noticed Philune's less than gracious welcome. I suppose I understood it—in a matter of seconds, Axon had arrived and usurped his leadership. But I was still shaken by the attack, the loss of a friend, and the fact that we were so ill-prepared for this expedition. Philune made it clear to us through whispered words that we would not be turning back. Not without the Shield.

And then Pilot perked up. He overheard Philune and mentioned that their group also sought the Shield. Well, next thing anybody knew, Philune and Axon were in a heated argument.

Vost stopped talking as eyes settled on Axon once again.

"And what was said during this argument?" Zev asked.

Vost shrugged. "Once it was clear they were not happy with each other, the two of them took their fight privately into Philune's tent. We could hear the tone but not the words. You'll have to ask them."

Zev sat forward and gestured toward the door. "Then I thank you for your time. You may go back to the ballroom."

FURTHER WITNESS ACCOUNT OF
AXON COPONIV

Before this gets twisted any further, allow me to explain what actually happened.

Mr. Duke flapped a hand at the empty interviewee chair. "It's been made quite clear. You and your team went in and saved the lives of these Easterners. They owe you a debt of gratitude, at the least. Then you had an argument with Philune. It is to be expected. Nobody wishes to give up their power in any situation, yet you deserved to be the leader of that group. No need to explain further. We support you."

While I appreciate your words, Zev does not necessarily agree with you. Isn't that right, Zev? I can read a face, too, and I see on yours that you're more interested in that argument in the tent than you're letting on.

"If you have something to say," Zev said, "I'm happy to hear you out."

I...that is...you're making this so difficult. We argued because Philune was determined to continue on his journey. Vost and the others were defeated. They all wanted to go home. It was that simple. He had to turn back, yet he would not agree to do so.

Then when he realized that I wanted to take the book and map from him so that my people could retrieve the Shield, he lost all sense of decorum and proportion. He screamed and howled and moaned about all the injustices he had faced in his life, about how he was feared by his men because he punished them when they deserved it, how he had a reputation for torture, how—I can't even remember all the bizarre things that spewed out of his mouth. He wouldn't stop rambling, so I tuned out a lot of what he had to say.

Pilot came in, thankfully. To make sure he gets full credit for what he did, it was Pilot who saved the entire mission. He entered that tent all full of smiles and generous laughter and, well, you know Pilot. He has a way about him that can relax any situation.

He calmed the two of us down—which was good because I had started thinking the best route forward involved taking my Water Blade and killing the rest of the Easterners. Pilot listened to our gripes and suggested that we work together. The Easterners had the knowledge to find the Shield, but they could never survive without our knowledge of the wild, of survival. I won't say Philune and I were happy about the compromise, but I will give the man this much praise —he had the sense to listen to Pilot.

We spent the next several hours burying the dead and re-setting the camp in a more strategic manner with a proper rotation put in place for night guard. But I'll tell you—I could have been the guard the entire night. Didn't sleep for a single moment. Every noise made in the camp perked my ears. I wondered who made the noise, why, what they were doing, and if that noise had attracted more unwanted attention.

By the morning, I felt exhausted. I did my best to hide it, and we headed out.

Despite Philune's protests, we left most of the ridiculous supplies behind. But again, I'm willing to admit that they had brought many useful items, especially their firearms, which we made sure to pack on our horses. Philune led us forward—after all, he had the map—and I kept close behind so that at least one of us had eyes on our surroundings as we headed north.

"Thank you for the clarification," Zev said. "We'll take a break now. I need to consider all that I've learned."

CHAPTER THREE

When Zev stepped into the hall, his attention immediately turned to the far corner. He held still and listened. No sounds of breathing or scuffling of feet. No indication of the spy he knew he had heard before.

With as soft a step as he could manage, he headed down the hall. He halted right before the corner and once again, listened. His own breathing filled his ears.

Better to deal with the problem head-on. He whipped around the corner, raising his fists, and found an empty space. However, further down, stood a woman in a black robe with white trim.

The godwalker of Pralma, Goddess of Man.

She faced the wall with her head bowed. Her arms moved in slow, graceful motions—arms out wide, arms above her head, arms at her sides.

Zev observed her, wondering if all those motions were necessary to creating her spell or were merely ritualized movements evolved over years. If necessary, did they have to be synchronized with the other godwalkers? If so, how did each godwalker know to move when they were all spread throughout the castle?

Zev chuckled. His mind loved to think on varying subjects, and it sought a more palatable problem than the one he had been sent here to do. He strolled down the hall, and several feet beyond the godwalker, he found an open door that led to a balcony overlooking the city.

The fresh air satisfied his lungs and lifted his spirits. He set his elbows on the stone railing and watched toy-sized people and carts rummaging about the late-night streets. What a strange view from so high up.

All those people—none of them knew what went on at the castle. They probably thought the evening progressed with music and dancing and drinking and perhaps even debauchery. The idea that peace for the entire region hung in the balance would be furthest from their minds. And beyond that—the idea that a failed farmer from Fernbund could tip the scale either way, all based on what he could deduce from a story in which he questioned the truth of every word told him—his head throbbed.

"You okay?" Bellemont said as she stepped alongside.

Keeping his view on the city, he said, "I suppose I have to be patient. I just thought that somebody would have confessed by now."

"That fast? Really? I assumed we would be talking with them for the rest of the night, possibly throughout tomorrow and into tomorrow evening."

"Perhaps. It usually doesn't take me this long to figure out an answer for our normal clients."

"The problems of Fernbund are far smaller. I'd be worried if you took this long to know that young Kyle Turnko left a pasture open, lost all the family's horses, and blamed it on two men passing through town. This—you've never had to deal with something this serious before. Well, except Xarad's murder. But not before or since then."

"Maybe I'm not as smart as everyone thinks. With the godwalkers and the guards shutting down this castle, the thieves should be easy to find."

"Even if the thieves were working under the pressure of a tight schedule like you suggested, they would still have to be skilled, talented, and somewhat prepared before attempting a theft of this magnitude. At the very least, we should expect them to be good at hiding their crimes. So, no, this was never going to be easy. You just don't like being forced to work this hard. You don't like being forced into anything. Isn't that a part of why you chose to come here instead of visiting your father?"

Zev turned around and faced the castle. He refused to take the bait. Focus on finding the thieves and the Shield—that's what he needed to do. And when it came to that, more than anything, Axon troubled him.

Could she have changed so much in two years? Or perhaps she was the same and he had changed. Something was off, and he could not pluck it out of his mind. He felt it, but he did not like to rely on feelings alone.

It suddenly hit him that Bellemont was on the balcony and not at her post in the ballroom. "Has something happened?" he asked.

She laughed. "A lot. Philune decided to take the initiative. Purely political step, but he offered to allow the Dacci witches a chance to look in the coffins. He said it would prove the innocence of the East, but of course, in return, he expected for his people to inspect the Virgin Cart."

"He's gambling on the fact that they won't actually agree to do it. They look bad for refusing and he looks good for offering, even though everybody knows it was an empty offer."

"Now you're starting to understand politics."

"That's not something I'm going to be proud of."

"Anyway, negotiations failed over the handling of the coffin."

"It got that far? Does that mean the Dacci agreed?"

"Of course, they agreed. They couldn't allow Philune to win."

"Ah. They called his bluff."

"Which is why he then added the obstacle of how the coffin would be handled. Each time they agreed to his terms, he amended things—always over the concern of maintaining the sanctity of the dead. As a result, tensions are worse than before."

Zev rubbed his palm against his forehead. "Was that Philune's intent? Why would he be trying to make things worse?"

"I don't quite see how this helps him, but to find any answer in politics, you merely have to figure out what somebody has to gain by their actions. Once we understand what Philune stands to gain, we'll understand why he acts as he does."

"Show me," Zev said.

Bellemont led the way back to the ballroom.

Seven months earlier, Mayor Adler bumbled through Zev's door flustered and frightened. Somebody had broken into the official Mayoral office and defiled it. That was the word he used—defiled. When Zev entered the Mayor's place to investigate, he found that feces had been splashed on the walls and floor—not in an effort to set blame on Dacci witches, but rather to mock the Mayor, to suggest that he and his office were full of crap. Fortunately, the culprits were not bright. The messages they had written on the walls using the feces were misspelled, and they signed their work with handprints. Before the end of the next day, Zev had found the two boys—Jek Hoolk and, not surprisingly, Kyle Turnko. While blubbering snot and tears, they claimed to have performed their destructive acts merely as a prank. But even after it all had ended, after the boys were properly punished, after the office had been scrubbed top to bottom, after life had settled back into routine, the Mayor never seemed comfortable in the office again. The violation had broken the bond he had with that space.

At the time, Zev thought the man acted rather foolishly. But now, as he followed Bellemont into the ballroom, he sympathized a little with what the Mayor had experienced. Only a few hours earlier, this ballroom had been a magnificent splendor to behold. It radiated such grandeur and promised to be a cherished memory for decades to come. As much as Zev scoffed and complained, he could not deny how impressive the ballroom had been.

But now—now, he saw the true face under the makeup. The wrinkles, the lines, the yellowing teeth. Nervous eyes observed tense postures. Women fanned their skin while their necks looked strained under the weight of their massive hair creations. Men itched their sides, their mouths drawn into firm lines. Witches narrowed their eyes as if sighting targets.

Walking on the ballroom floor no longer required the skill of weaving around people. The East, the West, and the Frontier had all sectioned off, leaving gaps of floor space between each group.

The quiet struck Zev more than anything. No music, no excited conversation, nothing but stressed silence. Any talking that needed to be done occurred in harsh whispers.

A group of Eastern men sat at a round table covered with half-eaten dishes and several empty wine bottles. The men had an exhausted glaze about them. Sitting in the middle of the group, Philune whispered in the ear of another—a dark-haired man with a dark-tinted cane dressed in a stylish black and gray suit. Though he clearly wanted to be seen as relaxed and in control, Zev did not miss the man's darting eyes.

At least Zev could use the quiet to his advantage. He stopped near the rotating platform for the band, inhaled deeply, and in a brash voice said, "Philune Baxtery, it is your turn to be interviewed. Please follow me."

He did not look back to see how Philune reacted. He knew the man would follow. No choice, really. It was one thing for him to stall or deflect while Zev handled matters elsewhere and a general chaos permeated the building. But now, in that tense quiet, all ears heard Zev's voice, all eyes looked upon Philune. If he refused, he would look petty and possibly guilty.

As Zev walked by Bellemont, she snickered. "And you say you don't know anything about politics."

WITNESS ACCOUNT OF
PHILUNE BAXTERY

Before we begin, I should make two points clear to you—important points. Primarily, I want you to know that I am not here because I am willing to help. I am here because, like my compatriots, we're being held prisoner.

"That is not a fair characterization," Mr. Duke said. "King Robion has locked in everybody, including his own people, so that we may identify the culprit or culprits, find the Shield, and restore some sense of order and harmony amongst our peoples. Would you rather have a blood-soaked mess on the ballroom floor?"

That is why I am cooperating. Because, secondarily, I am one of the few people out there who is maintaining any aspect of the calm you may have noticed. There is stress, yes, but all the people from the East are either seated or standing at ease. They are not lined up in a militant formation nor are they threatening to cast spells. Like others.

Zev said, "Is that why you were whispering orders to your man?"

I am doing everything I can to placate them. It's difficult when others such as Lord Radugo want to rile up the situation. Of course, you have the benefit that all the people from the East are gentlemen and ladies. I can't speak for the Dacci or your own from the Frontier, but Easterners of this high quality won't bloody their hands unless absolutely necessary. Still, I warn you, keeping me here too long means those like Radugo don't have any voice to counter their own. These people locked in a ballroom are scared. They're scared because they don't know what is going to happen the rest of this evening nor what King Robion's plan might be. They are even more scared because they don't know what the ramifications of this theft will become. Most of all, they are scared of the Dacci. Most Easterners have never met a Dacci witch in person. Aside from the pungent aroma and distasteful behaviors, the Dacci strike an intimidating figure. Until you know the truth about them.

"Truth?"

That without their spells, they are nothing but paupers ripping out their teeth and playing with their shit. You fine people from the Frontier—you are strong, resilient, knowledgeable of the civilized and uncivilized worlds. Hardy and loyal with an honorable culture. We of the East are brilliant—no, no, I am not being arrogant. Look at all we have invented. Not only the incredible tools and weapons, but the advances we have made in government and behavior. We have studied and applied so many lessons in the way people react to danger, to love, to stress. It is quite astounding. And government—I mean no offense but you still have a king. As if the Cassun Nine could truly dictate who would be the best ruler. But not us. We rule ourselves. We vote for our leaders. A far better system.

Please, no need to argue. I have heard all the debates, and now is not the time for such a discussion. I merely point out that both our countries are sophisticated and noteworthy in their own ways. But not the Dacci. They live in a place called the Feral Lands, after all.

"And yet, if I understand things correctly, the remnants of your expedition eventually teamed up with several Dacci witches."

Is that what you want me to sit here and discuss? That was more Axon's doing than mine. Though, I suppose it is interesting enough. But how would that have anything to do with our current predicament? No, no, don't bother with an answer. If it is what you want me to regale you with, then so be it. The sooner we can begin this tiresome exercise, the sooner I can return to my people and perhaps accomplish something of value to maintain decorum.

Philune paused while his eye lingered on Axon.
"Do you have a problem with her being here?" Zev asked.
Philune shook his head.
"Then please, tell us what happened after the argument with Axon in your tent."

Well, let me see. I am confident you know by now that it was Pilot who saved the expedition. His wisdom allowed me to see a way forward—alongside Axon, of course. After they removed themselves from my tent, I had nothing to do the rest of that night except sleep.

However, to nobody's surprise, sleep would not come. I was far too agitated by the bowback's attack. A lot of good people died, yet I was expected to go on.

I felt horribly for the survivors. I'm sure they had the same sentiment as myself—to go home, return to civilized life, and to do my best to remember the dead in the clearest of light. They would not want us to dwell upon their actual moments of demise.

I remember closing my eyes and trying to will myself to sleep. I could hear the crackling of the campfire, and I could hear the soft whispers of those still breathing. In the wind, I swore I could hear the breath of the dead, too. A rustle of leaves, a snap of a twig, any sound really, they all forced me to stay awake.

I remember thinking I would never sleep again. I even tried—

"You've made your mental state quite clear," Zev said. "Perhaps it would be more beneficial to continue from when you awoke the next morning."

Of course. I apologize if my attempts to provide the clearest possible picture for you is not something you require.

The next morning, I left my tent having not slept at all. Our two groups now merged together to form a single eight-man team. Only eight. So many lost. At least ten of them worthy of being mourned. But even the deaths of the servants weighed on my thoughts. A little.

We began packing the horses. Axon demanded that we prioritize certain pieces of equipment. The items she thought held lesser importance were to be thrown aside. My men looked at me, unsure if they should follow this newcomer's rules. While I disagreed with her, and while I understood my own people better than she ever would, I also saw the value in staying with her. At least, for that moment.

About an hour later, I suppose, we had packed up as much as she would accept, and we headed out.

That first day of travel was disheartening to say the least. Only four Easterners left. Vost had proven himself invaluable so many times. But the real surprise was Tagge. I had known him before we left. He was not part of the group that applied for the position. In fact, I had known him since I was a child.

Tagge was what we call a Kitence.

Zev turned to Axon and Mr. Duke. "It's a person whose position is greater than a servant but far less than a Lord or master or even a family member."

Ah, yes, I had forgotten. You were originally from the East. Then perhaps you understand. As the Kitence on my family lands, Tagge meant the world to me. Growing up, he was a friend, a confidant, and always fiercely loyal. When I was given the opportunity to form this expedition, Tagge was the first one I called upon. And though I gave him the choice to refuse, I knew he would accept without hesitation.

The other survivor, Sekat, joined the expedition because Tagge had invited him. I had never met the man before—he worked on the Baxtery lands as an autocart driver but took on the position long after I left the house. Tagge knew him, of course, and the recommendation of Tagge meant everything.

That was the group. Many of the others I had barely begun to know and they were now buried beneath the cold dirt of a foreign land.

Well, you can be sure that as the days progressed, I made an effort to get to know Vost better. I would have preferred to have known more about Sekat, but I could not do so. Though he was a friend of Tagge, he truly did not rise above the level of a servant. No matter how large or small an army may be, one still has to follow certain hierarchies.

It took us several days to work around Mount Sputra and over the Darkened Ridges. Then we were into uncharted lands. Uncharted, that is, except for the map I held.

The ground sloped sharply downward. The low vegetation disappeared, although the number of trees thickened. They had unusual trunks with sleek bark that had a rather metallic sheen. The branches twisted, intermingling with those of other trees, to form a thicket overhead. I have never seen anything like it.

It was one of Axon's men—Kapa, I believe—who suggested we start naming the trees and insects and whatever other items we wished. After all, as he pointed out, none of our people had ever seen such things before. None of it had been named. I remember laughing. Not hard, but enough that I realized it was the first true laughter I had enjoyed since setting out on this adventure.

"I think it's a splendid idea," I said, and I suggested that we name these unusual trees in his honor—Kapa trees.

Despite such moments of levity, however, we were quickly reminded of the threats surrounding us. Our horses tensed up, and one of them bolted. It belonged to Sekat, and he struggled to calm the horse enough to return. Axon pulled out her Water Blade while Pilot unsheathed his own sword. I had my hand pistol as did Vost. Tagge, of course, carried his rifle with him always.

I have no idea how long we remained there staring into the shadows of the forest. I could feel the fear of those behind me, and I knew I had to lead by example. I sat straighter on my horse and pointed my weapon into the dark forest. "There's nothing to fear," I announced. "We won't be taken by surprise ever again."

That simple declaration seemed to be what the men needed. Sekat returned, and even the horses appeared to have eased.

Taking a more relaxed pace, we guided the horses through these shadow-filled woods. Each one of us did what we could to keep our horse calm, whether petting or murmured words or even a gentle tune, but the animals remained agitated. They snorted and stomped on the ground as they walked. You could feel it on your legs—a growing urge within the horse to tear off at a full gallop in an effort to escape this unseen force. Had I not been sitting in the middle of it, I might have found it fascinating.

Now, from my understanding, Mr. Duke is the only one in this room who lacks any real combat experience, so for the rest of you, it is not a surprise at how time shifts and changes during the intensity of battle. There's a clarity of the moment that is something only those who have experienced it could ever possibly understand. So much of our journey had that kind of clarity.

In this case, our battle was not direct. Yet, before I fully grasped the threat, all eight of us were galloping through these thick woods, none of us daring to look back.

Still, we heard it.

If you doubt me, and there is no reason to doubt, take one look at Axon's face. She remembers it well. An enormous beast smashing through trees and branches, growling as if the ground itself had awakened. We galloped as hard as we could push our steeds, yet the beast's snarling and grunting grew louder, even shutting out the thunderous hooves on the ground. No matter how fast my horse charged through those woods, the sound always felt right over my shoulder. I heard it with such clarity that I became convinced that any moment I would feel blade-sharp teeth ripping through my flesh.

Thankfully, that didn't happen. I don't know what that creature was. I don't need to know nor do I desire the knowledge. I do, however, understand one thing—it lived in that forest, and it would die there, too. It would never leave. Because as we blasted along, as I felt the branches stinging my skin when they flicked across me, I saw up ahead a pinprick of light that grew larger, brighter. I hoped a clearing neared, but the result proved even better—it was the end of the forest.

We broke through the tree line and raced into an open field of blue and green grasses. Our horses bolted straight up along the hill until finally, near the top, we were able to regain control. Only then did any of us dare to look back. The vicious sounds echoed into a dim rumble. Whatever that thing was, it would not follow us into the light of day. We had survived.

We made a short camp to allow the horses time to calm and graze. I suppose several of us needed to calm as well. It was during that break that I had one of many enlightening conversations with dear Axon.

Don't look so surprised? Just because we do not agree on many things does not mean that I cannot value your thoughts. You may not encounter this under the leadership of a king, but I assure you in the politics of Eastern government, nothing of value could be accomplished without people of vastly different opinions coming together and seeking out common ground.

"You still haven't answered our original request—that you tell us how you came to meet with the Dacci," Zev said.

You must forgive me for saying this, but I have absolutely no desire to return to this room and answer more of your questions later. Thus, I have chosen a tactic of giving you the most detail possible in hopes to avoid any further inquiries. So, please, ask me questions if you need clarity about anything. Unlike many people in this castle, in this world, I have nothing to hide.

Anything? No? Then I shall continue.

While we relaxed, Axon approached me. I was going over my map and quickly stuffed it away—my trust in her had only begun and I worried that if any of the Frontier group got hold of that map, they would have no use for us Easterners. We'd be abandoned, and we'd probably die out there.

A grin of acknowledgment crossed her face, and she settled next to me. I think that grin gained her more trust from me than anything. That grin not only said that she understood why I hid the map, but also that she approved, and possibly, that in time, she hoped I would not feel the same. All that from a simple grin. Then a unique thought struck, one that had not occurred to me until that moment.

I turned to her, and I asked, "Why haven't you killed us yet?"

She did not act taken aback or surprised which confirmed to me that she had considered the idea previously. She said, "I've glimpsed enough of your book to know that I will not be able to decipher the key. Maybe Pilot could—he has a lot of experience with the East. But that's a chance I'm not willing to take."

I almost asked her what chance she referred to, but then I already knew. If she killed us, her team would have to turn back. They could take a stab at deciphering the code and reading the map, but if they ended up wrong, if they made one mistranslation, they might never find the Shield. Of course, if they killed us, they would prevent us from getting the Shield and they would acquire the map and book, but then they would have to return to the Frontier. King Robion would, no doubt, have scholars who could eventually decipher the materials —over the course of years, maybe. He would form a new expedition, one that may or may not involve Axon and Pilot and the others.

The truth covered her face just as her grin had told me so much already. She refused to take that chance. She wanted to see the Shield for herself, even if that meant working with us.

I laughed. Quite hard. Actually fell on my back and held my stomach. I don't normally laugh like that.

I explained to her what I had determined, and she laughed as well. "So, you're stuck with us, and we're stuck with you," she said.

"I promise it won't be so bad," I said. "Vost is well-traveled and has had some experience as a chef, although he is more comfortable working with better ingredients, and Tagge is a gentleman of the first order."

"And you?" she said. I thought I saw a glint in her eye.

I said, "I don't think we would match well."

She then surprised me. She told me of her distinguished lineage, of her brother who studied at our university in the East, and of her sister, married to a prince, I believe. But even as she informed me of her eligibility as a woman of note, she made it clear that I had misread matters. She had no interest or intention of marrying anyone.

Still, I did not take offense. In fact, I found the conversation both illuminating and encouraging. As we cleaned up, mounted our horses, and continued on her way I thought over that short exchange, and I smiled. I wondered if those of the Frontier and those of the East could find other ways to help each other. If we could do it with our knowledge of the map and language mixed with her knowledge of survival and the wild, then our countries could do it as well.

I hope I have not embarrassed you.

Axon shook her head. With a slight gaze at Zev, she said, "Mr. Asterling has requested that we do not interfere with his interview. That is the only reason for my silence. Do not misinterpret anything more as you are so prone to do."

I will try not to disappoint.

Let me see now… ah, yes—the land that stretched out before us was unlike anything I've ever experienced. As far as was visible, rolling hill after rolling hill. Each one covered in the same green and blue grasses, yet no herds of animals grazing, no evidence of people like farmers. Just untouched land. Always to the right, the forest. And to the left, more of these hills. Behind us, Mount Sputra hovered in the sky never letting us think we had gone too far. Even as the cold worsened, the lush grasses remained. How they survived such harsh cold is beyond me.

We traveled for most of the day and once dusk arrived, Axon suggested we camp for the night. She explained the proper way to set up a safe camp along with a proper guard rotation so that no surprises came our way. My men and I were eager to learn and benefit from her expertise, and since we had already experienced some of what she could offer us, we did our best to be good students. I don't think we gave her too much trouble with our ignorance, and we all managed to get some rest through the evening.

The next morning, we rose to continue our journey—and that's when we discovered the horrible truth. Tagge's friend, Sekat, was the first to alert us of the issue. I remember his words and the haunted way he said them. "Isn't this the same hill we rested at yesterday?"

Indeed, we all scanned the area. There was no mistake. Hills rolled ahead of us, the forest to our right, more hills to the left, and directly behind us more forest—the one we had burst out from. At the same distance from where we made our first rest.

Axon frowned at me, her eyes accusing me of incompetence. But I swore, and she knows now I spoke truthfully, that I had not taken us the wrong way. I made sure to keep the forest on our right and never to stray too far into the endless hills on our left, never to lose sight of the forest. According to the map we merely had to go straight for several days, and we would reach the next part of our journey. Yet here we were back at the beginning.

Axon commanded that we set out again, only this time everybody would pay attention to our progress. If anyone noticed us drifting off-course, we were to stop and regroup. We spent the entire day walking through those hills. Always with the forest on our right and the hills on our left. Whenever I glanced behind, I saw the tree line receding until only hills remained. And when we decided to set camp, we took a clear look around. We had definitely made progress.

But come the morning, we had returned to where we began.

Pilot snapped his fingers at one of his men—Feddi—and ordered the man to check the edge of the forest behind us. Like a dutiful soldier, Feddi hustled down to the tree line. Well before he hit the actual forest, the creature slumbering in there made itself known. A horrible roar wrestled from the dark forest sending a flock of gezzit into the air.

Feddi glanced back, clearly not wanting to go into the forest alone. Pilot, in his great wisdom, waved the man to return. No sense in losing another member of our diminished team over this.

Axon pointed to my saddlebags where I kept the book and map. She said, "What does your book say about this?"

I remember that distinctly because I found it to be such an absurd question. It suggested that I had the answer in front of me all the time yet decided to waste a couple days playing games. I suppose I could understand the attitude if I had not lost well over half my men. But in our state at that moment, I found the question ridiculous and some-what insulting.

We all sat and tossed about ideas of how to handle the matter. I'm rather proud of that. Other fools would have tried to race faster through the hills, go back into the forest and die, or any number of useless notions. We simply put out ideas and quickly dismissed them without wasting days of travel. We could do this because it was evident that we would always end up right back to where we were. Naturally, the only logical explanation was that we were lost within some delusional spell. The question wasn't how do we escape it, but rather how do we break it?

Unfortunately, for all our intelligence, we could not come up with an answer. As another day neared its end, I decided to search through my books even though I knew no answer existed there. It merely gave me something to do.

That night, as I looked for possible mistranslations of the text, Axon pulled back my tent flap and entered.

Axon shot straight up. The screech of her chair knocking back matched the grinding of her teeth. "Enough."

FURTHER WITNESS ACCOUNT OF
AXON COPONIV

I know that Philune has more to say, but if he will kindly step outside for a few moments, I have some private matters to speak with this panel.

Axon made no attempt to hide the grit in her voice. Though her words were polite enough, none missed the venom in the air. After a short pause, Philune wiped his hands and stood. "I don't suppose I have much more to say, but I always believe in being a gentleman. If the esteemed lady requires a private moment, who am I to deny her this? I'll be in the hall."

Axon held the door for him. And when he left, she slammed it shut.

This entire exercise is a ridiculous waste of time. Time in which we are allowing the thieves to think, plot, and possibly even escape.

Did you listen to what he said? It was nothing but lies to make himself look better. Same with Vost. And I imagine everybody else we listen to will have their own version filled with lies and deceptions. Which means that any real truth is unattainable. At least, through listening to this garbage.

Zev gently placed his hands on the table and with a peaceful tone, he said, "I am not ignorant. I know that many who come before me are going to lie. Some of them will lie on purpose with the aim of deceiving me. Others are simply shading the truth in hopes of looking more favorably in our eyes. That is part of my job, though—to listen and separate truth from fiction."

That sounds delightful, but this is not like what we dealt with before. Back then, you had many days to observe, to question, to learn the truth. We are running out of time, and you've barely made it beyond the first few days of our journey.

What really galls me is that you won't even let me tell you the truth. Pilot and I are the most trustworthy of this entire interview process, yet you barely let us speak. Meanwhile Philune rambles on and on. His self-aggrandizing is enough to make me vomit.

"Unfortunately, I don't see another way for us to find the answer. You say you want to tell me the truth, but that is not quite accurate. You only want me to hear the truth to a point. Until you're willing to tell me the full truth, I have to question everything I hear. From you, from Pilot, as well as the ones I truly expect deceit from."

I cannot allow this to continue. I'll shut this whole process down, grab together Pilot and the Royal Guard, and we'll force out the thieves.

"Will you now?" Mr. Duke said. Despite an appearance that Zev often found comical, the man threw all the weight of his office into those simple words.

Well, that is to say that I would of course request King Robion's support for such an action.

"Request denied."

I'm sure you wish to lay down the law, but we both know I have a friendship with the King. I think I'll go talk to him personally.

"Of course, you are welcome to do that. But you should be prepared to answer his first question—why did you not ask Mr. Duke about this since he was right there in the room with you? And you, being a loyal and honest member in the King's service, will tell him the truth. At which point, he will become quite angry. He will yell at me for not stopping you, he will yell at you for not

listening to me, and he will yell at every single person within hearing about how you have wasted his time and slowed this entire process when—as you so astutely pointed out earlier—time is something we don't have a lot of. Therefore, I strongly suggest you sit down and let Mr. Asterling continue his interviews."

By Sazieck, I hate politics.

Axon returned to her seat, and Zev waited in silence, allowing them to recompose. Then he called Philune back in.

The man had enough sense not to gloat as he settled in the chair, cleared his throat, and continued his story.

RESUMED WITNESS ACCOUNT OF
PHILUNE BAXTERY

I shall do my best to conclude this as rapidly as possible. I entirely understand and sympathize with Axon's position. Yes, the walls are thin enough. I could hear you all. But you should know that my goals coincide with yours. We all want to see justice brought to those who have caused this unfortunate evening.

While Axon and I do not share the same views on many topics, we have been able to find common ground before. And while she may not appreciate the manner in which I convey our story, I have not lied or embellished or intentionally deceived any of you. Even if I wanted to, I live by a code of honor. I am the Captain of the East—a title I take seriously. It requires me to be tough, fair, sometimes brutal, but always honest. I would expect Pilot, as the Captain of the Royal Guard, or Axon, as a leader among leaders under King Robion, to share my devotion to duty, truth, honor, and loyalty.

Zev patted the air and said, "It's okay. Coarse words were exchanged, but I think you can understand that everybody is concerned for the outcome. If you would please continue so that we can understand how you ended up joining with the Dacci."

Certainly. As I was relating before this interruption, Axon entered my tent that night. She told me that she intended to perform a ceremony of prayer to her gods and goddesses, asking for divine intervention, I suppose. She wanted to know if I had any requests of the Nine.

I said nothing. I was bemused that she thought I served any deity. But I did not wish to be rude. Everybody has their individual beliefs, and I do not think mine superior to any others—mostly any others. While I did not have any requests of her superior beings, I did have a request of her. I asked if it would be okay to watch. I had never seen this personal prayer ceremony, and I thought it might be educational, at the least. Plus, to be fully honest and transparent, I was no closer to an answer from my book and map, and I wanted a distraction. I have found in the past that divorcing myself from the immediate problem can often allow my thoughts to work in a less aware manner, and oftentimes, I'll produce an answer where brute force of thought would have failed. Do you find that to be the case, too?

> *"At times. But it first requires your mind to have the information it needs. As I do, at the moment, need to know how you encountered and ended up working with the Dacci."*

Yes. My apologies.

Axon surprised me by agreeing to my request, and we strolled one hill over. We could still see our camp from that distance which I found reassuring. I did not want to even think about what might happen if we got separated.

She lowered to her knee and placed a square cloth over her head. One hand grabbed her necklace with nine strands for each of the gods and goddesses.

You see, Axon, I paid attention.

As I understand it, under normal circumstances, one would pray to the specific god or goddess depending on the situation at hand. This unique ceremony involved setting out a prayer for each of the Nine. One at a time. Starting with Tiq, the goddess of birth and continuing all the way to Wiq, the god of death. Then Tortu and

Pralma, the god of woman and goddess of man, finally culminating with the Lord of All Existence, Qareck. Each prayer involved Axon mumbling quietly to herself and then raising her head, opening her heart up to the sky, and calling out the god or goddess directly.

It was actually quite moving. Her fervor, her depth of belief, struck a part of me that did not often awaken. I could see through her why religion is valuable to many people. But I did not truly believe it would help us in any way other than emotionally.

That is, until the next morning came.

The sun rose golden on the hills, and we all stood around the morning campfire barely eating our breakfast. We stared at each other with hollow eyes. Not a word was spoken, yet volumes passed between us. We had reached a defining point. We could not continue the path we had gone. That much was clear. We could not stay there forever. We would perish. And we all feared trying to go back through the woods. Not with that beast lurking in the dark. Thus, we were stuck.

Kapa stood opposite me in our circle, so I watched the change come over his face. He perked up. His entire face widened. He dropped his food and pointed beyond me.

"People," he said.

Just that one word, yet a magical energy shot through us all. We whipped around, and one hill over, near the exact spot where Axon had prayed, we spotted them.

Even from a distance, we recognized that they were Dacci. Those dark rags they wore stood out against the clean fields. And I don't have to tell you about the smell. There were five—Thalia led the way —though, of course, we had no knowledge of their names at the time. The other four carried the Virgin Cart—the very one sitting in the ballroom right now.

In as strong a voice as I could muster, and I suspect Axon would suggest I yelled out of fear, I commanded my men to arms. I admit that it would have been better had I given my orders quietly. As it were, my voice carried across the hills. The Dacci heard me and froze.

Axon pulled out her Water Blade, and at the sight of the fabled

119

weapon—one that had in recent times slaughtered many of their people—these Dacci set the litter down and prepared for battle. We checked over our weapons, making sure we had enough ammunition and that we were properly loaded. Across the way, the Dacci formed a straight line while one of them knelt before the others. Even from such a distance, I could smell the excrement she poured from a vial in her pouch. She then set small animal bones on this pile of waste.

Axon and I mounted our horses while the others approached on foot. We moved at a steady yet measured pace. As Axon would explain to me later, since we were the ones approaching, we would be forced to climb uphill. This gave the Dacci a slight advantage.

As we moved onward, I saw this witch pull a metal tool from her pouch that she then used to extract one of her teeth. Several of my men groaned in disgust. She spit blood onto that horrid pile and placed the tooth atop of it all.

You must understand, we had never experienced anything like this. Oh, we had been exposed to stories about the Dacci. Most of those tales came in the form of fables designed to teach children a lesson or that we told each other to give a fright. You know—don't go strolling alone in the woods or the Dacci witch will get you. Eat all your vegetables or you'll lose your teeth like a Dacci witch. That sort of thing.

Obviously, we knew the Dacci existed, that they were real, but the idea that their spells were anything more than a bunch of rituals and superstitions seemed ludicrous. Until that moment, of course.

No, I've misrepresented things. Because even at that moment, as we settled near the bottom of the hill, I still thought I gazed upon a bunch of mad women. Mad women playing with their feces and ripping out their teeth. If anything, the fact that Axon took it far more seriously than I expected gave me pause. But then, I reminded myself, according to legend, she had faced these Dacci for real.

So, I decided to be cautious. I pointed at Tagge. He raised his rifle, took aim, and squeezed off a round. A rifle creates an obnoxious racket, and I expected the Dacci to scatter at the noise. I did see them flinch, but none of them moved. More importantly, none of them fell either.

I looked at Tagge. I knew he had excellent aim. While this may have been a bit of an awkward angle, we were close enough that he should've hit one of them. He shrugged, settled the weapon in the proper position, aimed, and shot again.

Once more, nothing happened.

Axon leaned closer to me and said, "We'll have to fight them one-on-one. Once we're close enough, he might be able to shoot them, but not until we understand what spell they're using."

I remember those words clearly because I thought to myself *spell?* Surely, she cannot mean it literally. That's the stuff of religion. But then, I'd spent all that time the previous night watching her pray. And before my mind could go wandering the path of connecting her prayer with the arrival of these Dacci, she lifted her Water Blade overhead and commanded a charge.

The eight of us tore up that hill, yelling as if we were hundreds.

The Dacci stared at us and did not move. The one on her knees, casting the spell, lifted her head and removed her veil. Large gaps in her mouth suggested she had pulled out many of her teeth in the past. To my mind, she looked insane.

But in the next seconds, my view of the world changed forever.

You see, we slammed into an invisible wall. Hard like stone we smashed into this nonexistent barrier. We stumbled back, blood dripping from our noses or gashes on our heads. Tingling numbness rolled out from the center of my head until my arms and legs felt it, too. The woman I thought insane pointed at us and laughed.

That was when I learned spells were real. The Dacci witches were real. More than just a cult, they wielded powers through their disgusting practices, and we would have to find a way to defeat them or we would end up dead, our bones used for whatever spells their demented brains created.

I was grateful that I sat atop my horse, for if I had stood, my legs might've given out. I am not ashamed to admit that I held to my share of fear at that moment. I looked to Axon for some idea of how to handle the matter. I don't know what she saw, but something happened that made her change tactics.

She put away her Blade and ordered the rest of us to lower our weapons. We hesitated, of course. But her stern voice suspended any argument. Once we complied, one of the witches stepped forward from the line.

At the time, I had no way of knowing who this was, but it turned out to be Thalia—the leader of the Lost.

Without bothering to knock, Bellemont burst into the room. The strain in her eyes and the strands of displaced hair said far more than her shaking words. "It's all falling apart."

CHAPTER FOUR

As Zev and Mr. Duke jumped to their feet, Axon and Philune remained seated. Zev watched a battle of looks between them. Mr. Duke cleared his throat, and both rose.

The group followed Bellemont toward the ballroom. Zev noted that the few godwalkers he had seen before no longer occupied their previous positions. Bellemont kept several paces ahead, no doubt trying to avoid questions from Mr. Duke or the others. Zev closed his mouth. The answers would be coming soon enough.

They entered through the backstage door, and when Zev finally observed the ballroom, his teeth clamped tight and his fingers rolled into fists. It had only been a few hours, yet these three groups of supposed leaders could not hold themselves together—not even for an opportunity at peace.

On the Eastern side of the ballroom, they had commandeered an adjoining room intended for the kitchen staff to prep serving dishes. All the well-coiffed ladies had been ushered into this room while Lord Radugo and several other men guarded the front with rifles. In the actual ballroom, the dark-haired man with a dark-tinted cane, the same one Zev had witnessed Philune whispering to, organized the construction of a wall of tables and chairs. He had a chest of armaments before him which he handed out to all the Eastern Lords.

"I see," Zev said as he faced Philune. "Your long-winded speech, your little tangents, your desire to tell us as much detail as possible— you were keeping us from knowing what your man had put into motion."

Before Philune could answer, Zev turned back to the ballroom.

Most of the witches stood back by the Virgin Cart. But three of them, including Red Veil, boldly knelt before small mounds of bone and bile near the front. The shimmer of a protective wall surrounded them.

"How is that possible?" Zev asked, not sure who he intended the question for.

King Robion stepped closer. "Godwalkers are not nearly the accomplished users of spells that the witches are. While the godwalkers' spell has kept things relatively calm, it was only a matter of time before the witches decided to combine their forces. When the Easterners sequestered their women, that witch in the red veil assigned two of their own to cast the spell. It wasn't enough to overcome my godwalkers, so she added a third."

Those representing the Frontier had pressed up against the stage. On the edges, a handful of the King's attendants helped the ladies onto the stage proper and ushered them toward the back.

Bellemont said, "You should keep your godwalkers doing what they can. The more the witches must work to perform even the most basic spells, the better our chances will be."

"I can keep some of them on that task, but if this is going to break into violence, I would rather have the godwalkers preparing a more advantageous spell."

Zev scanned the crowd for the leader of the Lost—Thalia. He did not see her among those of the West. Of course not. Axon and Philune had spent most of their time on the stage along with Thalia. Zev turned around—sure enough, the Lost witch stood in the back corner, her dark clothing helping her blend in with the shadows.

To the King, he said, "Don't give up on me yet. There's still time."

King Robion clasped Zev's hand. "You came through for me once before. You have my full faith now. I will do all I can to keep this situation from getting worse, but it will get worse. Hopefully, I will find the right words to push that moment back as far as possible. But please, by Qareck, move quickly."

Zev approached Thalia.

He wanted to order her into the interview room, but her eyes warned him off. The Lost witches and the regular Dacci witches did not get along. In fact, the only reason the Dacci witches agreed to be in the same room with the Lost was because the Lost witches helped acquire the Shield. Thalia would not leave the ballroom, not leave her witches alone with the other Dacci. Whereas Philune might not like Lord Radugo, the two would set aside their differences and fight together against a common foe. Zev could see in Thalia's eyes that she did not hold the same belief of her own people.

"I need to hear your side of the story. If I can find the thieves, we can avoid any bloodshed out there. Please, I understand that you don't want to leave here, but help me."

Thalia stood still, holding the tension of the room between her eyes. At length, she cocked a glance toward Bellemont. "Have her go down on the floor. She can exchange herself with Ashturov. Make sure she only talks to my people—the Lost."

"Can you do that?" Zev asked Bellemont.

She nodded, of course, but there was no mistaking the shudder in her shoulders. She stepped onto the floor and walked up no man's land in the middle. Wearing her Frontierswoman sundress but also the veil of a Dacci witch, neither side knew what to make of her. Her reputation and her connection with the events of years before gave her the respect of the Frontier and the East but also the animosity of the West. However, as Bellemont approached the barely visible wall, Thalia nudged her way to the edge of the stage.

With a strong timbre, she said, "We are not here to fight each other. The situation exists because of the theft. And we, the Lost Dacci witches, will continue to do our best to help discover the criminals. Ashturov, you will go and answer Mr. Asterling's questions. Let the Stolen witch stand in your place."

For three interminable heartbeats, no one breathed, no one spoke, no one moved. The ballroom stood still as a painting. Finally, Red Veil walked forward. She tapped one of the kneeling witches and made a quick nod of the head.

Zev could not see what changed in the witches' spellcasting, but in the next instant, Red Veil motioned toward one witch standing near the Virgin Cart. This witch approached Bellemont with a firm stride and a proud head. She stepped through the barrier and gestured for Bellemont to enter. As this witch, Ashturov, then approached the stage, the spellcasting witch presumably returned to her previous spell, locking the wall back in place. And Bellemont—she stood alone. The surrounding witches gave her as much distance as they could manage, acting both afraid and disgusted by her.

Bellemont turned her back on them. She had no interest in sensing their scorn. Instead, she stared at the stage, at Zev. And he felt her. He felt her eyes upon him with all their concern drilling into his bones. He wanted to cry out *Don't worry, I will find these criminals, you won't be harmed.* But he could say nothing. He had no idea if those words would have been true.

Thalia turned toward Zev. "Hurry, Frontiersman. Whatever you hope to get from my witches, you don't have much time left."

Hoping he communicated to Bellemont as much reassurance as he could manage, he touched his forehead and smiled. Then he turned away. Axon and Mr. Duke followed step as well as Ashturov. When they returned to the interview room, they each took their seat and waited.

"You have one chance to help your people." Zev poured a mug of water and set it on the table. "Don't test us." He sipped slowly from the mug, trying to clear his mind so that he could listen and listen carefully. "On the hill of green and blue grasses where you met Axon, Philune, and the rest—tell us what happened from that point on."

WITNESS ACCOUNT OF
THE WITCH ASHTUROV

I do not like talking, but Thalia tells me to talk, so I will talk. This woman sitting next to you and the Easterner in the ballroom, they led the group to attack us in the hills. Thalia ordered Barna to cast a quick protection spell. If you understand the Dacci at all, you know asking one to cast a spell is serious. She must sacrifice a tooth—one less spell she will ever cast. But Barna willingly did so, happily in order to protect the group. We Dacci are not like you. We have seen how you in the Frontier and the others in the East—you will destroy each other over nothing. We work together.

Zev nodded as if he agreed yet raised one finger and scrunched a look of confusion. "But you all belong to a group called the Lost. Didn't you break away from the Dacci?"

Dacci witches are the lost ones. We broke free from the boundaries. They only cast as far as Nualla can reach. But Nualla graced us with part of his wonderful being. As long as we carry him with us, we can cast spells wherever we are. You should all be grateful that we are more peaceful. For if our sisters ever grasped the great power we held, there would be no more Frontier, no more East.

That is how Barna cast her spell to protect us from your rifles and swords. This woman, Axon, she had the sense to stop the pointless fighting before it became dangerous to her people. The one called Philune was not so smart yet acted as if he was in charge.

"What are you doing here?" he asked, and we could hear his sneer.

To our surprise, Thalia answered, and answered truthfully. "We are in search of the Shield of Taladoro."

I'm sure you can imagine how your people reacted. Or you can ask Axon. And why is she here but not Thalia?

"Thalia sent you in place of her. She feels it is more important to watch over your sisters during this delicate time."

She is a wise woman. That is why I honor her wishes.

Axon and Philune spent time talking with Thalia. She had to explain what should've been obvious—that the hills were under a powerful spell. Any who entered would forever be adrift. But, of course, that did not hold true for us. We had our own spells to counter the hills. So, the Lost were the only ones not lost.

"If only that were the truth. But it's not quite, is it?"

You surprise me. Very perceptive. It's true that while we were not disoriented by the spell, we had not found the Shield. It became obvious quite quickly that Philune had a book and a map to guide him to this fabled Taladoro. It was equally obvious that he had joined Axon because she knew how to handle the treacherous wilds, and along with her team, they were good fighters. But without us, they would never make it out of the hills.

I believe it was Axon who suggested the three of us work together. She said, "We all want the Shield, and none of us will get it by ourselves."

She was right.

We formed an unlikely band. At first, Thalia led the way. She had sacrificed a tooth many days earlier so that we would not fall victim to the spell. She had to sacrifice one more to include the addition of your people. But she did it. Two days later, we were free of the hills. From that point, Philune led the way.

Each morning, he climbed his horse and trotted ahead—consulting his book and map as we weaved our way through colder and colder weather. Each night, we set camp. Those of the Frontier and the East built one camp, and we built our own separate camp. We left one communal fire in the middle. There was little trust between us all, though some individuals broke ranks. Inx, for example. I saw her scurry off to talk with the Easterners. She always had an interest in other cultures. I also noticed that Axon often visited Philune.

Does that satisfy you? I do not know what more I could possibly add that's valuable.

Zev started to ask a question but pulled back. He weighed out the possibilities and finally nodded. "I suppose you're right. As I understand it you, Thalia, and Inx were the only survivors from your group. Since you have no more to offer, and I'd like to honor Thalia's decision to stay in the ballroom for now, would you please send in Inx?"

I will put the request to Thalia. If she approves, then Inx will arrive.

WITNESS ACCOUNT OF
THE WITCH INX

I don't understand exactly how this is meant to proceed. What is it you want me to say?

Zev wrinkled his nose at her caustic aroma. "Simple enough. In your own words, start from your travels with the other groups. Perhaps tell us what you were doing at night when you left the Dacci side and went to the others, and beyond that."

Beyond that?

"As best as you can remember."

Okay.
Um...
I'm sorry. We of the Lost don't spend much time talking. It's rather strange.

"You're more of a meditative group?"

Exactly. Besides, there's not much to talk about when you under-stand your sisters so well. When you've spent so much time with them that you can predict their words before they're even spoken. I suppose that's why I spent some of my nights in the other camps. It was refreshing to hear other voices saying words I could not anticipate. Many times, I simply sat at the communal fire and listened to Kapa or Feddi or Vost as they chatted back and forth about things I had never seen. Sometimes I asked questions and they'd laugh, but I never felt they were laughing at me in a mocking way. Rather, I think they enjoyed introducing me to new ideas.

Zev grunted. "You've never seen the ugly history of our societies before? But surely in your own life in the Feral Lands, you came across many of the things that would've been talked about."

The Lost have existed for generations. I was born into this. I only know what it's like to travel the empty parts of the world. I only know the Virgin Cart and my sisters.

"Then perhaps you can tell us about your travels with the group."

Most of it was quite peaceful. We would break camp in the morning and spend much of the day walking according to Philune's map. At some point, we would halt for a rest and food. At another point, we would pitch camp for the evening. It went on like that for a long time. Long enough that I stopped counting. I trusted Thalia would not let us fall prey to the spell that makes one lose their way.

There were a few times when we thought we heard something in the woods or spotted something off in the hills, but nothing ever came of it. I suppose many from the East and the Frontier found the days boring, but for me and my sisters, it was delightful. Peaceful, quiet— the perfect kind of environment to fall within one's thoughts as we walked.

That all changed when we reached the foot of Taladoro.

I had a sense that morning we would be finding something new. The weather had been getting colder and colder all along, but we finally had to put on our heavy furs. Those of the Frontier and the East had to wear their own veils to protect their faces. Winds blew hard, spraying crystals of ice and snow as if they were sand. The sun burned bright, blinding against the white ground yet not melting anything.

It's strange when you take a long journey and finally reach your destination. It happens in no time. All those days of moving, hiking, trudging, and then suddenly you're there. Taladoro stood before us. It was a wide section of mountains all smashed together into one giant endless wall of rock and snow. The clouds cut through and obscured the snowcapped peaks. I remember thinking that if we attempted to climb those spires, we might die.

But we never had to get that close.

As we neared, we learned that our thoughts were mistaken—that is, we thought all of that mountain was Taladoro, but no. Taladoro really was a small section, a temple of sorts, waiting for us ahead.

We took a break to eat and care for our horses. Then we made our final push. When we laid eyes upon the open temple, I admit I found it impressive. Though not as honest and wholesome as any offering the Dacci Lost make in their travels, this temple contained that same reverence for those things greater than ourselves. It created an awe that prickled my skin far more than the cold.

Carved into the mountainside were four enormous figures. Each one depicted a giant—one man, one woman, and two other figures that had the body of the man and woman but the heads of other creatures. Ones I had never seen before. Things with large teeth and long snouts. Between the feet of the statues, wide blocks of stone had been placed. Bones of long dead sacrifices rested atop these blocks. The dark stains of blood trailed from these sacrifices downward until buried by fresh snow.

But it was clear the direction they went. Four streams of blood that collided into one thicker stream coming towards us directly. Until they reached the gaping hole in the ground.

I could picture the past so clearly. Long ago, the people that built these statues and worshipped these creatures would honor their gods, perhaps even cast spells, by sacrificing animals or perhaps other people. The blood would stream together until it dripped and poured into that hole and what awaited beneath.

"And what was that?"

The Shield of Taladoro, of course. That blood merged with the melted waters coming off of this temple and slowly drifted through the mouth of that cave. Somewhere below it fell upon the rock and over centuries and centuries, drip drip drip, little by little, carved out the great Shield, infusing it with blood, sacrifice, and a cast spell.

The mere concept of it was enough to fill my heart. I yearned to jump down that hole and find the Shield. I could feel the energy in my sisters, too. In all of us—in Vost and Kapa, in Philune, and even in you, Axon. I could feel it all. I could see the way Pilot had trouble holding still or the way Feddi kept looking to Axon for an order. We all desired to see that Shield.

But a lone figure stood before this hole.

He wore no clothing. With skin so white, we did not see him until we were nearly upon him. He simply blended in with the snow. He did not move, and I remember having the thought that he might not be real. He might be a smaller version of one of the giant statues. But he was less like a man and more like a creature. He had no eyes that I could recognize, but his face protruded like an animal snout. His legs, though straight at that time, appeared to have extra joints. And he had four strong arms that hung motionless at his sides.

A hard-shell carapace began at his head and dropped down behind him forming a cape, but one that did not flow. Instead, this cape clung to his skin. From the front, we could not see any of it. He was simply a snow-colored statue creature.

Axon—she and Thalia stared at him in silence. They looked around the area and attempted to understand the situation before they acted. But they never had much of a chance. Philune blundered ahead.

"Ho there," he said. At least, that is what I heard. His words were very strange.

Ashturov stepped in front of me, her bone armor clinking in the wind. It's a beautiful sound, even at a tense moment such as that one. But the others did not hear it like me. They all feared the creature and missed out on the glorious gifts of Nualla. Pilot placed his hand on the hilt of his weapon. Even Tagge and Sekat pulled out their rifles.

I don't know what Philune thought he might accomplish, but he strode forward, talking the whole time. Something similar to—*We're looking for Taladoro. Could you help us? We'll be happy to reward you for your service.*

If not for the other members of the team pulling out their weapons, I would have laughed. It would have been a better response than the one he got.

The creature said nothing. But once Philune stood close enough, one of the creature's arms snapped out to the side. It had three long fingers that ended in sharp nails that glistened in the sun as if they were ice.

Philune had the sense to step back. Amazing he had any sense at all. "We don't mean any harm," he said, and I heard the quiver in his throat. I recall his words perfectly because I did not share the sentiment. To me, this creature looked full of danger. I would not hesitate to harm it if necessary.

Apparently, the creature felt the same way about us. What I had mistaken to be its mouth did not move, but lower down its pale body, a long and large mouth opened. Not much for teeth—it could never become a Dacci witch—but its dark, pink flesh rippled as a grating shriek spewed forth.

Philune stumbled back and fell into the snow. While the rest raised their weapons and prepared, Philune fumbled out his handgun and fired off two shots.

The creature hurtled through the air, its anger directing straight to Philune. Tagge let loose his rifle, but the bullet pinged off the creature's hard shell. He left a mark like a scratch, but it did not slow the creature at all.

Faster than I could follow, Axon whipped out her Water Blade and started swinging. The creature respected that weapon. It dodged her attacks, arching back as if it had no spine. It rolled away only to hop to its feet and shriek at us once more. Its shell shifted around its body. I had never seen such a thing. It was as if the shell had a mind of its own, as if it was a second creature clinging to the pale creature's back, and now had decided to act as frontal body armor.

Ashturov held tight to her bone spear, but the rest of us turned toward Thalia. If she commanded us to cast spells, we would not hesitate.

No such command was given. Instead, Pilot said he had an idea. With his sword pointed in the creature's direction, he strolled toward the edge of the open hole in the ground. Though the creature had no eyes, it appeared to be watching him. Around the same point that Philune had reached, the point which set this creature off, Pilot halted. He watched the creature carefully and then took one further step forward.

The creature bolted after him. Swinging his blade with wild abandon, Pilot hurried back toward the group. He laughed off his experiment as he reset his wide-brimmed hat, but we could all see the anxiety on his face. He was lucky to make it back alive.

And the creature—it had resumed its original position. Although now we knew its purpose. It guarded Taladoro.

Philune's face twisted in fury. He stomped over to his men and commanded them all to fire at once. "It can't dodge every bullet," he said.

Vost, Tagge, and Sekat obeyed orders. They all took aim and waited for Philune to give the final word. He did not hesitate, and neither did they. Shots ripped off into the air, their loud cracks echoing into the distance.

The creature's shell armor covered it completely. Bullets dinged off, leaving their scratches but doing no measurable harm.

Philune commanded the men to reload as he complained about how ridiculous the whole situation was. He suggested we simply walk around to the other side. But of course, we all understood that the creature would follow the rim of the hole. And while we could have fanned out and approached the circle from multiple directions at once, somebody would then have to face the creature almost one-on-one. I didn't see Philune offer to self-sacrifice.

Simple enough—there was no getting in without dealing with the creature.

Philune did not like hearing that. He suggested that Axon should attack with her Water Blade since the creature clearly feared the weapon. Axon did not answer this. She merely stared at him until he finally stopped talking. It was a relief to us all.

After a moment, Pilot turned to Axon and Thalia. He wondered if there would be any room to reason with this creature. Thalia shook her head. Though we had never seen such a creature before, we had encountered other beings of the North. We had yet to find one that would talk with us. In fact, if this creature had any way of speaking beyond that terrible shrieking, we did not know it.

Pilot tipped his hat back and grinned. He said, "Then I guess we'll just have to figure out how to kill the darn thing. Because there is no way any of us are leaving without the Shield." We all agreed.

"It seems that you got along with Pilot," Zev said.

He's a very likable person. Lost witches do not often see men. Dacci men want nothing to do with us, and most other males in the world fear us. Unfortunately, the majority of those experiences we have had with non-Dacci men were unfavorable. But a few of the men in this gathered group surprised us—or, I should say, me. The others did not share my interest. As much as one can say, Pilot certainly led the pack of decency when it came to your gender.

"I take it that Philune did not garner the same respect."

Certainly not for me.

In fact, I suspect that if anybody other than Pilot had suggested what he did, none of us would've followed. Definitely not if it came from Philune. But as it happened, Pilot was the one who brought us all together. He pointed out that just as we had relied on each other to come this far, we could further rely on each other to overcome this creature. We knew bullets would not hurt the creature and none of the witches would sacrifice a tooth to cast a spell unless it was our last resort. Pilot assured us that would not be necessary. He even gave Philune credit for pointing out the way the creature evaded Axon. Pilot felt certain the Water Blade could cut through that carapace. We merely had to make it possible.

The plan we settled on was simple. I'm told that's a sign of a good plan.

Every one of us had a task involving attacking the creature. Though none of us expected to actually strike the thing, that was not our intent. The Easterners took up positions creating a half arc in the back. From there, they would repeatedly shoot at the creature, forcing it to react with its carapace. At the same time, the witches would make as much noise as possible while we ran at and dodged around the creature. Finally, Pilot and his men would swipe at the creature with their swords.

The idea, and the hope, was that in all of this attacking we would confuse the creature. Axon would wait for the proper moment, and when she spotted a good opening, she would fly in fast with her Water Blade to skewer the creature and destroy it.

"Is that what happened?"

No.

It began that way. Philune marched back and forth behind his men calling off a firing order. My sisters and I did our part running circles around the creature. Pilot and his men made their moves like the trained professionals they were. All seemed to go well.

The creature did not stay in one place, of course. It moved at us, and we jumped and ducked. It had the grace of a dancer with speed like a bullet. We thought we were herding the creature closer towards where Axon hid amongst the horses. But we were fools to think we had any control in the situation. It was the creature who had been moving us.

You see, at first it lunged at me. At anybody who was close. But it soon realized it would not be able to get to us without exposing itself to the others. Which meant that it needed to thin the attackers in some other manner.

So, it moved closer and closer to the guns. At one point, Vost was in the process of reloading his weapon when the creature made its move.

It swept across a swath of snow. Vost reacted fast and almost got away. But he slipped on the wet surface, and the creature latched onto his arm. He screamed out as blood spurted.

It was not how we planned things, but the creature's momentary attack on Vost gave Axon all the opening she needed. The Water Blade sliced through the creature with a hot, sizzling sound. It let go of Vost, screaming as it rolled on its back, exposing its soft white underside. In its pain and confusion, the carapace did not know where best to move to protect it. A downward thrust, and Axon ended the creature's life.

Philune started offering congratulations, but Axon raised one hand to quiet him. She listened closely to the wind. The rest of us understood. This creature could not be alone. There had to be others. We had to move fast because at some point in the future, its replacement would arrive.

Zev let those words hang in the air. "Thank you for your helpful answers." He put on a show of deep concentration before speaking again. "Tell me, do you have any cuts or wounds on your arms perhaps?"

No. Nor on my feet. I was not involved in that fight directly or any of the other fights. That's not my purpose with the Lost. Ashturov wears bone armor and carries a spear. She is a warrior. I focus on casting spells.

"I see. You also help carry the Virgin Cart. You must be quite strong."

No more or less than any of the other sisters.

"You carry that Cart everywhere. I imagine that after all the time you spent lugging it around, you could probably carry a lot of heavier items, too."

We can carry anything we are asked to carry. If we come across something too heavy, we always have spells to help us.

CHAPTER FIVE

As Zev stepped into the hall for a break, he could feel Mr. Duke's eyes on his back. He had to give the King's Aide some credit. The man had kept quiet for the most part, and though his looks grilled upon Zev, he refrained from outright saying anything. That didn't change the fact that Zev felt the pressure.

He needed to come up with a solution, but these interviews brought up more questions than answers. If he had more time, three days would do it, he knew he could solve this matter. With that much time, he would be able to hear each person tell the entire story from beginning to end. The omissions, the mistakes, and the blatant lies would present themselves like a blazing fire in the dead of night. But even at a pace he considered rushed, time unraveled too fast.

Leaning against the hallway wall, he covered his face with his hands and tried to block the world for a moment. Something in his mind wiggled like a loose tooth—a thought he could poke but not dislodge. He wondered if he had already heard the key details he needed but missed them. Or perhaps it had been something he saw.

"Or perhaps I'm just wishing with empty prayers," he muttered into his hands.

He heard a muffled cough from down the hall. His head snapped up—the spy. Zev hurled down the hallway. Dashing along the wood flooring, he could hear the spy's rapid footsteps diminishing in the distance. When he turned the corner, he found only an empty hallway.

Not entirely empty. On the floor, near the edge of the wall, his eye caught a small, pink dot. Lowering on his hands and knees, he crawled up to inspect this little thing. A flower petal. A small flower. Like an appleday or a pink rumple.

"Or the flower of a Feral Moon."

Lady Jos.

Sitting back on his heels, Zev stared at the empty hall. How could a woman in a formal gown possibly have sprinted down this hall and escaped before he even reached the corner? Of course, if she knew the castle well, then she would know which doors would be unlocked and which ones led to access passages for a fast exit.

Zev stormed back to the interview room. He did not like being toyed with under any circumstances, but using his old friends for the purpose went beyond the line. To Mr. Duke, he said, "Go to the ballroom, find Bellemont, and have her escort Lady Jos to meet me near the King's Gardens. I'm pretty sure I know how to get there, but you can show me on the way."

Mr. Duke snorted. "Don't you dare speak to me like that."

"You're one of the ones demanding answers fast. This is going to be a big help in that direction."

"That's no excuse for rudeness. And if this Lady Jos will help matters, then I think you would be wise to—"

"Either do it, or I'm going to that stage and ask the King to provide me with another Aide. You can deal with the repercussions on your own time. I'm out of patience."

With a roll of his eyes and a flap of his arms to suggest he did not care, Mr. Duke led the way. But Zev could see the flush on the man's face, the shiver in his eyes, and the twitch of his lips. After a few hallways and a flight of stairs, Mr. Duke indicated the passage toward the Gardens. "Lady Jos will be with you momentarily."

"Thank you," Zev said, with as much sincerity as he could muster.

Once Mr. Duke had walked away, Zev let out a long-held breath.

He suspected that waiting for anything important would never get easier. The mind refused to allow it.

He paced by the Garden's iron gate. During the day, the maze of flowers and bushes filled the air with fragrant aromas and created a colorful sensation for the eyes. Or so Zev had been told. Bellemont raved about the dazzling experience on several occasions, but during his previous visits to Ridnight Castle, Zev never had the opportunity to behold the sight himself.

Looking into the Gardens now, he saw only the dark. Perhaps if he succeeded this night, the King would invite him back again, and he could finally behold this wonder. On the other hand, if he failed, he would be lucky to see anything ever again.

No, he couldn't think like that. King Robion had proven on numerous occasions to be a thoughtful, fair, and just king. Zev did not believe the man would punish him if he could not find the thieves or the Shield.

Still, all kings had to play politics. If things went bad—really bad—it may turn out that the best move would be to sacrifice Zev. A scapegoat could be a wonderful thing for those in power.

Before his thoughts could darken further, the soft steps of Lady Jos echoed from the hall. She approached with the same glittering smile as if the party had continued and nobody felt a single bit of tension in the air. Swishing her dress playfully with one hand, she offered a formal curtsy before giggling.

"I didn't think I would see you again so soon," she said.

"I didn't think you had it in you to spy on me."

Her expression never broke, even as she looked away. "Oh. You found me out."

"Not many people here wear such expensive flowers."

"Of course they do. I would be willing to wager that the cost of all the flowers worn tonight far exceeds whatever your king paid to feed us all."

"Perhaps. But you're the only one wearing a flower as unique as the Feral Moon."

Gazing upward as if she could actually see the towering artistry of her hair, she said, "I'll have to remember that for the next time."

"Do you understand what's going on here?"

"Of course."

"Then how can you stand there and smile at me? I know it was you in the hall spying on me, and you at least have given me the courtesy of not denying it. My job tonight is hard enough. I don't need spies making me worry about the different factions claiming parts of the ballroom as if it were the world itself. I'm surprised that Philune put you up to this. As much of a fool as he appears to be, he should have tasked one of his men for the job." Zev caught the shift in her expression. "I see. Philune didn't put you up to this. Then who?"

She turned several steps away. "Please, be kind. Don't embarrass me."

"If not Philune, then one of his men? No. Even Vost, who probably has the most clout at the moment with Philune, even he wouldn't go behind the Captain of the East's back. It would have to be somebody who chose to send a Lady despite all the gowns and flowers. Somebody who would trust that, as a gentleman, I would not cause too much trouble if you were caught."

"I beg you," she said, though her voice remained firm.

"There's only one other name that makes any sense—Lord Radugo. He would want to keep his men close by so as not to cause suspicion. But why would he need to know of my progress? None of the people coming tonight knew about the Shield until they were here. Lord Radugo might be simply trying to take advantage of the situation. If he found out any small bit of information—especially information that pointed at the Dacci or the Frontier—he would want to capitalize on it before Philune or the King could make a move. Is that it?"

He took Lady Jos by the shoulders and turned her gently. "Tell me. I could've gone into that ballroom and questioned you in front of everybody, but I brought you out here so that your reputation would be protected. I won't betray you. But I need to know moving forward who my enemies are."

With a bitter chuckle, she dabbed a lace cloth at her eyes. "Enemies? You have it all wrong."

"Don't play games. I know what I saw."

She placed her gloved hand on his cheek. "So smart, yet so thick."

Zev yanked her arm down. "There are lives in danger here. If I've missed something, then tell me. I don't have time for this."

She wrenched her arm free. With a pout devoid of her usual glimmer, she said, "If you remain this stupid, you're never going to get a wife."

Zev stepped back, trying to comprehend this sudden turn. "What is getting a wife have anything to do with the theft of the Shield?"

"Absolutely nothing." She turned and walked away. But after a few steps, she whirled around and stomped right up to him. "Not everything is about your hunt for a thief. I'm sure tonight seems like it's so important, that the fate of humanity hangs together by the thinnest of strings, but the truth is that I've sat in many fancy ballrooms and seen many of these political ploys, and in the end, they don't amount to much. A lot of posturing. But some of us have other interests. Some of us have spent years dreaming about our futures—real futures beyond who gets the most money. And some of us were left behind while others went off into the world to go adventuring."

"Are you talking about yourself?"

With a groan toward the sky, she walked away. Over her shoulder, she said, "You're so worried about enemies? You've got another one now."

The wind picked up for a moment, and the sweet scent of flowers from the King's Gardens drifted by. Or perhaps it was the sweet scent of Lady Jos. Zev tried to come to a quick conclusion about her, but nothing about her offered fast answers. He opted instead to tuck this moment away for later thought. He needed to prepare for his interview with Thalia.

With a sigh, he turned in a short circle. He knew which direction he had come from, but his thoughts had been upon the spy and not the exact path he had followed Mr. Duke. Drooping his shoulders, he shook his head. He would have to locate a guard or somebody else to help him find his way back.

Then he heard the shouting.

An uproarious chorus that echoed in a cavernous room—it had to be the ballroom. Heading off in the direction of the noise, he followed it as it grew louder. Two wrong turns, but otherwise, he found his way. It did not take too long before he stood at one of the side entrances to the ballroom.

The guard at the door blocked his entrance. "I'm sorry, sir, but nobody's allowed in or out."

Zev put on a friendly grin. "I'm the Master Solver. The one King Robion assigned to fix this mess."

The guard hesitated. "I'm sorry, but I was not informed of anybody with permission to enter. And I've not heard of a Master Solver. I can't let you in."

"That's okay. It doesn't sound like I want to go in there anyway."

"No, sir, I don't think anybody would want to."

Zev made a show of checking that they were alone. "You smoke? If you want, I'll watch the door for you while you go enjoy a swig."

The guard chuckled. "No, sir, I've avoided the habit."

"You're a good man. I'll make sure King Robion hears about you." With a more relaxed posture, he asked, "How bad is it in there?"

"Getting worse and worse," the guard said, his stern stance easing back. "If you really are here to fix things, you better do so fast. I had to go in there a short while ago to break up a fistfight."

"Truly? They're throwing blows at each other?"

"Two of them."

"I can't imagine someone from the East attacking one of the witches? Not those pompous men. Or was it someone from the Frontier?"

"Nobody from the Frontier would dare defy King Robion. Especially in his own home."

"My apologies. You're absolutely right."

"It actually was two Easterners. One of them wanted to go fight the witches while the other demanded patience. Apparently, patience didn't last long."

"Any idea who the two Easterners were?"

"One of them works under the Captain of the East. I don't know about the other, but he appeared to settle down near the one in charge with the big mustache."

Zev thanked the guard and headed down the corridor. Sounded like Philune and Lord Radugo were forming two factions within the East. Probably Philune's man was the same one he had stalled for. Lord Radugo's man could be any of them.

After turning two corners, Zev came upon what he thought was the backstage door. It banged open with Thalia slipping out like a dark shadow breaking from behind a dark cloud. Mr. Duke followed.

"You," she said when she spotted Zev. "You said I would not have to be interviewed."

"I said that you wouldn't have to be interviewed at that moment. But that eventually you would. That time has come."

From behind her, Mr. Duke gritted his teeth and clenched his hands. "She refused to come, even with the King watching, but when I explained to her that if she failed to talk with us, many of the people in the ballroom might die. She finally agreed."

"It is clear to me," she said, "that if I can be of any help, I will. That bag of lifeless, soulless cloth is going to open fire at any moment."

"I believe she's referring to Lord Radugo."

Zev moved in closer, trying not to wrinkle his nose at her sharp stench. "Then I am sorry that I have to call you in, but I'm glad you are understanding about it."

"Let's get this over with. Now."

The King's Aide led the way back—thankfully. With only a few turns and a short walk, he had them at the interview room. Zev laughed. Had he been on his own, he would have spent the rest of the night searching for that room.

As they settled in, he whispered to Mr. Duke, "If I'm ever invited back to this castle, please provide a map."

Mr. Duke smiled—a genuine smile.

Thalia sat and set her eyes upon Axon. Neither woman flinched. Zev put on another performance—this time pouring yet one more mug of water and doing everything he could to let the two women continue their stare-off. He did his best to surreptitiously observe each woman's face and body posture. Axon appeared as she always had. Sitting straight and firm, keeping her face as stoic as ever. Thalia's eyes, however, seemed to be asking a question yet not receiving an answer.

"Do you have specific interests, or should I just talk?" she asked. Away from the noise of the ballroom, her voice surprised Zev with its soothing, natural tone. Not the sharp honed weapon of a leader. Certainly not the frightening, toothless sound of a seasoned witch.

The more he watched her eyes, the more he thought she was both a strong leader and quite seasoned. In fact, if he were a witch and had been raised to hide his mouth so that others could not know how strong he was, it would be smart to hide the sound of one's voice for the same reasons. For casting spells, he would start with the teeth in the back, preserving his front teeth as long as possible so that the most obvious speech issues would not take form until his final spells.

Zev shared a knowing grin. "By now, you must have heard from the others what to expect in here. So, whenever you're ready, please begin."

WITNESS ACCOUNT OF
THE WITCH THALIA

After dealing with the creature guarding the entrance, we regrouped. I ordered Inx to nurse Vost's injured arm while the rest of us explored the cave beneath. I needed Ashturov and Barna because they were my strongest witches. Doz was a good follower. But Inx did not have much fighting skill. However, she is an excellent spellcaster. She would be able to attend to Vost, and should more of those creatures arrive, she would be able to protect them both.

All three groups had the foresight to bring rope on our journeys, so we were well-situated.

Zev leaned in closer to listen. She had an unusual way of talking as if she not only chose her words with care but the very shape of her words, too.

As we tied off on large rocks surrounding the rim, Philune kept poking at the creature's carcass.

"Crayten," he said.

Axon asked him before I could. "What you talking about?"

"That's what we'll call these things. Crayten." My confusion must have shown because he laughed. He said, "After my ex-wife."

His men forced a laugh. Axon's people, too. I understood the joke but did not find it amusing. I did tell Inx that should she need to cast a spell, she could use the corpse of the crayten. Its connection to that particular location might give her extra power.

Axon stopped everybody from moving. She suggested that only two of us go down at first. After all, we had no idea what to expect. She suggested she be one of the two. I immediately volunteered to join her. I expected Philune to complain that his group should be represented as well, but he said nothing. I admit I was still a bit surprised. I thought his greed would overcome his cowardice.

As for my people, I thought it a wise decision to have them wait. In addition to caution, I expected we would need the Virgin Cart lowered into Taladoro if we were ever going to get this Shield out. After all, if finding and taking the Shield were easy, it would've been done centuries ago. My instincts and my logic told me that we would need all the spell power we could get.

Then, with the help of Pilot and Kapa, Axon and I stepped through the hole into the real Temple of Taladoro.

As we lowered, we witnessed an amazing sight. A kind of artistry that astounded me far more than the impressive statues in the mountainside above. Columns and sculptures had been carved directly into the walls of a large cave. The air around us was notably warmer, enough so that it melted the water on the edge of the opening above— water that dribbled on my head as we lowered. The sound of these drips plinking against the ground created a music that echoed around us and filled the room with endless, delightful sounds.

We Dacci are not known for being appreciative of such beauty, but I admit that I held my breath in awe.

Mr. Duke sat forward. "Forgive me, Mr. Asterling, for interrupting, but these words are the first I've heard of this. Not the cave, but the details. Why was King Robion not informed? Such a great find requires further study. Clearly, this Temple is a relic from some past civilization. We need to send a team up there at once."

I don't see why you would be so interested. It's just an old room. Lovely, yes, but of no value anymore.

"Is that why you didn't tell the King? Want to save the riches all for yourself?"

You misconstrue my words.

Thalia turned her eyes to Axon. Before Mr. Duke could get in more of a huff, Zev shifted in his chair so that he faced Axon, too. "You did not mention this to the King, did you?" he asked.

"That's because there's nothing to inform the King about," Axon said. "Thalia is describing the room as she experienced it, as she saw it. But that is through the eyes of a Dacci witch. One who has been roaming the empty lands of this world with a handful of sisters and no other contact. Believe me, it was not as impressive as she makes it sound."

Mr. Duke leaned on the table. "Then what was it like?"

"There were a few carved columns in the walls, but the level of artistry was paltry compared to even the furniture that had been in this bedroom earlier. Thalia is correct in detailing the sounds of this warm cave. The melting snows made an unusual music. But it went no further. Most of the walls were too dark to see. In fact, the only true treasure was the Shield itself."

Before Axon or Mr. Duke could go further, Zev rapped his fingers against the table and sat back. "Yes, Thalia, please continue from when you landed on the ground and found the Shield."

My apologies. I did not mean to cause any problems. Hearing Axon describe the cave in her words, well, that is more accurate.

"It's okay. I think I understand quite clearly. Just continue now."

At the bottom, the Shield stood like a soldier at attention. A shaft of sunlight through that opening illuminated all its glory. This one spot had been carved out drop by drop. From my guess, there had once been a large column of stone reaching from the floor to the ceiling. Something caused it to fall, ripping that hole in the top, and leaving behind a mound taller than I could reach with my hand. That was the beginning of the Shield.

You could see where the stone had fallen aside. It stood out because most of the ground was fairly smooth. Soft ground. And I remember thinking how strange that was. But I dismissed the thought because we had this incredible Shield in front of us. The goal we had sought.

We quickly signaled for the rest to come down and to bring the Virgin Cart. On sight alone, I could tell the Shield was enormously heavy. Plus, the bottom was still partially built into the stone it had been carved from. We would need a spell to set it free and float it to the top.

It took a while, of course, but eventually we lowered the Virgin Cart on the ropes and set it in front of the Shield. All but Vost and Inx then came down to help.

"Why did everybody need to come down? If you were simply going to use a spell to lift this giant Shield to the top, why go through all the effort of having everyone descend?"

Because Axon is a smart warrior. She insisted on the rest coming down, fully armed, fully prepared. Like you, I thought it was silly. We needed our soldiers up top for when more craytens arrived. But where I had discounted the smooth ground, Axon saw danger.

After Pilot descended to us, finishing our complement of the team, I found out what Axon feared. I heard a strange click—like two hard surfaces bumping each other. Then I saw—the dark shadowed walls moved. Everywhere I looked, everywhere I thought was shadow or empty space, the dark carapaces of the craytens moved. They were the walls, and they surrounded us.

"I think that is plenty," Zev said. "Thank you for your time."

What? I need to tell you about—

"You made it quite clear that you did not want to be in this conversation, and I'm trying to respect that. You need to get back to your people and help keep things calm in that ballroom. I've acquired plenty of information from you, and if you would be kind enough to have Pilot return once you get to the ballroom, I believe he can provide what happens next."

I suppose. But—

"There is one more thing. Did you suffer any injuries during your fight with these craytens?"

No. Part of our plan was—

"Thank you."

As Thalia left the room, Zev made sure to watch Axon's face. She held still, clearly aware he observed her.

FURTHER WITNESS ACCOUNT OF
PILOT

Wanted me back, huh? I guess you know who to call on when you need the truth. So, where are we picking up this time?

To Zev's surprise, Pilot's eyes fell upon Axon. Had he done that during their first interview? Zev couldn't recall. But now, it seemed evident that several people were taking cues from Axon.

"Just a moment," he said, turning towards her. "Would you please step outside? Once we're done with Pilot, I'll need you to fill in the final gaps."

"Me? I thought you didn't trust me anymore."

"Because we're under a time constraint, I'd appreciate it if you collect your thoughts so that we can speak as fast as possible when the time comes." He

hoped his excuse did not sound as absurd to her as it did coming out of his mouth.

With a tilt of her head, she said, "Of course."

Whether or not she accepted his reasons rested entirely on her state of mind. Clear-headed, she would see right through the deception. But Zev saw more concern and confusion in her eyes.

Nobody spoke while she exited the room. It was a strange silence. Not comfortable—more awkward than intense.

With the thump of the door closing, Zev nodded to Pilot. "Now, please continue from the point that the craytens revealed themselves down in Taladoro. I believe Thalia was using the Virgin Cart to release the Shield."

Oh. I see.

"Is there a problem?"

Just not something I want to think about. It was…an unpleasant time. The kind of thing that made me wish I was back in the Feral Lands with you fighting off an army of Dacci.

These craytens, they moved fast. It had been tough enough fighting one in the open air and sunlight. Down in that cave, they moved in and out of the dark, at times flashing their pale white bodies, at other times they were shielded by their hard, black carapaces. It was disorienting. And even though we were in a large cave, it had its limits. It was still a confined space. Even more confined because we couldn't go fighting off into the distance of the cave. We had to stand our ground to protect Thalia, the Virgin Cart, and the Shield.

So that's what we did.

We divided our circle around the Shield into four quarters. Axon led one quarter, Philune another, Ashturov another, and I led the last. With our backs to the Shield, we stood there and waited. Any crayten that dared come our way, we fought with everything we had.

It was a brutal experience.

These creatures moved in strange patterns. It seemed like they were crawling over each other, sometimes on the walls, sometimes on the ceiling, sometimes on the ground. If they'd simply stormed forward, I don't think we would've survived. Their numbers were too big.

On the way back, Thalia suggested that they must have had some experience with the Dacci before. They must've sensed her ability to cast spells and knew the dangers. So, they were cautious.

Maybe.

"You don't sound convinced."

I think Thalia has an inflated sense of her importance. Animals behave in all sorts of ways that don't make sense unless you think like they do. Doesn't matter, though. They did as they did.

"Don't dodge the real question. Why do think they held back?"

I happen to think they didn't know what to make of us. Nobody had been down there in ages. They may never have seen another creature like us. That made them cautious. No less dangerous, though.

And it's a pointless debate. Thalia needed to put all of her energy and focus into getting the Shield free. She couldn't be casting spells to aid the fight. Ashturov, Barna, and Doz—well, they were mostly fighting. Casting spells is not an instantaneous thing. We often didn't have a moment with enough rest for one of the witches to extract a tooth, create a pile of waste, and cast a spell. Remember, they have to concentrate on that process. It's difficult to concentrate when craytens are leaping at you without warning.

"I thought you said they weren't attacking you like that?"

Oh, they attacked. I just said that they didn't all attack at once.

They kept circling us, darting out an attack at different times. Sometimes only one crayten. Sometimes two or three. We would get one in Philune's quarter and one in Ashturov's quarter at the same time, or three would attack my quarter all at once.

We fought fierce and strong, blocking with our shields and counter-attacking with our swords. The Easterners knew from the fight above that their guns would do no good, but they proved to be quite capable with more basic weapons. And Axon—I could hear the Water Blade sizzling through the craytens' shells. They learned quickly to avoid her. But that just meant more came upon the rest of us.

Kapa fell first. I saw it happen. He had locked into a pattern of blocking and slashing, blocking and slashing. In battle, a rhythm can be very useful, very effective, but a pattern is something your enemy can take advantage of. That's what happened.

The creatures showed us at that moment they were smart. They picked up on his pattern, and they slaughtered him for it.

Three of the bastards charged us. I slammed my shield against the hard shell of one, knocking it aside. Absorbing that blow sent me off my feet. They knew it would. That was their intent. As Kapa used his shield to shove off the crayten on his left, he followed his pattern and immediately swung his sword. That motion exposed his right flank, and with me out of the way, the third creature leapt upon Kapa with ease.

The rest happened too fast. Kapa barely screamed. Worst of all, as those three craytens retreated back into the swarm of others, they dragged Kapa with them. We listened to them feast on his body, crunching his bones. We saw the thicker mass of black shells forming a ball around what was left of Kapa.

That first loss—seeing it, hearing it in that way—hit us like the wall of a violent storm. But we couldn't stand there too long. More craytens shot out of the dark and attacked.

As best we could, we closed ranks to cover the gap. If the creatures weren't making slobbering, eating sounds, they were shrieking like beaten children as they whipped around us. And the smell—first off, they smelled like the inside of your boot after you've been riding a horse all day long in the hot sun. Disgusting. But then we had a bunch of Dacci witches periodically trying to cast spells. I don't need to tell you what that smells like.

"But you said they couldn't take the time to cast a spell."

Didn't stop them from trying. With three witches together, Ashturov decided two could defend while one cast. I heard her order Doz to cast a barrier.

For a bit, nothing attacked us. Well, nothing attacked our side. Behind us, on the other side of the circle, I heard the sounds of an attack. I want to look back, but I didn't dare take my eyes off the enemy in front of me. Besides, I could hear enough.

Doz shouted for a brief moment. Then I heard nothing. Then I heard a feeding frenzy.

Axon tried to give orders, but the general chaos of battle coupled with the fact that I couldn't even see who she spoke to without taking my eyes away from possible attack, made the whole thing ridiculous. I did hear her shout at Thalia, asking how much longer we were going to have to hold this. Never heard the answer.

As the fight wore on, we began to tire. That much was to be expected. But a strange development took place—the bodies. We killed so many of these craytens that their corpses began to pile up. Not terribly high, only up to our shins, but enough that the new attacks had to step over in order to reach us. That helped us by slowing them down—even just a small bit. But it also meant that when a crayten attacked, it stepped up and came down at us.

The whole thing was insane.

"The fact that you're sitting here tells us you survived. How?"

I'm getting there. This was not an easy time. I want to make sure you understand clearly what happened. After all, of all people, Zev, you should understand that if you weren't there, it's near impossible to describe it to somebody else. But I understand the situation we're in right now, and I'm trying to do my best so that you get to the answers you're looking for.

And yes, it was bad. We closed ranks again, tightening our circle, doing our best to provide as much cover as we could for Thalia. But things fell apart quick.

I think the creatures could taste our desperation. They knew we were weakening. They probably could see it. If they had eyes.

Whatever senses they have, something in them figured it out. They did exactly what I feared—they attacked in large numbers. Not all of them, thank Qareck. If they had done that, I wouldn't be here talking with you. But they did attack in a coordinated way. Seven of them shot straight at us. Feddi was on my left end, and before I knew what had happened, they dragged him away. I fought hard against one of the creatures directly in front of me. To my side, Tagge tried to fill in the gap. I remember turning my head to him while shoving my shield forward against a crayten. I wanted to tell Tagge to pay attention and not worry about Feddi. My lapse gave the creature all it needed.

In an instant, it had ripped my shield down and launched at me. I pivoted out of the way, but it still latched onto my arm. Its skin was cold and clammy like somebody that'd been sick for days—I'll never forget that feeling. It surprised me because I expected it to be hot with all this energy and effort of battle. But no—that creature could have been filled with snow instead of blood. And it didn't bite me. I expected that, but instead, it just pulled. It wanted to bring me back to feed with the others.

Now, I'm not boasting when I say this, and Zev can back me up— I'm a strong man. Not indestructible, but I can hold my own. I'll tell you that vicious beast pulled with such hunger, with such ferocious need, that I could barely stay on my feet. And while I didn't fall, I still stumbled forward.

I thought for sure it was over. I was going to die. Tagge roared like a goddess angry with an offering. He slammed down with his sword, and he got his weapon wedged between two parts of the creature's shell. It let go of me, wailing and flailing, and as I fell backward, it twisted its body toward Tagge. That motion ripped the sword out of

Tagge's hand, and by the time I clambered back to my feet, Tagge was gone.

The man died saving me.

"You okay? Do you need a break?"

Axon called to shore up the circle again, and we could tell it was over for us. We were doomed. When faced with that type of situation, people react in very different ways. Sometimes strange ways. Sekat bellowed like a hibernating bowback awoken too early. "Save yourselves," he shouted so that his voice echoed off the cave walls. He raised his sword and charged forward.

He swung wildly as the craytens formed a hole to swallow him in. I did look over my shoulder to see who we had left. Just me, Axon, Philune, Thalia, Ashturov, and the Virgin Cart. And Barna. I missed her because she was on her knees casting a spell. Only she failed. Lost in the concentration of her casting, four of the beasts launched forward—two to distract Ashturov, and two to haul Barna to her death.

Now, I don't like Philune. Not at all. But from what I could see, he fought hard. There's a vicious side to that man when he's got no way out. And he finally did something worthwhile. He turned to Thalia and said that it was over. We had to leave. There was no way to stop all these creatures.

Thalia lifted her head, for the first time seeing the carnage we had endured, and she commanded that we all get behind the Virgin Cart.

"Nobody look inside," she said, and you could hear in her voice that this was not superstition. This was not religion. This order was designed to protect our lives.

I crouched near the middle of the cart. From there, I had no fear of accidentally looking inside, but I could see the roof and edges. I watched as Thalia crawled up over the top and unlatched the doors. With her eyes closed, she swung the doors open and dropped back next to me.

Zev, Mr. Duke, I know you've heard the rumors about what is

inside that palanquin. Everybody's heard. The Lost believe it contains a piece of Nualla. Now, Zev and I have both seen Nualla work through its people. I can tell you I have no doubt that thing was part of Nualla. Maybe it had something else in there, too, but I know what I saw.

These snakelike arms shot out with such force—they were like spears made of lightning. They slammed through every creature in its way. The craytens behind us, the ones that could easily have attacked us, didn't dare move. They cried out and scattered toward their brethren. But they only met a similar fate.

I didn't count how long we huddled behind the Virgin Cart. It couldn't have been more than three or four breaths. Then that thing retracted back inside and closed the doors on itself. Thalia scrambled up top and locked it in.

There were still craytens around us, but they pressed against the wall as if trying to slip through the cracks to escape. They were not going to move against us again. Still, Axon kept her Water Blade at the ready while Thalia finished the spell.

And that was it.

Soaked in blood, shaking from the energy of fighting, we waited until the Shield floated up to the surface. Ropes were dropped for us to climb, and we headed back.

None of us had the victory march you'd expect. We weren't celebratory, weren't full of mirth and battle stories we wanted to share. We had been lucky, and we knew it.

The whole time, Thalia had a powerful weapon at her disposal, but she could have chosen not to use it. She clearly never wanted to use it. If not for the Shield, I think she would have let us all die.

Zev could see the struggle on Pilot's face. "I'm sorry to have asked you to recall that pain, but I needed somebody I could trust."

Pilot flinched as more thoughts of battle appeared to cross his brow.

"Axon is waiting outside. Let's get this finished. Pilot, I hope you and I can have a drink when this is all over. For now, though, I'm sure King Robion wouldn't mind if you took some time to yourself in one of the empty rooms."

I might just do that. I suspect he wouldn't mind if I liberate a few jugs of wine, too.

FURTHER WITNESS ACCOUNT OF
AXON COPONIV

I still don't understand why you're letting me do this. I didn't think you would believe anything I said.

Zev clasped his hands in his lap and lowered his head. "I have never once doubted that you have told me the truth. I have only said that you're withholding information. Maybe I'm wrong. Or maybe whatever is causing your strange behavior has no bearing on the current question. But right now, I need to know what happened on the way back to the Frontier."

Nothing. We didn't encounter anything. Even the giant creature in the forest—we never saw it. It was as if by defeating the craytens, all the other creatures gave us a respectful distance. But Pilot could've told you that already. So why am I here?

"Because there's only one Shield and three groups. At some point, you and Philune and Thalia had to have discussed how to handle that situation. I don't trust Philune or Thalia to give me the full truth about that conversation. I'm hoping you will."

That? That's easy enough. The first day of travel, we did not talk about it at all. We wanted to, but everybody was physically exhausted and emotionally demoralized. We had lost so many lives.

But on the second night, Philune took the lead in bringing Thalia and I together with him. We met in his tent, and he wasted no time in raising the question that you're asking. Before I give you the answer we came up with, I think it's important to say that nobody tried to swipe the Shield from the others. Nobody tried to strongarm the others. We all understood that the only reason that Shield was with us, strapped to the top of the Virgin Cart no less, was because we all had worked together. Each of us, on our own, could never have succeeded.

And I think it was the fact that we realized this which made our decision fairly easy. While we understood that our respective governments and religious leaders would want to use the Shield's power for the glory of themselves, we thought it could do better by not being used. We thought it better to create a symbol out of it. So, we agreed to share the glory of attaining the Shield and hoped that by taking it here to Ridnight Castle, the center of our country, by inviting all our peoples together, we might take a step toward uniting us, instead of fighting.

Now I know that must've sounded strange coming from me. Just a few years ago, we invaded the Feral Lands and struck a blow against Nualla. But that did not get us anywhere. It delayed a larger fight and angered our enemy. After spending only a short time with Thalia and Philune, I questioned whether we had any enemies. The East—they want to make money. And while there is always plenty of money to be made in war, it's only for a select few. If everybody wants to benefit, peace is the only way. And the West— they want to follow Nualla, cast spells, and do what we all want, live peacefully.

So that's it. The conversation did not take long that night. We were of the same mind to begin with. We merely had to agree on where to take the Shield to start.

"And you convinced them to come to Ridnight Castle?"

Thalia suggested it. Philune, of course, wanted to bring it to the East. I could not decide what made the most sense. But Thalia understood the situation best of all of us. If our goal truly is to unite our peoples, it would not happen in the Feral Lands. Those of the Frontier and of the East are too prejudiced against the Dacci.

Zev, you know—we've both been to a Dacci village in the Feral Lands. That's no place for an Easterner. Could you imagine those ridiculous women with their overdone hair and enormous dresses?

They would turn their noses up and never hear a word that was spoken.

The East? The moment Philune showed up with the Shield, they would take it away from him. Either the government would confiscate it and not let anybody use it until they had found a military application, or the businessmen would grab hold of it and fight each other like slobbering beasts until somebody ended up with it in their sole possession.

The Frontier? We have one thing that separates us—King Robion. We had a short window to bring him the Shield and show him the potential for uniting our peoples. Ridnight Castle has the benefit of being appealing to the wealthy of the East yet rustic enough to make the Dacci somewhat comfortable. At the very least, it was closer to their homeland.

So, it was settled. We would take the Shield to Ridnight Castle, invite leaders from all over, and it was our hope to let the Shield become a symbol of peace and unity.

Unfortunately, that's clearly not what happened.

Axon stopped speaking and stared at Zev. He could feel the challenge in her eyes, the line set between them, daring him to cross, daring him to ask one of his small questions. But he refused to be pulled into that. No good would come of it. Besides, there were only two reasons to ask those questions. Either he already knew the answer and wanted to see if the person being asked would tell the truth, or he didn't know the answer, but the answer did not matter. Rather, he wanted to see how the person answered, how they reacted.

Those kinds of questions did not pertain to Axon anymore. He had already observed her throughout the night.

He noticed a little twitch at the corner of her mouth. Had she figured it out? Did she know that he had been watching during the interviews and all the storytelling that had occurred? Or perhaps she recognized that he had no answer for the King. Still.

"I really wish that we were both on the same side of this," he said.

Perhaps we are, and you just can't see it yet.

Zev cringed as his fingers tightened against each other below the table. He considered a handful of tactics but decided there was no more to gain with these questions. She had told her story, and he needed to digest it.

Setting his chair back, he rose and nodded at Axon and Mr. Duke. "I think we can adjourn."

"It's over?" Mr. Duke said. "Then who stole the Shield?"

He doesn't know. Not yet. But give him a little time. King Robion was right to put him in charge of this investigation. Zev is one of the most intelligent people I've ever met.

Zev barely heard her words. His mind had already begun to replay the various portions of the story each surviving member had shared. But before he could get lost in those thoughts, he heard three muted snaps.

He suspected the nature of the sound, but Axon's face confirmed it. Yet still he asked, "Was that—"

I'm afraid it was. Gunfire.

PART IV
WAR

CHAPTER ONE

More cracks of gunfire reached the interview room. Each shot struck at Zev's mind as if he stood in front of the bullets himself. They sounded like defeat, his investigation murdered by the impatience of others.

"We must get to King Robion," Mr. Duke said, drumming his hands on the table. "His safety above all else."

In one swift motion, Axon pivoted out of the chair and opened the door. "The two of you go help the King if you can. I must get to the changing room and retrieve my Water Blade." She did not wait for a response.

Mr. Duke led the way, and Zev continued to be grateful for that. Though he recognized some of the passages to the ballroom, so much of the castle looked the same—gray, stone corridors with the sharp lines of Frontier architecture. More than that, though, Zev could barely concentrate on where his feet took him. While his task had not been simple, it had not been something out of reach. Not for him.

What could have set this off? It had to be more than mounting tensions. Especially if gunshots were involved, because the Eastern lords and ladies were not warriors. Their weapons were more ceremonial than useful. If they wanted battle, they would have sent others to do the work for them.

The witches? They were certainly capable of instigating an attack, but his experience with the Dacci suggested they were more strategic. Breaking out into violence while locked within a confined space did not seem like an intelligent way to start a fight of this magnitude.

As they hurried down the corridor running the side of the ballroom, Zev noticed the godwalkers at every door. They stood with their arms out and their heads arched back. Could King Robion have started the battle? He mentioned having the godwalkers prepare for this very occurrence. But of all the players involved, King Robion least wanted a war involving all three groups. After all, the Frontier was sandwiched between the East and West. He would be stuck fighting on both fronts. He could never win.

They turned the corner and rushed up to the backstage door—the only door without a godwalker. Strange. A moment later, Zev understood why.

They stepped onto the stage where they found two more godwalkers in similar positions—hands out, heads up—facing the main ballroom. All the Dacci witches and Eastern lords below stood motionless. Locked in battle, the godwalkers had also locked them in tableau like statues depicting a great and tragic moment in history. But then Zev noticed tiny movements. So, not frozen but slowed. As Zev's eyes adjusted, he saw that, yes, the entire battle played out but moved far slower than normal. Slow enough, in fact, that he could watch the path of a bullet as it burst from the flames of a rifle.

"You're here. Good," King Robion said, bounding toward Zev. "Don't be deceived by what my godwalkers have done. It won't last for long. And while it might be slow for them in there, it is still progressing. They can still hurt each other."

Zev could see the face of Lord Radugo—eyes bulging, cheeks red, spit flying—as he jabbed a thick finger toward the enemy. On the other side of the room, several witches knelt before piles of waste as they cast their spells. Red Veil strode behind them, her eyes piercing through the slow time, directly at Lord Radugo.

The Frontier guests that had been on the stage earlier were nowhere to be found. King Robion must have had them escorted to a safe room. Others of the Frontier lining the bottom edge of the stage were caught in the slow time. Several of them gawked at the battle, pointing in different directions of horrors they witnessed. A few faced Zev, reaching up in hopes of getting help onto the stage to escape. The fear frozen in their eyes penetrated like a gruesome painting of an artist's nightmares.

Bellemont approached from behind. Zev had missed her when he entered, but the sight of his assistant flushed warmth through his system. "I'm glad you're not caught in that mess," he said.

With a wink, she said, "As am I."

"How did this happen?"

Grabbing Zev's jaw, King Robion wrenched him over. "Stop jabbering. Those people down there are going to kill each other unless you pay attention."

Zev nodded. "Yes, sir. Of course."

"Tell me who the culprit is. Who stole the Shield?"

There it was. The question Zev knew had to be coming. The question that would ruin him. He sighed. Best not to make his failure more painful than necessary. "I don't know. I'm close to an answer, but I don't know."

"You must give me a culprit. Right away. If you don't, I'll have to fake one, and I do not want to condemn an innocent man. But if one life must be sacrificed to stop this escalation, then as King of the Frontier, I'll name that man willingly."

Zev stumbled back as the King's words struck him in the gut. This had gone beyond his own reputation and the glories that came with success. The King's eyes did not deceive. If necessary, he would have an innocent man executed for this crime to stop the bloodshed in progress below. Perhaps in the world of politics that made sense, but Zev wanted to throw up at the idea.

"Wait," he said, stepping in front of the King. "Just let me think. I've heard the entire tale, I've been to the crime's location. I know I have all the pieces. I only need to figure out how they go together."

King Robion pointed at the nearest godwalker—a woman repre-senting Bieck, Goddess of Adolescents. "Do you see the shaking in her hand? Do you see the sweat on her cheek? We have no more time."

"Then be quiet and let me think."

Both Zev and the King looked shocked at the outburst. In a softer tone, King Robion said, "I've already sent my men to the dungeons. They will grab one of our prisoners to blame. You have until they return." He turned away.

With a shaking breath, Zev paced the stage as he thought.

CHAPTER TWO

W here to start? Where to start? Zev paced faster, back and forth across the stage, his head down, his fingers tapping the side of his skull as if he could loosen the answer from all the information that had piled up in there.

He needed a clear mind and a quiet room. The latter would not be happening. The former—he moved close to Bellemont and whispered, "I need you to find the men King Robion sent to the dungeons."

"Of course," she said, her brow wrinkled tight. "What do you want with them?"

"Not to see them. Stall them. Get me as much time to figure this out as you possibly can."

Bellemont waited until he paced to the opposite side of the stage. When he turned around, she had slipped away. Good. One less thing to worry about.

What did he know? Three groups from three different regions were each set on a course that forced them to crash together. They relied on each other in order to succeed at finding the Shield. They fought against terrible odds and paid a steep price in lives. But they did succeed.

Their victory united them both in glory as well as tragedy. Yet while they talked a lot about unity and peace, they did not seem as closely bonded as he would have expected.

Still, with Philune and Thalia as the leaders of the East and the West, none of this should be happening. Except they were *not* the leaders—they were only the leaders of their expeditions. Thalia led the Lost, hardly a representative group of the Dacci. And Philune bore the title of Captain of the East—only a military rank. Not president. Not the head of a company. By Eastern measures, a military ranking was admirable but not particularly powerful.

Which meant that the real people in charge, at least those in charge of the attending guests this evening, would most likely be Lord Radugo and Red Veil. Lord Radugo had done all he could to provoke a reaction from the West. He was insulting to the entire idea of peace. Red Veil had more control over the witches than anybody else on the floor, and she had been anxious for a fight from the moment Zev saw her.

Zev glanced out at the ballroom. Why did that matter? Looking at the battlefield, it was obvious who was in charge and who was not. Yet his instincts suggested he should pay attention to these facts.

He saw another rifle spit out flame and bullet. Lord Radugo had dropped to one knee and struggled to get back on his feet. On the opposite side, thick tendrils of black smoke snaked up from the three piles of waste. Most importantly, Zev could see the movement of everybody clearly. They were moving a tiny bit faster. The godwalkers barely held control over their spell.

Resuming his pacing, he smacked his forehead, tapping out a beat that challenged his heart to see which could pulse faster. Thalia had been the one to cast the protection spell around the Shield—the same spell that not only failed to stop the theft but failed to blare an alarm as promised. But he did not think Thalia stole it. She never would have had the time. Not with all eyes being on her while on stage.

Zev glanced over at the empty seats where Axon, Philune, Pilot, and Thalia had sat. None of them were on stage now. He stepped closer to the godwalkers and looked out at the ballroom. He did not see any of them on the floor. He did spot Ashturov in her bone armor.

She had pulled a bone spear off the Virgin Cart and slowly hurled it into the air.

Then he caught sight of Vost and Inx.

They crouched near the main entrance of the ballroom. Vost had one hand on the door, trying to shove it open. But that was not what seized Zev's interest. Not at all. It was Vost's other hand. That hand reached behind. That hand held Inx's hand as she gazed back at the witches. And not only did they hold hands, but their fingers were entwined.

The answer. Zev tasted it. He had most of it now, but the small details, the ones that made everything fall together were close. He rushed over to King Robion.

"Sir, did you ever see the Shield when it came here? Or were you going to see it for the first time tonight like everyone else?"

With a confused squint, King Robion said, "Of course I saw it. I helped make sure it was secure in the holding room."

"Did you touch it?"

"Yes," he said as if Zev were a fool. "Why wouldn't I? Such a sought-after relic. Surely you don't mean to imply that my touching of the Shield, helping put it in place so they could cast a spell around it, surely that is not the cause for everything you see out there? Is it?"

Zev grinned. "Not at all. You've done nothing wrong. In fact, you've just helped me find a solution."

King Robion's face brightened. "Who? Who's the thief? And is the Shield safe? Or did they get away with it?"

"I'll explain everything. But we've got to stop all of this, and the only way to do that is to find the leaders of the expedition."

"I don't understand."

"Don't worry about anything else. Think for a moment. Where would Axon take the others—Pilot, Philune, and Thalia? Where would she take them so that they could discuss matters privately right now?"

"Well, in the past, I've let her use my conference room for private meetings. It's the closest such room to here."

With his heart hammering in his chest and his throat tightening with excitement, Zev said, "Take me there."

CHAPTER THREE

Zev

Although Zev knew King Robion was far from an old man, it still surprised him when the King tore off at a full sprint. A combination of urgency and anger thumped the ground as each step propelled him, and Zev could feel the King's heat in his wake. When they reached the private conference room, the King slammed the door open. Inside, amongst the plain wood table and sparse decorations, they all sat—Axon, Pilot, Philune, and Thalia.

Philune startled and instinctively pushed back in his chair. Thalia refused to meet King Robion's eyes, opting to focus on the wood grain of the table. But Axon and Pilot looked calm and composed.

"You knew we would be coming," Zev said.

Axon offered the King a respectful bow. "I hoped our guests in the ballroom would not go as far as they have. I did not want it all to end this way. None of us did. I told you that we wanted to unify this world, bring peace to our countries, and that desire has driven us during this ordeal."

"Talking with cryptic words does not create peace. Only suspicion." The King whirled on Zev. "We are all here now. No more stalling. I want to know who stole the Shield, where it is now, and why these four are conspiring while war is breaking out a few rooms over. I want an answer, Mr. Asterling, or perhaps you would like to be the scapegoat I'm looking for."

Zev clasped his hands behind his back and stepped to the head of the table. "I'll tell you everything, but first—"

"I am your king, and you will obey me. By Qareck, what is going on in my own kingdom?"

"Of course. My apologies." But before Zev could begin, the door opened, and Mr. Duke entered. The man's face paled under the King's angered words. Mr. Duke slid to the side, keeping his back against the wall. Zev cleared his throat. "This is complicated, so please, listen carefully. The thieves are two of the members of the expedition—Vost and Inx. No need to rush after them. They're stuck in the ballroom, near the main entrance, and I'm sure you can have guards posted to grab them."

"I will."

"Then they'll be arrested when they step out."

Mr. Duke cracked open the door and whispered to a guard. The sound of jangling armor told Zev the guard had jogged off. After closing the door, Mr. Duke said, "I don't understand how you know it's those two. I heard all the same interviews as you. What did I miss?"

"Quite a lot, I suspect."

The King pulled back a chair and sat. "Get on with it."

"To begin with," Zev said, "Vost and Inx have had a deepening relationship from the first time they met. While most of the others in the expedition hovered close to their respective camps during travel, Inx would visit the Eastern camp on many nights. She got to know Vost quite well. Enough so that she nursed him to health after he was attacked by the crayten."

Thalia said, "I ordered her to do that. It was not by her choice."

"She did not argue, either. Ashturov, Barna, Doz—they would've insisted on coming down to help with the fight. To them, helping the Lost get the Shield far outweighed the injuries of an Easterner. But even if you want to argue that fighting was not Inx's vocation, that it made the most sense to have her healing the injured man, she did not need to continue doing so while you all traveled back. So, tell me, did one of you take over the job or did she continue?"

Philune nodded. "She took care of him the entire way."

"While that may all seem circumstantial, it was seeing them in the ballroom holding hands like lovers that confirmed my suspicion."

"But why?" the King asked. "They helped bring the Shield back. Why steal it now? It would've been much easier along the way."

Zev said, "It would not have been easier. Not with Axon and her Water Blade nearby. Not when they were in the middle of a strange and dangerous territory. Even if they had managed to steal the Shield while everyone was asleep, even if they had managed to somehow get a half-day lead on the people sitting here, do you think any of them—especially Axon or Pilot—would have trouble getting it back? No, Vost and Inx must have known their best move was to wait until the Shield was out of such capable hands. Waiting also gave them the time necessary to come up with a solid plan. And that's all assuming they decided to steal the Shield right away. Considering the hasty execution of the theft, it's equally likely they did not choose this course of action until very late—possibly after they arrived at Ridnight Castle.

"Now, as to why they stole the Shield—I think they were motivated by a mixture of interweaving issues. They were angry, for one. Angry at the heavy losses all in the effort to get this Shield. They were angry that the Shield would come back at all and that they would be praised despite the slaughter. They were angry at the idea that governments and businesses and religious leaders would claim the Shield, would fight over it, would continue—one way or another—to cause bloodshed over this artifact. And like a serpent in the grass, their love slithered between all of that. It fueled their passion. It gave them a desire to strike back at the unfairness of everything. Because in the end, no matter what I say about noble causes or vengeance for those who had died or any of that, the most unfair thing of all to them was that they knew nobody would allow them to be together."

Pilot shook his head. "Love?"

"Or lust," Philune said.

Pilot chuckled. "They thought that if they stole the Shield, and if this Shield actually had the well of awesome power it's rumored to have, then with her knowledge of spells, Inx could use that power and, I suppose, make things perfect for them. They could skip off together holding hands. Is that it?"

Zev said, "That's along the right idea. But when they got to Ridnight Castle, the problems began to mount. Their main plan was simple enough—they would steal the Shield, get it to some hired fools to drive off with, and then meet up with these drivers once everything had settled down. Not a great plan but not complicated. Unfortunately, for them, they discovered that the castle was difficult to get around. They both admitted to me that neither had ever been here, and I know firsthand that it's a maze. There was no way they were going to navigate the place alone. So, they hired somebody who knew the castle well."

"The fake guard," King Robion said.

"Yes. A former servant for the castle who either needed fast money or relished the idea of messing up your big plans or both. It doesn't matter. That man had the job of taking out the real guards, posing as a guard himself, and waiting. Once the Shield was stolen, Vost or Inx would hand it to their new man, and he would get it to the drivers waiting at the stables."

Pilot stabbed his finger toward Zev. "But the guard never showed up to grab the Shield because you stumbled upon the real guards tied in the pantry. With the help of those guards, you ended up detaining this man."

"And while I was busy inadvertently destroying their plans, they were in the holding room stealing the Shield. Breaking Thalia's spell would not be hard for Inx. After all, the witches admitted to me that she was extremely skilled."

The King said, "But why did Thalia's alarm spell not ring out?"

"That's a good question. We'll get to that. But for the moment we only need to know that Inx succeeded in breaking the spell. The Shield, which had been suspended in the air, fell fast. It would have crushed Inx, but Vost lunged forward to grab it. In doing so, the

Shield smashed into his arm which had been injured back during the fight with the crayten. The blow reopened his wound. Not a lot, but enough to leave the blood trail we discovered.

"Now the problems were becoming more evident. They waited and waited, yet their man did not show. They could hear King Robion giving his speech. Time was almost up. They had to expect a swift reaction once King Robion unveiled the missing Shield. Maybe they didn't know about the godwalkers, but they certainly knew that soldiers or guards or anybody available would scour the Castle in search of the Shield and the thieves."

The King snapped his fingers at Mr. Duke. "How much longer until the godwalkers fail?"

Reddening around his fancy collar, Mr. Duke said, "That was partly why I followed you here. I've been informed that in an effort to halt they battle's progress for as long as possible, they would have to release some of the edges of the ballroom."

"What does that mean?"

"That we may have fighting in the corridors soon. But I did have a message sent to the godwalkers to keep the main entrance frozen, so we shouldn't have to worry about Vost or Inx escaping."

King Robion leaned on his elbows and scowled from Axon to Pilot to Philune to Thalia.

Philune raised his hand. "Perhaps we should postpone the remainder of this fascinating discussion so that more pressing matters can be attended to. In fact, might I suggest—"

"Unless you have the authority to surrender the entire East to me, I suggest you keep your mouth shut." Rolling his neck from side to side, the King shifted toward Zev. "Continue."

Zev wished he had that jug of water. Trying to summon enough saliva, he went on. "With no man coming to take the Shield and the castle about to be flooded with guards, Vost and Inx decided to push on together. They took their chances and carried the Shield out into the hall. With any luck, they would not be seen. If they were, they would act as if things were normal. People tend to accept strange occurrences when such things are presented as acceptably normal.

"Luck was with them, though. As they scurried through those twisting passageways, looking for some idea of how to get to the stables, they managed to avoid detection. In fact, they made it all the way to the top of the stairs that led into the kitchen. But they never went further. If they had only known they could reach the stables through the kitchen, they might have tried. But they did not want to be seen carrying this Shield by all the kitchen staff. As they stood there, unsure of what to do, all of their hopes and plans fell apart. Because that was the point where they lost the Shield."

"This is ridiculous," Mr. Duke said. "How could they possibly lose a Shield as big as that?"

A knowing grin widened across Zev's lips. "That very question has been bothering me throughout this night. It bothered me more than anything. From the moment we searched the holding room, from the moment I was told what this Shield looked like, I could not figure out how such a big object could go missing. They never escaped the castle with it, yet no guards uncovered it. So, where was it?"

"And?" Mr. Duke said with an exasperated flail of his arms.

"Axon, would you care to explain? No? Then perhaps Philune? Not interested? Pilot? Thalia?"

They all bowed their heads like students being reprimanded by the teacher. The King watched their reactions, and his face stiffened.

"It's okay," Zev said. "I'll explain. The reason they lost the Shield was because it disappeared. Vanished between their hands. Because the Shield was never there. Never real. The reason their crime went so wrong and was so difficult to detect afterwards was because the four people sitting here never brought the actual Shield back. They faked the whole thing."

Crossing his arms and legs, Philune said, "Why, that is the most absurd thing I have ever heard."

Zev waited for more objections, but thankfully, none came. The shame on Axon's face balanced by the relief in her relaxing shoulders confirmed everything. But not for King Robion.

"That is a serious accusation," the King said. "To suggest that not only my esteemed guests but my own people would betray us all like this—it's unfathomable. If anybody else had said this to me, I would have sent them to the dungeon already. Unfortunately, you are the one speaking. Which means I have to ask—how am I to believe this?"

Gazing down the table, Zev waited to see if Pilot, Thalia, or Axon might simply admit the truth and save him the trouble. But both Axon and Pilot refused to raise their heads. And Thalia stared ahead with cold menace.

At length, Zev simply rested his hands on the table. "There are many small reasons. For example, Thalia's spell meant to protect the Shield and sound an alarm should it be stolen. We've been wondering why it never went off. There are only three possibilities that make any sense to me. One, Inx is a superior spellcaster to Thalia. That does not seem likely. Simply listening to them talk will show you how much experience Thalia has. While Inx is considered gifted and has a bright future in casting, she has barely cast enough spells to develop a lisp. Thalia talks well, but during her interview, I was struck by her way of speaking. Clearly, she had worked hard over the years to overcome any speech issues to hide her true strength. The second option is that Thalia failed to cast the spell properly. That somehow, after all she had accomplished throughout her life and their journey, somehow she could not pull off a relatively simple spell."

Thalia said, "Who are you to judge what spells are easy or not?"

"Granted, I am presuming. But, if you want to deny what I've said, we can get Bellemont in here to tell us the truth. Or, if you don't trust her, any one of the witches in the ballroom at the moment could speak to the matter. Perhaps the one wearing the red veil."

"I only meant to point out that you should not draw conclusions without proper information. But, yes, the spell I cast was rather rudimentary."

"One you would not fail to cast properly. Which leaves the third option. You never cast the spell to do the things you told us it would do. It only looked like a massive spell of protection with an alarm, but really, it merely kept the Shield floating in the air."

King Robion rested his chin on his fist. "Why would she do that?"

"That is the part that only makes sense if we accept the simple fact

—she knew the Shield was fake. To cast this spell, to protect the real Shield, is not such a rudimentary thing. Remember, the Shield is thought to hold great power. That's what we've been told. In order to protect such a thing would have required great power as well. Perhaps even more than one tooth could provide. But I saw the pile that she left, and it only had one tooth. I also saw the pile that Inx used. Also, one tooth. This was another reason I suspected the fake. There were two piles."

"Shouldn't there be two piles?" Mr. Duke said.

"Not if Thalia had truly cast the spell as she had indicated. She would have cleaned up the pile afterward. She wouldn't want anybody knowing the kind of spell she cast. Not when the other Dacci were around."

"Ridiculous," Thalia said. "You cannot tell the kind of spell cast by looking at the casting pile."

"That's right. Bellemont made that clear to me. But I also learned that the Lost and the Western Dacci do not trust each other. If Thalia had used a proper amount of power to protect the real Shield, then at least two teeth would have been in that pile of waste. Any witch attempting the theft would see those teeth and know what they were up against. It would be a clue on how to defeat the spell. So, Thalia would take it away. Clean it up. Let the spell stand on its own.

"But why do any of that if the Shield is fake and the spell is fake? Why do any of that when you don't expect anyone to be bold enough to actually steal the Shield? I argue that she thought it better to leave the pile in place with her one tooth, to put on a show of the spell being there. The second pile, of course, belonged to Inx who simply had no time to clean up afterward."

"I still don't understand," Mr. Duke said.

King Robion gestured toward Mr. Duke. "I do. A Dacci witch wears a veil to hide her mouth so that the other witches have no idea how seasoned she is at casting spells. They wear dark clothing to hide in the shadows. Their entire way of doing things involves not letting others know how powerful they are."

"Exactly," Zev said. "All of that adds up to the point that Thalia knew the Shield was fake and did not want to waste limited teeth on a pointless effort."

"That's it?" King Robion punched the edge of the table with the heel of his hand. "An extra pile of crap on the floor is the reason you accuse my people of lying to me?"

"I said that was one small reason. Here's another important reason—throughout this night, more than any other detail, one could not be nailed down by me. The Shield itself. How big was this thing? What does it look like? How much does it weigh? And by the end, I realized where the truth lay. Not with anybody who had dealt with the Shield here in the castle. No. The truth came out in the interviews when they told me about entering the cave at Taladoro and how they fought the craytens. Because it was down there that Thalia and the creature in the Virgin Cart had to combine their power in order to break this Shield free and, using magic, get it out of the cave.

"That bothered me. Why did they do that? Vost and Inx were able to carry the Shield together. You, my dear King, admitted that you had held the Shield yourself. Pilot is strong. Philune is strong. Axon is very strong. Any one of them or combination of two could easily have carried that Shield out of the cave. Unless the Shield was different than what we were told. You see, the truth is that the Shield is much larger and much heavier than anybody could lift. They told me that when they found the Shield, it was still embedded in the stone it was carved from. I believe that to be true. In fact, I believe the Shield is still there—still in the cave at Taladoro."

King Robion and Mr. Duke gasped. Before they could bluster another question, Zev continued, "Note that neither Axon nor Pilot has interrupted me once with everything I've said. They've not denied it. They've not stood in anger. Thalia corrected me and conceded a point but otherwise has remained mostly silent. The only one to question me was Philune, and forgive my rudeness, but after an evening of hearing everybody speak, he is the least trustworthy in this room. Mr. Duke can attest to that."

The King turned to Mr. Duke, and the man nodded. Philune

wanted to speak, but a sharp look from Axon cowed him. The King's gaze then cast across the entire room. He said nothing. He waited.

Zev understood. The King hoped that Axon would raise her head and her voice to dispel these charges. But that never happened. His people continued to look away, as they waited to bear his punishment.

With an expression both haunted and horrified, the King stood, clutching his elbows. "Axon," he said with enough force that her face lifted as if he had placed a blade under her chin. "Is this true?"

They all knew the answer. The King had to know it, too. But he needed to hear it.

"Yes," she said, no waiver in her voice. "And I would do it again."

Axon

King Robion grabbed his chair by the back. With a burst of breath like a raging horse, he tossed the chair over the table. It smashed against the wall, splintering into several pieces. As it clattered onto the stone floor, Axon did her best not to flinch.

From the moment that the fake Shield had been stolen, she had prepared herself for the possibility that they would be discovered. Especially after King Robion assigned Zev to look into the matter. The situation could not have been worse. By reputation alone, she would have held concerns about Zev. But she had spent serious time with him, had seen his brain in action, and she knew that the chances of fooling him would be slim.

In fact, whenever she had a small success—such as maneuvering a position at the interview table for the entire night—she had to wonder if she had actually succeeded or if Zev had seen through her and merely played along. He clearly knew something was off. He had said so a few times. How she wished she could simply bash her way through the problem. Wield her Water Blade and cut down her enemies. But it would never be that simple.

With a painful roar, King Robion slammed his fist on the table. "All this bloodshed for a lie. For nothing."

The time had come. Though she had never spoken false, she had withheld the truth. She could do so no longer.

Holding her head firm, she rose to her feet. But King Robion jutted his finger at the chair. "You sit down. You have betrayed me. You have betrayed the Frontier."

"It wasn't supposed to be this way," she said, careful to shove back any sounds of pleading. "What's going on in the ballroom is exactly what we were trying to stop."

"You're a liar. Why should I believe you about anything?"

Licking his lips, Pilot said, "If you'll just let her explain, you'll understand."

"Oh? Is that what I have to do? Let her explain?" King Robion stormed over to Pilot, looming from behind his chair. "Do you know that I was seriously considering promoting you again? You? Of all people who have come through this castle, you would have been considered the least likely to attain any serious position. But you worked hard, you showed loyalty, and Axon vouched for you. How could I not instill my trust in you? So, I did. And this is the result. This is the gratitude. You make a fool of me." He slapped Pilot's head down against the table, hard enough to break the man's nose. Stomping around the table, he said, "I stood in front of leaders of the East and the West, I brought them here to share this wondrous relic which we thought could change the world, and the entire time you were making a mockery of us all. I was a dancing jester."

Breathing heavy like a lumbering beast, he continued to circle the table without a word. Philune cleared his throat and said, "If you've finished ranting, then perhaps now would be a good time to suggest—"

"Silence," King Robion said, his eyes wide as if he had been slapped. "You finish that sentence, and I'll have you executed. How dare you come to my castle, my country, my home and play this game with me. At least Thalia has the excuse that she's a backward-minded piece of Dacci trash. You—a civilized member of the East."

To Axon's surprise, Philune jumped to his feet. Standing taller than usual, he lifted his chin and leveled a harsh, fiery eye at the King.

"You forget yourself. Just because this is your castle and your country does not make me your subject. If you execute me, as you so flippantly suggest, then you should be prepared for the serious consequences of such an action. Especially with a country that has mastered the art of rifles. If you think that's the height of our weaponry, you are sorely mistaken. Now, I suggest you sit and listen to your own people. Let Axon explain to you why we did what we did. Because we still have a problem in the ballroom. All of us do. And whether you like it or not, whether you feel hurt or betrayed, does not matter. The fact is that we are all that you have to save this situation."

As Philune spoke, Axon checked her own assumptions. She should have realized that Philune was not a coward—not all the time. With the exception of political puppets, nobody achieved success in the world of kings and leaders through cowardice. Philune simply knew where his strengths rested. He was not a warrior like her. He was not a brain like Zev. But he had a vicious streak.

He had told her as much during their journey, and she had suspected it when the haycart drivers killed themselves. They took one look at Philune, they recognized him, and they knew that while he might not be a brave soldier, he was no weakling. Especially if he needed to extract information. Philune had the blood of a torturer and the mind of a politician. He could deliver a speech when necessary, he knew how to throw a political punch, and he knew just how to make the perfect, most dangerous threat to get what he wanted.

King Robion gestured to Mr. Duke, and the man relinquished his chair. "Speak fast," the King said as he sat.

Philune eased into his chair and crossed his legs in a far more comfortable manner. All eyes turned to Axon. She wanted Zev to explain it all. He clearly understood, and he thrived on this kind of speaking. But passing over the explanation was not an option—not with the King's attention pressing upon her.

"We did find that cave at Taladoro," she said, the sound of her voice stronger than she could have hoped. "And we did descend into it. The Shield *is* there. But it is enormous. Not some shiny piece of decorated metal as you would think of one, but rather picture a giant mushroom of stone."

"Mushroom?" Mr. Duke said, the sneer in his voice unmistakable.

"It's a wide-topped shield on its back connected to a column of stone that plunges into the ground. From a distance, it looks like a giant mushroom. The Shield itself is a massive chunk of rock. We *were* surrounded by the craytens, and we did fight them while Thalia attempted to break the Shield free. But though we fought off the creatures, there was no way to get the Shield loose. Hacking at it with weapons barely chipped away at the hard stone. Perhaps, given years, we could succeed in that manner, but I doubt it. The power infused in the waters that created this Shield left the stone harder, denser, tougher than normal. And as we stood there amongst the corpses of our enemy, we considered leaving. We could go back to our respective homes and report all that had happened—including our ultimate failure."

"But you didn't do that," Mr. Duke said. Axon noticed that King Robion did not stop his Aide. She had seen leaders do this before—use an underling to speak words the leader did not feel becoming to spout himself.

"I said that we considered it. However, standing under the shadow of this huge Shield, we could feel its power pulsing off of it. You could hear it running in your head. No doubt it attracted these craytens like a pond of freshwater will attract wildlife. They wanted it. Needed it. And recognizing this, we had to acknowledge that the stories about this Shield must be true. It held such great power.

"That's when Thalia pointed out the deeper truth to us all—that if we return and admit failure, we would also be admitting that the Shield exists. We could not choose to lie about the entire expedition because our leaders would question why we returned empty-handed. Even you, King Robion, would wonder what happened, why I did not bring back the book or the map, why I had taken so long, if I could not find Taladoro. Even if you believed some fabricated story, there would be questions that didn't quite sit right for you. That's the problem with a lie that deep—too many questions with reasonable but unsatisfactory answers, questions that eventually would gnaw until you were forced to look into it more, questions that would lead to the truth. So, either way we handled it, the result would be the same—all the leaders of the world would send more expeditions. But those groups would not work together like we did. They would be under orders to get to the Shield first. To find a way to bring it back."

"In other words," Zev said, "there would be a battle."

"There would be a war. Those snow-covered mountains would be painted in blood."

"That's why you formulated this plan?"

"We thought that if we gave the world a version of the Shield, we hoped it might have the same effect as the real Shield had upon us. That it would make you all feel the power and awe of the entire universe. Instead of fighting over it, we could revel in it as a group, as one. Earlier I said that we wanted to bring unity and peace, and that's exactly what we sought to do."

In a calmer yet still dark tone, King Robion said, "This doesn't answer why you lied to me. Why did you betray me in such a way? Why didn't you trust that I could understand what you have told me now?"

"I wish things had worked out differently with that. Our first problem was that Vost and Inx remained up above. They knew nothing about what we had discovered. Philune understood better than any of us the problem that posed. He suggested we create the fake Shield. If we left Vost and Inx out of our ploy, then they would not have to lie. They would believe the Shield to be real, and they would act accordingly. We never imagined they would attempt to steal the Shield."

"That's the problem with deceit," the King said. "One can never fully understand the repercussions."

"I suppose so. Once we got to the castle, Pilot and I discussed whether or not we should inform you, sir. You should know that Pilot believed telling you the truth was the right thing to do. I'm the one that failed you."

"But why?"

"For the same reason we lied to Vost and Inx. Appearances. If you believed that our fake Shield was the real thing, then you would not be forced to lie yourself. There would be no hint in your speech or in your magnanimity or in your graciousness or any of your behaviors that might tip off these other groups. Our goal was to bring peace to our countries. In doing so, we hoped to save the lives of thousands and thousands of soldiers from a bloody conflict far to the north. With that much at risk, I did not want to chance failure.

"Perhaps I was wrong, but I felt lying to you for the greater good was the better choice. My loyalty has always been to the Frontier first and a king second. That is why."

Axon sat back and waited. Nobody spoke. Most importantly, King Robion remained silent. She thought that a good sign. He had always struck her as a thoughtful man. He did not rush blindly into matters and rarely reacted out of emotion alone. Despite his recent outburst, she trusted that the King she admired still existed.

At length, he stood. "Master Asterling, I thank you for the service you have provided. I'm dissatisfied about the outcome, but that is not your doing. In fact, I am indebted to you more than ever for your honesty—something that appears to be in shorter supply than I had realized."

Axon tried not to cringe, but the words pierced deep. The King's disappointment might as well have been her parents rejecting her desire for a life of adventure instead of ball gowns and dancing.

"All of you found yourselves in a tough position," the King continued. "I understand your thoughts in the decisions you made. And while your intentions may have been noble, your actions were not. Your first mistake was to lie to your own members—Vost and Inx. Obviously, your next mistake was lying to me." He walked over to Mr. Duke. "Please get me a report on the situation in the ballroom. I need to know how bad things are."

Mr. Duke made a short bow before exiting the room.

Clapping his hands on the table, King Robion said, "How are we going to fix this?"

Nobody answered. A terrible thought weaved into Axon's mind.

She could offer herself as the thief. The King searched for a scapegoat —she could be it. She would admit to stealing the Shield which would stop the battle, and the King could have his revenge for her betrayal. The more she thought about it, the more it seemed an honorable way out.

But before she dared to open her mouth, Thalia rose. She sniffed as if everyone else created the foul aroma in the room. To Axon, she said, "On our return, I gave you something. Do you still have it?"

Axon frowned. "You mean that rock?"

"Yes. The rock. Do you still have it?"

"I suppose. Most of my gear has been piled in the corner of my room. I haven't had the time or the desire to go through it all."

Thalia cocked her head towards the King. "Then I have a way we can fix this."

The King looked from one woman to the other. "How?"

"We will use the power of the Shield—the real Shield."

"But you left the Shield in Taladoro. We don't have time to go all the way back there."

"That is why I'm going to need that rock and a lot of assistance. This won't be easy."

CHAPTER FOUR

Zev

After hearing Thalia's plan, Zev hurried out of the conference room. Mr. Duke stood outside with two guards and a recently bruised man wearing filthy rags for clothes—Kallot, the prisoner meant to be the scapegoat. Bellemont waited a few steps away.

"You again?" Kallot said when he noticed Zev.

"He won't be necessary," Zev said.

"Don't listen to him. I'm plenty necessary. I'm the most important part of the whole thing."

"You should be quiet. They want to execute you."

"This guy knows what he's talking about. I've nothing to do with none of this. Not necessary at all."

"You guards take this prisoner back."

"Oh?" Mr. Duke crossed his arms, his fingers tapping against his elbows as he pushed Kallot aside. Looming closer to Zev, he said, "Don't mistake your shining moment to mean you have any real authority around here. You do not get to order me or my men."

"But I do," the King said as he entered the corridor. "How bad have things gotten?"

Mr. Duke cleared his throat as he tried to save face. "Of course, your highness. By reducing the sphere of influence of their spell, the godwalkers appear to be holding quite well for the moment. I've been assured that is not an infinite situation. As feared, there are stragglers who were not in the ballroom and are now outside the spell's influence. They have been skirmishing throughout the halls. I believe some hold the misguided notion that they can find the Shield and bring success to their side of the fight—or perhaps they seek some personal glory."

Pointing to the two guards, the King said, "Hadlo, I want you to take this prisoner back to the dungeons. When you finish, go to the Gardens. That will be the rally point. Jocha, you are to accompany Mr. Asterling. He has a vital mission. Do as he says. Consider an order from him to be an order from me. Mr. Duke, by my side. Move."

As the men went off in different directions, the guard, Jocha, faced Zev with an expectant look on his face. Zev waved Bellemont over.

"I tried to stop them," she said.

"You did perfect," Zev said. "You bought us all the time we needed. But now things have changed. Jocha—you know your way around this place, yes?"

Jocha, a rotund and baby-faced man, nodded. His armor rattled. "Yes, sir."

"Then you lead us, and I'll explain on the way. We have to move fast."

"Yes, sir. Where am I leading you to?"

"First thing we need is a bucket. Where do we find one?"

Jocha gave it a moment's thought before jogging off. "This way."

Keeping pace at Zev's side, Bellemont said, "A bucket? What's going on?"

In as few breaths as possible, Zev explained all about the fake Shield and the group lie Axon and the others conspired about. "But it turns out, Thalia had an extra little surprise. Something she did not tell anybody. Before she left the cave, she cast a spell upon two stones.

One stone she gave to Axon. It acts like a key. And it can open the door to the other one."

"The other one is where I think it is?"

"Back at the cave of Taladoro. Thalia believes she can go back to the Shield and use its power to make all this trouble right."

The crack of a rifle echoed through the hall as a bullet cut a divot in the wall next to Jocha. They halted, and Jocha pulled out his sword. Another crack and another divot—this one far too high. Like a terrified animal that can't find an escape, one Eastern man shouted a war cry and charged. He held his rifle overhead like a club. Must have been his last two shots, and with no time to reload, he tried to use the rifle as a bludgeoning weapon.

Jocha held his ground. The guard had been trained well, and Zev made a mental note that, should they all survive, the King ought to know of the excellent job Pilot had done in preparing his guards.

Gripping the rifle by the barrel, the man from the East opened his eyes wide and shouted again. Jocha ducked just enough to launch forward and slam his armored shoulder into the man's exposed ribs. The rifle flipped through the air and smacked into the floor as air gusted from his stunned gaping mouth. He stumbled back, but Jocha did not wait. A quick motion of the sword and the man fell to the ground gripping his side in hopes of keeping his innards within.

"Let's go," Jocha said, and resumed his steady pace.

Zev and Bellemont had to step over the bloodied mass, but they quickly caught up with the guard.

"Storage room is up ahead," Jocha said.

In only a few steps, they reached the door. Jocha pulled out a bucket and handed it to Zev. "Are there more?" Zev asked.

Jocha pulled out another bucket for Bellemont and one for himself. "Where to now?"

"Outhouse."

Confusion crossed Jocha's brow. "Excuse me?"

"Do you know how the Dacci witches cast their spells?"

As the truth dawned on the guard, his body slackened. "Do we really have to?"

"Afraid so," Zev said with a little warmth and a chuckle. "Nobody said being a hero was a clean job."

From down the hall, they heard men scrambling. Jocha did not need instruction. Rolling his head, he indicated that he would continue to lead. They left for the outhouse.

Axon

Two Eastern soldiers who had been tending to several autocarts during the party now rested in crumpled heaps at Axon's feet. Her Water Blade dripped a small puddle on the floor. She paused long enough to make sure neither soldier moved again. Satisfied, she marched through the castle toward her quarters.

She wanted to be angry with Thalia for withholding the information about the spell until the last moment. She wanted to point a finger at the witch and accuse her of betraying the group. But the hypocrisy of such an act kept her still.

At the cave, after battling the craytens, their decision had made clear and perfect sense. They didn't want to battle each other for the Shield, and since nobody could wrest it from the cave, what would be the point? Bloodshed over an unwinnable prize—pure idiocy. But the moment they had returned to Ridnight Castle, Axon realized she made a mistake.

If only King Robion knew how many times she had wanted to tell him the truth. Zev, too. She valued him more than most, and now she wondered if he would ever trust her again. True friends were hard to come by in life, and friends that would fight while traipsing through the dangerous wilds of the world—those were almost nonexistent. Yet she had Pilot and Zev and even Bellemont. *Had?* No? She could not say.

As she approached the door to her private quarters, she had to place her hopes in Thalia's plan. If it worked, then perhaps she would have made great strides toward repairing the damage she had done.

But she opened the door to find a Dacci witch standing on her bed, holding the stone she had come for.

Axon strained against her instinctive desire to leap across the room and lash out with her Blade. Had she been facing an Easterner, she would never have hesitated. But a Dacci—until Axon knew whether a spell had been cast in her room, she had to be cautious.

The witch had curly, black hair that poked out of her headdress like broken springs. Her veil had dropped below her nose revealing a crooked, pimply mass with long nostrils. So many blemishes suggested this particular Dacci was in her teens.

"Why do you have thith?" the Dacci said, swimming the stone in a circular motion. Her heavy lisp pointed to a lack of front teeth. Young and brazen—not a good combination.

"It's a rock," Axon said. "And this is my room." She pointed her Blade at the Dacci. "Unless you want to die, you better put the stone down and leave."

The witch laughed. Axon had to take in the entire room without losing her focus on her enemy. She did not spot any piles of bone or bile used for casting. The smell of the witch overpowered any other scent in the room making it impossible to know if such a pile might be hidden under the bed or behind the chair. Beyond the bed and chair, Axon had a small table and nothing more. Not many places to hide things.

"You should not threaten me," the witch said. "Not unleth you mean it. Though, I shouldn't be thurprised if you bluff. All you ever do ith lie."

Trying to hide the shake in her voice, Axon said, "You know nothing about me."

"You are the wielder of the Water Blade—a powerful weapon that you point at me, an unworthy witch. Oh, I know you quite well. You invaded my homeland and killed many people I knew. You fought and thtruck against Nualla. And afterward, your king called a gathering under the pretenth of peath. But when we arrived here, what do we find? The betrayerth of our land—the Lotht. You—the one who came in and fought our people. And the heathenth of the Eatht who have abandoned all propriety. Yet, we did not walk out. We were polite. We came to hear your overtureth and we waited."

"You think we planned this?"

"I put nothing beyond your kind. You've betrayed all. Now the Dacci are locked in that ballroom, fighting to live, and you are here threatening me with your Blade while lying to my fathe."

"I'm not lying."

She shook the stone in her fist. "Nothing but a rock? I can feel the thpell thurrounding it. Why? What did you do to it?"

"It's what I need to fix things." Axon had spotted nothing that resembled a spell. She decided to put away her Water Blade. "I'm not threatening you. Please, give me the stone so that we can help your people and mine."

But the witch had no need for a spell. The moment the Water Blade no longer posed a threat, she attacked. Leaping off the bed, the Dacci wrapped herself around Axon's head. Though small, the witch had enough weight to knock Axon off-balance.

Stumbling backwards, Axon lost her footing. As she went down, she felt the witch push off. Rolling to her feet, Axon swung out with her Water Blade, but the witch was already halfway down the hall.

Unfortunately for this young Dacci woman, Axon was a superior warrior. She sprinted through the hall, maintaining tight control over her Blade. Before the witch could reach the end of the hall, Axon had caught up to her. The witch glanced back, and Axon bared her teeth. She felt the satisfaction of the witch's fear.

And she plunged the Blade through her enemy's spine.

Zev

"Through here," Jocha said, leading them down two steps onto wood boards caked with mud. He opened the door to a court-yard with the privies sitting at the opposite side against the castle wall. Two large braziers bracketed the wood path leading to these privies, providing light and warmth.

With a cocky glance back, Jocha winked. "I told you I'd get you here."

He jogged out into the courtyard. He only managed three steps. Rifle fire rattled in quick succession. With a gurgle, Jocha dropped.

Zev and Bellemont pressed against the sides of the alcove. Breathing tight, Zev turned his head. Jocha did not move. Blood pulsed out of his neck and his leg. His head had twisted enough that he faced Zev—blood flowing rivulets down his nose and across his cheek. Though his dead eyes stared into nothing, they still managed to accuse Zev, to blame him, to peg him as responsible.

Zev looked away and listened. He did not hear footsteps. He did not hear running. Only the soft clicks of rifles being reloaded.

In a harsh whisper, Bellemont said, "Take my bucket. I'll cast a shield around us and we can walk over to the outhouse."

Zev shook his head. "You shouldn't waste a tooth on this. We'll find another way."

"We don't have time to go searching for another outhouse. We have a job to do."

"No, we don't." Zev battled the urge to push off the wall and pace as he spoke. "We've not been hired for this. It's not our job. We did what we was asked of us. What we should do is go back into the castle, find a way to the stables, and get out of here. None of this matters. I didn't even want to come here in the first place. We should be back at our small little business in our small little town."

Bellemont smirked. "I know you want that, but you also want everybody to know who you are. You want all the adulation of being the hero."

"I don't care about that kind of stuff."

"I've known you for too many years now. You can't lie to me, even if you want to lie to yourself."

"I'm serious. I don't care about adulation. If anything, I want respect. That's all."

Bellemont pointed at him but quickly snatched her arm back against the wall. She waited, and when no gunshots pinged off the stone, she said, "Why do you think you're here? It's out of respect.

King Robion, the King of the Frontier, the entire Frontier—he respects you enough to invite you to this very special event. And when things fell apart, he entrusted you with finding a solution. How much more respect do you need?"

"He only respects me because he's benefited from me."

"I don't know what that is supposed to imply. Of course, he benefits from you. But that doesn't mean he doesn't respect you."

"It means that we shouldn't be here. This is a bunch of rich people patting each other on the back, and then when things go wrong, look how fast they want to kill each other. And the only thing that slowed down the entire process wasn't me running an investigation, but was the fact that they all hoped they would get out of the situation fast enough to muster their troops and make a bunch of less fortunate people fight for them. It's insane. We should go back to Fernbund where things make sense."

"Okay," she said.

Zev paused as if she had spoken in a foreign language. "Now I don't understand."

"You want to leave here? You want to abandon Axon and Pilot? Okay. You go back to Fernbund and hide out there. We'll have failed here or we'll have won. Either way, your reputation will go into that outhouse."

"My reputation as the Master Solver will be perfectly intact. I solved this matter."

"And then did nothing about it."

"That's not our job."

"Maybe not for you, but I fell into all of this working with Axon. You helped us then. In fact, Axon and Pilot and me—none of us would be alive if you hadn't joined us into the Feral Lands. We would've been betrayed and murdered. And now, this night would have ended in war, guaranteed—but you discovered the truth. You have given us an opportunity to survive that fate." She dropped her angry scowl and sighed. "You need to accept it. You need to understand it."

"Accept what?"

"That the very things that will bring you the respect you want are the very things you do for the King. The things you do for the Frontier. For the whole world. When you hide in that little town, you waste the gifts you were given. For some, solving the mystery of who stole the farmer's plow is the limit of their gifts. And in doing that job, they are serving all of us. That is the level they're worth. And that is admirable. Respectable. But you—your gifts exceed most. If you don't use them for that purpose, then you don't deserve the respect you seek."

"And running out there to get shot is what I'm supposed to do?"

"You always use your brain to solve a difficult puzzle. Then you use that same brain to make your solution matter. You didn't just uncover the traitor in the Feral Lands. You helped fight Nualla, bring us all together, and save our lives. You were part of that solution. That's what you can do here. That's why I will use a tooth to cast a spell so we can cross to that outhouse and fill these buckets with crap."

Bellemont's words hung in the air until Zev laughed. Her cheeks raised, and she snickered.

Rubbing his forehead, he said, "I'm sorry. I don't know why I got like that."

"I imagine the men with rifles waiting to kill us had something to do with it."

"Of course, but I don't know what to think about everything you said. I do agree that if we leave, if we don't help Thalia succeed with her plan, then the likelihood of war is almost guaranteed. Okay. We go ahead. But how can you cast a spell here? You're not going to tell me that Nualla is underneath this castle?"

One of the riflemen yelled across the courtyard. "You got an eye on them?"

"I got nothing. You think they ran away?" another said.

"Let's be sure. I don't want any surprises."

Bellemont slid back along the wall until she reached the two steps leading into the main corridor. She dropped to her knees and pulled out her small bag of animal bones. Piling them in front of her, she said, "It never stops amazing me how little you all understand about

Nualla. He's not an animal burrowing through the mud and grime only to reach up to our offerings and grant us our spells. Nualla is so much more. Nualla is the ground itself. Nualla is the mud and stone and trees. Yes, the solid creature that you fought lives under the Feral Lands. But the energy, the spellcasting energy, lives throughout all. For there was a time long ago when Nualla was everything."

"Is that Dacci theology?"

She shrugged. From her pouch, she produced a small glass vial. She removed its cork stopper and poured a dark liquid onto the pile. While Zev did not know the vial's specific contents, the nauseating aroma clued him in enough. Last, Bellemont brought out her metal tool used for extracting teeth.

"I will only be able to hold the spell," she said. "I'm sorry, but you'll be the one filling the buckets."

"Just get on with it before I get crushed under the weight of all this wonderful respect."

Bellemont folded her hands over the offering pile and closed her eyes. Zev tried to calm his rapid heart in order to listen for the enemy —the soft footsteps, the clicks of rifles, the rustle of fancy clothing. Those men approached around the corner, sliding along the wall, trying to summon the courage to burst into the alcove. Probably the only way out of the courtyard.

Zev white-knuckled the two buckets. Sweat trickled down the side of his face. Cornered both physically and mentally, he bit back the desire to yell. Worst of all, his thoughts continued to return to Axon.

King Robion's rage at her betrayal did not compare to the gut punch he felt when he heard what had been done. Axon had sat next to him in interview after interview. She had numerous opportunities to confide in him. But she thought she could ride it all out, that she could fool him.

No. She never would make that mistake. Perhaps she actually gave him the respect he spoke of. Perhaps she recognized that he was smart enough to figure everything out eventually, so she chose to stay silent rather than risk giving herself away too early.

"Anybody in there?" one of the men said, attempting an authoritative voice but sounding unsteady. "We don't want to hurt you, but we will shoot."

Bellemont rose to her feet. She positioned her hands out to either side. Like a princess on her wedding day, Bellemont placed one foot directly in front of the other, walking forward with poise and grace.

"Last chance," the rifleman said.

As she stepped in front of Zev, she kept her focus forward. He knew enough to fall in behind her and stay close.

From over her shoulder, he watched as two riflemen spun into the entranceway. They glimpsed Bellemont, yelped, and jumped back. Though Zev could not see the other riflemen, he heard the clanking of their equipment as they rushed back to their previous positions. The two in front lifted their rifles and shot.

Zev dropped to his knees, but there was never any danger. The bullets made blue circles in the air in front of Bellemont. They did not shriek off into the distance. No spark, either. Just blue circles and the bullets vanished.

Picking up the buckets again, Zev pressed his head against Bellemont's back and followed her into the courtyard. To his right, three riflemen took up positions behind thick bushes. To his left, two more hid behind the wood storage structure.

All the riflemen opened fire. Several shots never came close. These men were trained in politics, not warfare, but the few that landed their targets only created more blue circles that dissipated into the air. Zev fought his instincts. He had to trust Bellemont's spell and ignore what his eyes told him.

They continued their walk across the courtyard while the riflemen shot uselessly. Each hit became a blue pinpoint, a star in the sky, before vanishing from sight. Zev could not relax but he could keep moving. When they reached the outhouse, Bellemont turned to the side, allowing Zev to enter.

He had expected this next part to be unpleasant, but when he realized they had forgotten to bring a rope with which to lower the buckets into the pit, his stomach threatened to create more of a mess. Part of him wished he would throw up. He could empty his stomach into the bucket and be halfway done. But his constitution held—queasy but firm enough.

Peering down the circular hole in the wood bench, he saw the muddy slop glistening under the flicker of torchlight. He rolled his lips in and shook his head. Breathing through his mouth—not much better than smelling the horrible stench—he lowered one bucket. At least, the gala had been going on a few hours before the godwalkers' lockdown—a lot of people had used this outhouse.

Unfortunately, not enough. He couldn't reach the surface by simply sticking his arm down. He glanced at the wood door. Perhaps they should retreat, find a rope, and return. But Bellemont's spell would not hold on forever, and he could not ask her to sacrifice another tooth because he felt squeamish.

"Qareck, if you really are watching over us all, you owe me one for this." Zev gripped the edge of the bench with his left hand and bent over into the hole. Stretching his right arm, he managed to get the bucket into the vulgar muck. It filled fast.

The added weight made pulling himself back difficult. The muscles in his arm complained and his fingers gripping the bench burned. He thought about those small joints and muscles and bones—four fingers kept him from dropping headfirst into the revolting pool of filth below him. Muttering a quick apology to Qareck for his impudence, he pulled again.

With a few sharp muscle clenches, he managed to extract himself and set the bucket on the floor. He dropped to the ground. Sweat covered his body, and he leaned his head against the wall.

"I got one bucket," he said, gasping for air that didn't have a taste. "Can you hold on for me to get the second?"

Through the door, Bellemont said, "I'm fine. But these gentlemen are trying to figure out how to kill us. Let's not give them too much more time to think."

Flexing his sore fingers, Zev returned to his feet and picked up the empty bucket. Thinking that he would never complain about mucking out an animal stall ever again in his life, he gripped the edge of the bench once more and lowered down.

As with most skills in life, repetition made things easier. Like a diver plunging beneath the surface, Zev inhaled deeply before plunking his head through the reviled hole. He made quick work of filling the bucket, and though his muscles angered at the effort—his fingers, too—he managed to pull out of the hole with surprising speed.

When he stepped from the outhouse, he found all the riflemen approaching with great caution as if they were coming upon a poisonous lapsnake and feared startling it. As they moved closer, they spread into a half-arc, cutting off all routes. A few men made sour faces when they saw what filled the buckets.

One man with a bushy mustache said, "It's all just a waiting game now, gentlemen. Eventually, that witch is going to tire. When she lowers her guard, we shoot."

Without looking at Zev, Bellemont asked, "Are we ready?"

"Yeah," Zev said, still carrying the buckets at his sides. "Any bright ideas on how to get out of here?"

"Set those down. When I make my move, we should be fine, but just in case, I want you prepared."

Zev bit back the urge to ask *prepared for what?* He wanted Bellemont completely focused on whatever she planned to do. Especially since the riflemen were close enough that he could see directly into their eyes.

Bellemont curled her fingers into tight fists. "I need you to step in front of me." Zev did as she asked. Her eyes were closed, so he said, "Okay. Now what?"

"Remove my hat, please."

Zev reached up and took of the wide-brim peach hat she wore.

"Now, remove my veil."

For a breath, Zev forgot about all the weapons pointed at him. For a breath, memories of a teen discovering an intimate act for the first time prickled his body. For a breath, he dared not move, fearing he would collapse the reality around him.

Even as his hands eventually rose, they did not feel like his own. His fingers reached under her dark hair, and the thin strands tickled his forearms. As his fingers fumbled with the ties, he could feel her breathing—warm and steady with only a hint of the strain of her spell.

He pulled the veil down, revealing the soft skin of an astonishing face. Her tender lips lifted into a tiny grin. Zev had the brief thought —a good man would be lucky to meet her. He would see her beauty, but her strength and bravery would win him over.

She opened her eyes. Vicious, cold eyes. With a tilt of her head, she motioned for Zev to step back.

One step. That's all he managed.

She opened her mouth, and he could see the gaps in the back. But only for a second. Because the blood flowed. She hissed and the blood sputtered. The rifleman screamed as Bellemont's sundress became a blood-splattered mess. She snarled at the riflemen, and a few uttered strangled cries.

With a rapid motion, she brought her hands onto Zev's shoulders and shoved him downward. He could feel the protective barrier around them dropping as his knees hit the grass. From the ground, he gazed up. He heard the shots—only they sounded strange. They lacked the percussive blast but included the dull thump usually heard at the end. The little blue circles appeared around her.

"Check that they're all dead," Bellemont said as she fastened her veil over her mouth once more and picked up her hat. She must have seen the confusion on Zev's face. "My spell did not destroy their bullets. It absorbed them. It held them in stasis until I dropped the barrier. Then it simply shot them back outwards. I needed a moment to line up my shots, and I used the horror of my face to cower the men in place."

Zev had no words to respond. In a numb daze, he walked from body to body to make sure the men would cause no trouble. When he confirmed that she had been successful, that all were dead, they each grabbed a bucket and headed for the King's Gardens.

Axon

Over the last two years, Axon had visited the King's Gardens on numerous occasions. It was an unlikely place for most soldiers to frequent during their off-duty time, and for that reason, Axon found it the perfect respite. Nobody to bother her. Nobody to ask for a little extra bit of her time. Just quiet, peaceful land. Acres of growing life. She had a feeling that after this night, she would never want to step into a garden again.

The King's Gardens began with a long rectangle of low-cut bushes and small flowerbeds. Stone pathways in perfect, straight lines led the way deeper into the gardens. The King had ordered the first section lit up with braziers and torchlight. In case one of the roving bands fell upon them, two guards stood at the entrance way to the castle.

When Axon arrived, the evening's colliding groups had self-segregated. Thalia sat on a stone bench looking over the beautiful flowers. On another day, Axon would have suspected she had stumbled upon an old lady enjoying the colorful bounty of the King. Philune walked back and forth at the far end. He appeared to be in conversation with himself. Halfway along the path, Pilot stood in a soldier's at-ease stance. On the opposite side of the Garden, the King and Mr. Duke conferred in controlled bursts of movement, murmured words, and the occasional outburst.

These are the people who had to save the world. Axon scoffed a chuckle. *They can't even stand in the same place together.*

She settled on the edge of the stone bench and placed the rock next to Thalia.

"Thank you," Thalia said.

"I had to kill one of the Dacci."

She picked up the rock and held it against her chest. "I suppose you had no choice."

"I'm not sure. She was running away with it. Maybe I could've wrestled her down. Maybe I could have knocked her unconscious. I think I simply took the fastest route available."

"I see. But I have to wonder why you're confessing this to me."

Axon stood. "Secrets are what got us into this trouble in the first place." She stepped away.

When Zev and Bellemont entered carrying two acrid buckets of outhouse slop, Axon attempted to catch his eye. She had hoped that she could ask for forgiveness and gain absolution through a mere glance. Foolish, of course, but that didn't stop her brain from seeking the easy way out.

With the arrival of the buckets, everybody gathered around Thalia, wading in from the various spots in the garden. The time had come.

Thalia faced the group. "It will not be an easy spell to cast. Be patient. Once the path is open, Philune, Axon, Pilot, and I will enter. Bellemont must stay on this side and help maintain the integrity of the connection. Do not make a sacrifice to keep it open, though. If Zev is successful, you'll have an ally who knows how to get to us."

Zev stepped forward. "I don't understand one thing. If I'm supposed to protect Ashturov, even get her out of the ballroom, how do I do that when I'll start moving slowly if I enter?"

"Thalia asked that I take of that problem, and I have," King Robion said. "One of the godwalkers will cast a spell over you to make you immune."

"That'll work?"

"I suppose we'll find out. Mr. Duke and I are going to the ballroom stage to prepare. Don't be too long."

The King looked over everybody and for a moment, Axon thought he might make a short speech. Some words of encouragement for those about to leap into a deadly situation. But her betrayal and his pain wrestled across his brow. With a rough spin toward the stairs, he re-entered the castle proper, quickly followed by Mr. Duke and his guards.

Philune said, "Well then, it appears that we are on our own."

"He has every right to be angry with us," Axon said. "I suspect the only reason he's agreed to any of this is because he doesn't have much choice."

"Now, now," Pilot said, reaching out to place one hand on Axon's shoulder and one hand on Philune's shoulder. "There's no reason to get all testy. We screwed up. But it was for a good reason. The King is a fair and just man. If he wasn't, I wouldn't be here. I'd never work for somebody that I couldn't respect. So, let's stop the complaining and get on with the fighting."

Thalia took a bucket from Zev and dumped its contents across the marble steps leading down to the Garden path. Axon could not decide which urged her to vomit more—the vile stench or the sight of unidentifiable lumps in the slop. Pilot appeared a bit green in the cheeks, and Philune turned towards the bushes, pressing the back of his hand against his mouth.

"Over here," Thalia said. "If you want to throw up, you shouldn't waste it."

Her comment sent Philune over the edge. He threw up in the bushes. After, he wiped his mouth with a handkerchief and said, "I'll remember where to aim for next time."

With a shrug, Thalia took the second bucket and added its contents to the muck. She then knelt before this murky pool and pulled out her pouch. She added two small bones into the wet ground. Then she pulled out her tooth extractor.

She moved with a strong, practiced hand. Axon could recognize skill anywhere. She often had walked along the training grounds to pick out the new recruits who already had some basic skills. It only took her seconds to spot them. The way they balanced, the way they moved, the way they gripped a weapon—every aspect of their breath and muscle gave evidence to their experience. She saw the same with Thalia.

In a handful of seconds, Thalia pulled out one tooth. Then a second. Then a third.

Three teeth. Thalia acted calm and bland about the whole thing, but Axon knew the meaning of three teeth. They all did. Seriously difficult spellcasting.

As Thalia lowered her head and mumbled, Bellemont gestured for everybody to back up—give the witch space to concentrate. They all complied.

Before Axon knew her mind had decided to act, she walked over to

Zev. "I'm about to step through a spellcast tunnel to a cave sitting months away from here where I'm going to try to use one of the most powerful artifacts we've ever known about. You are going to go jump back into a ballroom where there's a war going on, albeit slowly. Do you think I could have a little bit of your attention to talk things through? It would be a shame for either of us to die with this thing hanging between us."

Zev's mouth opened and closed several times before he finally managed to say, "Certainly." He gestured to a stone bench on the side opposite the rest of the group. With his back to everybody, he sat. Axon settled next to him.

They stared at their feet in silence. She recalled the dates her parents would set up for her—princes of small towns, a mayor with the King's favor, or any number of sons of prominent figures in the Court. She would be dressed like a doll. They would find themselves sitting on some bench at some fancy location, and neither would know what to say. Neither wanted to be there. At least, she knew she didn't. Perhaps the boys had some interest in her or her family's money. However, she often got the sense that they disliked these arrangements as much as she did. The only difference this time—she had arranged it. Not simply by asking Zev to talk, but by causing the situation which required Zev to talk.

"I'm sorry," she began. "I know that isn't enough, but I think it's the most important way to start this. I want you to know, to understand, that I am deeply sorry."

"It's not that easy."

"I know. I just wanted you to understand—"

"You wanted me to forgive you for lying this entire evening, for putting everybody in such a dangerous position, for possibly speeding up the road to war this country has been on." When he faced her, she expected anger—maybe even hatred—but a different emotion resonated. She could not place it, and part of her wondered if this unnamed feeling pointed to a lack within her. He continued, "Do you realize that, in the last hour, Bellemont and I were shot at? That I was forced to dive into an outhouse so we can try to dig out of this disaster you've created? Or that a young guard named Jocha who woke up this morning thinking he was simply going to be bored all night while a bunch of rich people had a party—that he's dead now? This has gone far beyond saying you're sorry."

"Which is why I am willing to jump through Thalia's spell and do whatever I need to do in order to save people. I'm not apologizing to you because of everything that's going on. I'm apologizing because it hurts to think that you feel like King Robion. Betrayed. I can see how wrong we were about what we chose to do—a blind man could see that—but my decisions never came from selfishness. I tried to do the best for us all. Can you understand that?"

Zev grew quiet. She had seen him dive deep into his thoughts on several occasions, so she felt an ember of hope. He appeared to silently argue out the various angles—weighing her words against her actions against the larger events swirling around them.

She wanted to say something more, anything to give her argument more credence, but she had whined too much. She heard it in her voice every time she spoke. That needed to shut down. She knew how to be better—to clear her mind and become a warrior again. But first, more than anything, she needed to hear his answer.

At length, Zev stood and gazed down at her. "No," he said. It looked as if he might say more, but the break in his voice restrained him from adding another word. He walked away.

A loud sizzle followed by a crack as if lightning had struck overhead caused a shudder among the group. Thalia stepped back. An opening rose out of the ground as if a door lifted from deep waters. By the time it finished forming, the door shed away and an open tunnel stood before them.

Axon's mouth fixed into a firm line. She would not give up on Zev, but she had to focus on the task at hand. Without that, there wouldn't be anybody around to offer apologies to.

As Pilot and Philune stepped closer, Thalia gestured toward the tunnel. "When you're ready," she said, "we only have to walk in."

Axon pulled out her Water Blade. "I'm ready."

CHAPTER FIVE

Zev

He noticed the cold first. It blasted in through the passageway in the air and brought recognition that on the other side of this spellcast tunnel stood a cave far to the north of Ridnight. Zev wondered if he closed his eyes, would he be able to smell the fresh snowcapped mountains? But of course, he couldn't. Not with two bucketfuls of outhouse slop covering the way.

Besides, he did not want to close his eyes.

Standing behind Bellemont, he peered through the tunnel and marveled at the sight. Like viewing a painting that moved, he saw Axon lead the others through into this massive cave. With a slight dome shape, the cavern reached further than Zev could see. Somewhere up top, the hole they had originally descended through allowed the bright moonlight to shine down. It formed a pale beam in the darkness that splashed upon a magnificent stone structure—the Shield.

The interviews did not do justice to this miracle of geology. From where the tunnel looked out, Zev had to agree with only one part of the account—it was mushroom-shaped. But its size defied their weak descriptions. Though he could not tell how tall the structure was, he guessed most of Ridnight Castle could fit under the main part of the Shield—the mushroom cap. The top glistened in the moonlight, wet from the melting snow above. It had a smooth texture and the waters streamed down to dribble off the edges creating the tinkling of raindrops on the cave floor. If he thought of it as an actual shield, only a giant of giants could wield it. And even then, Zev could not be sure.

Bellemont turned her body towards him, but her face twisted over her shoulder to keep looking into the tunnel. With visible effort, she finally turned her head away. "You have to go. You have to do your part."

"I know." He did not move.

She clapped her hands as if angry at a pet. "You've seen it now. It's time to do your part."

"I will go. I promise. I only want to stare at it a little longer."

With a stern tone that reminded him too much of his father, Belle-mont said, "Zev Asterling, you have a job to do."

When he managed to shift his gaze elsewhere, each step became easier. He had witnessed some amazing moments in his short life, but nothing as wondrous as that. As his pace steadily increased, he allowed thoughts of their success to enter his mind. After all, if simply seeing the Shield instilled him with such emotion, maybe it really could stop the battle in the ballroom. But if it could not, he would have to do his part.

Don't lie to yourself, he thought. *I have to do my part no matter what.*

Once he stood inside the castle and felt the stone surrounding him, Zev's mind cleared. Strange. Perhaps Thalia's spell had side effects. How else to explain the way the tunnel had mesmerized him? With each head-clearing step, he moved closer to the ballroom. Though he still found it difficult to navigate the castle as a whole, he had travelled this particular path before. It would not take long.

Halfway down one corridor, he heard two gunshots followed by a snarling, snorting growl. There were shouted commands and the clapping of running feet. It all grew louder.

Zev did not want to get caught in another skirmish. He tried the nearest door on his left. Locked. Jumping across the corridor, he pushed the next door over. It opened. He stepped into an unused bedroom—bare bed and dresser drawers open to show they were empty. He closed the door, leaving a crack to watch.

Three Easterners backed into view. Two were soldiers, most likely part of the contingent maintaining vehicles outside, while the one barking commands was either a high-ranking officer or one of the Lords that had managed to escape the ballroom. They wielded their rifles like spears. As they backed further down the corridor, Zev witnessed a green- and black-striped arm whack at the spears. It had three clawed fingers, a deformed texture to the skin, and it connected to a half-human and half-monstrosity form—a Dacci witch transformed into a beast of rage and power.

With a swipe of her arm, she batted away two of the rifles and launched forward. The Lord moved too slowly. He shrieked as the witch-creature's jagged teeth ripped out his throat. The other two soldiers made a hasty retreat.

Zev held his breath. He did not know how clearheaded a witch transformed into beast would be, and he did not want to test her. She paused, lifting her head and sniffing the air. No doubt, she could smell the outhouse retch all over him. With a loud bark, she leapt ahead, the sound of her padded paws slapping the stone as she raced after the remaining soldiers.

Zev allowed himself a shallow breath. He counted to thirty before he dared set one foot into the corridor. The Lord's mangled body bleeding across the stones stared up at him. The dead did not bother Zev. He'd seen them many times before. He turned away and rushed for the ballroom.

Dashing the final length of hallway to the backstage door, Zev halted sharp. Lady Jos stood in the middle of the hall, her gown torn at the side and stained with dirt, her hair coming undone. She stumbled in a daze.

"What happened?" he said as he approached. "Are you hurt?"

"Zev?" She sounded far away.

He looked over her, searching for injuries—no blood, no bruises. If she had seen the witch-creature, that alone could account for her shock. If she had stumbled into a skirmish, that would also explain the dirt and torn gown. But other than experiencing a terrible event, she appeared fine—physically.

Taking her arm in his, he said, "Come with me. I'll take you to a safe place."

She leaned her head on his shoulder as if they were enjoying a romantic stroll on a warm afternoon. "That sounds lovely. You know, you've always ignored me too much. A lady deserves better from such a handsome man."

"I'm terribly sorry," he said, hoping all his tension did not play out in his voice. "You always have been one of the people I've missed since I left the East."

"I should say so. You know our fathers wanted us to match."

"Really?"

"Don't sound so surprised. My money makes me quite a catch."

"Your beauty does that just fine."

She nuzzled her head and breathed in his scent. Her nose wrinkled. "You need a bath."

"I'm sure I do."

Though he wanted to move faster, he kept a steady, gentle pace down the hall. As long as she remained calm, he kept talking as if they had no worries around them. They walked toward the ballroom and through the backstage entrance. Once on the stage, he offered her a chair near the far wall. "I've got to talk with the King and handle some matters. You stay here and you'll be safe from everything going on. Okay?"

"Will I see you again?"

He bowed over her hand and kissed her knuckles. "It would be my pleasure."

She placed her hand across her wide grin and batted her eyes at him. With a smile, he turned away and approached the edge of the stage. He gazed out across the ballroom. Despite the godwalkers' spell to slow time, the battle had progressed more than he expected. It corkscrewed the worry in his chest.

Spears of gray smoke rose from the witches' spell mounds. Several spears hovered over the Dacci heads. Others had swept across the room leaving a gray trail in the air. Yet more vibrated from hitting walls, tables, and people. In fact, Zev spotted two young men on the ground with spears planted in their chests.

In return, the Easterners rattled off gunfire like drummers attempting to fill every beat with as much noise as possible. Even slowed down, the air flashed as if caught in a massive storm. While the Dacci had put up an energy field which deflected the majority of bullets, no protection could be flawless. The barrage of rifle fire meant that at least one or two bullets would sneak through. The end result—one witch sat behind the Virgin Cart attending to a wounded shoulder. Another witch folded over as if in prayer, but a pool of blood formed around her.

Some Easterners had run out of ammunition and batted at nearby witches with the butts of their rifles. Blood sprayed slowly from a head strike. A Dacci rushed to help, swinging her bone blade and slicing through the arm of an Easterner. A graying Lord leaned back in a chair and popped bullets off with a handgun. On the Western side, crouched under the statue of Orlar, goddess of the elder years, a wrinkled Dacci cast a spell transforming herself into a muscular, furry beast with a ridge of spikes along her spine.

Zev looked closer—the Dacci casting herself into a beast had set her veil on the cast pile. A red veil. Blood dribbled from her mouth. As she hunched over to extract another tooth, a blast of gray energy threw several tables into the air. The screams and cries and guttural roars pattered through the room, echoing off the high ceilings all several octaves lower as even sound had been slowed.

"I know it looks bad," King Robion said as he came alongside Zev. "Imagine how much worse it would have been."

"I'm more troubled about after." Until Zev had seen this, part of him thought they would be able to stop the war. Not just save those in the ballroom but stop the entire thing from even happening. "Was there ever any real chance of avoiding war?"

"That was the point of this gathering. If Vost and Inx had not stolen the Shield—even though it was fake—we would all have believed it. Seeing that symbol of unity might have brought everybody together long enough to at least discuss matters. I did not fool myself into thinking it would be easy or instantaneous, but I had hopes that at the very least, everybody would have walked away agreeing to hold off on the fighting. We would all pick another day to meet and continue talking. That's how peace is achieved. Step-by-step. Little by little."

"But this—is there any pulling back from this?"

The King sighed like an exhausted horse. "No. Not now. Now, the best we can hope for is to minimize the casualties. Everybody will retreat to their borders, and plans will begin."

"You mean battle plans."

"Indeed. Peace will come eventually. It always does. Just as war seems to always follow...eventually. Back and forth. Like the tides. But it will be a lot of time and a lot of deaths before anybody in that ballroom is willing to consider peace."

Flicking his hand open to gesture at the entire ballroom, Zev said, "Then what's the point? What does it matter if you stop these people from killing each other? They're just going to try it again later."

"For me, as King, the point is how much time it will take me to restore peace and how many lives will be lost of my own people. If I let the godwalkers stop their spell and we watch these two groups slaughter each other, the tragedy of this day will become a rallying cry for both sides. They will fight longer and harder, and with the Frontier caught in the middle, there will be far more deaths than I can accept. Especially when we have a chance right now to make this war a minor entry for historians instead of a major event. I have no idea what the point is for you or them. I only speak for myself."

Zev glanced back at Lady Jos. "So, in a way, this is all about mercy."

"I suppose so."

Turning his back on the ballroom, Zev crossed his arms and gave the King a stern glare. "Then perhaps you should extend that mercy to Axon."

The King's eyebrows rose as his head pulled back. "I didn't think I would hear you coming to her defense."

"Don't read too much into it. I'm still angry with her. But all of them went back to Taladoro for us. They're trying to redeem themselves and fix the mistakes they made. They're trying to do the same thing you want to do—make this battle a minimal matter instead of the start of a major war."

"I know." King Robion bowed his head with a shake. "I wish it were so simple. But she's betrayed me, broken my trust, and in the world I live—the world of a king—trust is a rare commodity. It's a fragile one, too."

"I'm sure you can come up with lots of reasons to continue hating her. Have a few of my own. But clearly war is upon us. I should think you'd want the greatest warrior you have at your side."

Ducking his head, a tall man entered wearing the floor-length cloak of the godwalker. He approached the King, his white cloak with black trim denoting him as one of the Deities of Life. Zev noted that the godwalker's sleeve bore the image of a healthy, strong tree—the symbol of Sazieck, god of adulthood.

Gesturing at Zev, King Robion said, "This is the man who needs your spell."

The godwalker moved in front of Zev. He spoke in rich, smooth tones with an ease that did not fit the dangers surrounding them. "I want you to understand what you will face in there."

"I've already seen it. It's going on right behind me. What more do I need to know?"

"For you, I have been pulled away from helping the other godwalkers maintain the current spell. Thus, that spell, which is already creating an enormous strain upon my brothers and sisters, will fail even faster."

Zev rolled his eyes. "Because why should it ever be easy?"

"I, too, am exhausted. I will create a spell for you that will allow you to move in there freely, but my own power may fail before the rest of the godwalkers."

King Robion said, "Yes, yes, he understands. He's not going in there because he thinks it would be a good idea and a rollicking time. He's going in there because we need him to go in there. And right now, I need you to make that possible. Stop with the warnings and get to work."

"As you wish." The godwalker bowed before splaying his fingers in front of Zev's face.

Before he had time to calm, Zev felt a strange tingle across the skin. Then the godwalker dropped to his knees and began the spell in earnest.

Axon

Passing through Thalia's spellcast tunnel, Axon felt unusual ripples along her skin. An odd odor filled the air. Something had burned, but the smell did not match anything she had ever experienced before.

When they entered the cave, she discovered the tunnel exit had formed over a stone Thalia had left near the wall opposite the Shield. Axon paused. Looking back, she could see Bellemont standing in the King's Gardens. *Unsettling*—that word bounced around Axon's mind.

Up ahead, the Shield stood like a monument to gods and goddesses long forgotten. The moonlight shining down set the Shield apart from the dark walls behind, giving it an even holier gloss.

With his eyes wide as if he saw the Shield for the first time, Philune said, "It really is awe-inspiring. I must say that your King has no right to be angry with us. Not if he could lay eyes on this."

Snapping his fingers, Pilot said, "Why don't we do that? We can go back and bring him here with us, through this tunnel, let him see what we see. Surely, he would understand then."

"And who's going to cast that spell?" Thalia asked. "I only have so many teeth left, and I have no intention of losing another three to travel out here once again."

"We all got here without your teeth the first time."

Philune said, "You would never have found this place without me or Thalia. What makes you think you can get your King here without one of us?"

"Oh, I don't think you contributed that much. Axon and I could do it ourselves."

"Of all the impudent, naïve, frankly addlebrained things to say."

"Enough," Axon said. "We created our lie to bring peace to our peoples. Now you want to start attacking each other? Go back through the tunnel and fight it out in the ballroom with the rest of them, if that's your intention. If you stay here, you work together."

Pilot lowered his hat and his head. "Yes, ma'am. Sorry."

Philune stepped back and made a slight bow. "My apologies. Lead on, Madam Coponiv."

Axon resumed walking. "Don't be an ass."

With a gentle gasp, Philune hurried to join Axon up ahead. "I do have a question—how exactly are we going to use this thing? We know it creates a lot of power, but—"

"I'll use it," Thalia said. Before any objections could be formed, she went on, "I'm the only one amongst us who can cast spells. I understand how to utilize the energies that surround us."

Pilot said, "Not meaning any offense, sweet lady, but it took you three teeth just to open that tunnel. How many teeth you got left in your mouth for that Shield?"

"I'll give them all if I must. For the rest of you, this may simply be a way to postpone a war. You expect to go back and deal with your governments and your companies and try to help navigate them back to peace. That's not why I'm here."

Axon stopped the group. "You better explain that. The closer we get to the Shield, the closer we taunt our demise. If you're not trying to accomplish the same thing as the rest of us, we need to know."

Thalia moved several steps towards the Shield and closed her eyes as if basking in the warmth of the summer sun. "All of you belong to your people. Philune is a man of the East. Axon's a woman of the Frontier. Even Pilot has found his place starting in one world and ending in another. But I am only of the Lost. The Dacci want nothing to do with me. Yet here, in front of me, is a majestic source of gigantic power. My only experience with such strength until now has been Nualla himself. Such glorious power, yet most of my sisters are dead or about to be dead. There is nothing left to return to. By connecting to this great force, this Shield, perhaps I can also connect to Nualla—not a small severed part of him carried around like a prisoner in the Virgin Cart, but the real thing. The creature that brings us power from death. That gives the Dacci meaning. That is life." She met eyes with every member of the group and crossed her arms as if hugging the moonlight. "Don't worry. I will see to it that the Shield's one great burst of energy will do what we want it to do—protect all the people. I'm simply willing to sacrifice myself to the experience."

Axon did not like the words she heard. They sounded rogue and uncontrolled. But she recognized that she had little choice. Thalia had spoken the truth—she was the only one who could cast a spell.

Speaking with a tremor in his voice, Philune said, "Perhaps we should rethink our plan."

Axon did not need to look at what caused Philune's sudden fear. She could hear the sound of those hard shells clicking back against each other. From the darkness behind the Shield, from the shadows, a mass of craytens crawled forward.

Axon checked the surrounding walls. Nothing. After defeating them the first time, the craytens appeared to have found safety beneath and behind the Shield. Of course they did. It's a shield, after all.

Only now they appeared to be acting as a shield themselves. Instead of stampeding forward to overwhelm Axon and her team, the craytens climbed atop each other. Their dark hard shells faced Axon's group as they piled higher and higher. By the time the noise of their movements quieted, the craytens had formed a black wall completely encircling the base of the Shield.

Pilot pulled out his sword. "I kind of thought we might have to fight these bastards again."

Philune said, "Really? I assumed this place would be empty."

Axon chuckled. "You expected them to make it easy on us, did you?"

CHAPTER SIX

Zev

L eaping off the stage, Zev tried to move with speed and efficiency. He had no idea how long the godwalker could hold out, and he had no interest in testing the man's limits. But the moment he hit the zone of slowed time, he needed a few breaths to acclimate.

The air felt like a liquid—thick and muddy. Each motion of his body had to be pushed through with an effort. He could feel the air slipping between his fingers like egg yolks—gooey and wet.

Yet he had no time to dawdle in amazement. The slowed-time spell continued to weaken. He could see the battle in motion now—slow, true, but not slow enough.

To the left, a young Easterner charged forward with his weapon held back like an axe. To the right, a Dacci witch attempted to limp toward safety. With her attention focused ahead, she had no idea this young man rushed towards her.

As he dashed across the main aisle, Zev grabbed the young man's shoulders and spun him so that he faced the Easterners' turf. Zev expected the man to run on a few steps and either halt in confusion or perhaps trip and roll onto the ground. Instead, the young man arched back and screamed. The bones in his shoulders visibly snapped, and the way his waist twisted, Zev thought he may have cracked a hip, too. As the boy dropped to the ground, he looked back—straight at Zev.

Zev did not move. He stared in horror, trying to understand what had happened. Then he noticed several other Easterners pointing in his direction. Starting to run toward him. Barking orders at each other.

Of course. He was not invisible. Merely fast. They must have seen a streak arrive in the ballroom and attack one of their own. And that attack—Zev had learned long ago that there were only two ways to hit harder. Either build up muscle or build up speed.

While he had intended only to spin the boy around, the difference between his normal speed and the boy's slowed time meant that his touch happened at far greater speeds. He broke that boy's shoulders and wrenched him around hard enough to have shattered the hip, as well. He would have to be more than careful. He would have to think of himself as a living weapon.

He also had to use his speed to his advantage—especially when Easterners were raising their rifles to shoot him down. He jogged ahead toward the bandstand as they blasted in his direction. But he no longer stood where they thought. He had a short time before their eyes would catch up with him, and if he kept on the move, they would never be able to figure out where he would be.

He needed to find Ashturov. She should have been by the Virgin Cart, but he did not see her anywhere near that palanquin. He did lay eyes on Red Veil—what was left of her. The creature she had become fought two Easterners, her beast body smashing them with strength far beyond any person could possess.

Then Zev's eyes fell upon Vost and Inx.

Still clutching hands, they tried to wrestle the door open. The guards refused to let the door budge. They had a major advantage— they were not slowed by the godwalker spell. But, of course, Vost did not know this. To him, only a short time had passed. His mind had yet to give up on overpowering whatever blocked the door.

Zev knew he had to move, had to find Ashturov, had to keep her safe in case she was needed. Logic and reason told him to leave Vost and Inx alone. He bounded towards them anyway. Fury heated his skin. These two—they were responsible for all the deaths surrounding the evening. They were responsible for all the future deaths this war would bring. Whereas Axon, Pilot, Philune, and Thalia had conspired to deceive everyone as a means of planting seeds for peace, these two sought only selfish ends.

Inx's eyes widened as Zev approached. She must have seen a blur of color grow in front of her. Her mouth gaped wide, and a slow scream built in volume.

He wanted to punch them both, to release his rage, and though his fingers rolled into fists, he managed to hold back. If he punched them, he might rip right through their bodies. That was not the way. He would not become a murderer. But he would not let them escape, either. They had to face King Robion, the Dacci, and the Easterners. They had to be held accountable.

Bending closer toward to them, Zev reached out with two fingers locked tight together. Vost had his shoulder shoving the door. His legs stretched out bracing against the floor. Two quick taps behind the knees, and Zev sent the man down in agony. He would not be walking again anytime soon.

Zev shuffled to the side and tapped Inx's legs as well. Tears flooded her eyes as the pain registered. Though he loathed the truth of it, he had to admit that breaking their legs gave him a small amount of satisfaction. To be safe, he snatched Inx's casting pouch. He didn't want her throwing a spell upon him. Or anyone.

He had spent too much time in this one spot. If any of the riflemen had continued their search for him, they would be taking aim by now. Zev hopped to the side, jumped into the air, and jogged off. He hoped the erratic movement would confuse his enemies.

Facing the Dacci side of the ballroom, he scanned for Ashturov once more. Like a dark statue emerging from a gray fog, she appeared as he shifted his angle of view. Crouching behind the Virgin Cart, she aided one of her sisters. Blood spurted out of the injured witch's chest, and as Ashturov applied pressure, she searched for help.

He could do that. In fact, if he controlled his muscles, he might be able to put the exact amount of pressure to stop the witch's bleeding.

But as he stepped toward the Virgin Cart, the battle around him erupted. The blasts of gunfire grew to full volume, everyone moved at full speed, the smells and shrieks and war cries echoed around him.

And then it stopped. Everything returned to the slow pace of before.

This is not good, Zev thought. The godwalkers were losing control of their spell. He looked to Ashturov. She seemed to be gazing in his direction with confusion. She stood completely still, completely exposed.

Not good at all.

Axon

In all her years of battle, Axon had never experienced anything so unrelenting. She had charged straight to the wall of craytens, hacking away with her Water Blade. Yet each time she cracked through a shell, each time a bloodied body tumbled to the ground, another crayten took its place.

Pilot and Philune protected her flanks. She could hear them panting as they smashed their swords against one crayten after another. Thalia wanted to assist in the fight, but Axon ordered her to stay behind—this would all be pointless if the witch died before she even got to cast her spell.

At first, Axon thought the battle would be a simple matter of attrition. Slice through enough of them, and they wouldn't be able to replenish the wall. But they simply took her beatings and died and more came in. When they appeared to realize she would not be leaving, only then did they attack. Without Pilot and Philune, she would have perished already.

The clanking of steel against hardshell blended with the death screeches of the craytens. Axon could feel the sounds pounding in her head. Raising her Water Blade, exhaustion set in. Her muscles would not last forever, and already, each strike against those hard carapaces reverberated through her arms.

Kicking an impaled crayten off the end of his sword, Pilot said, "This isn't working. We need to regroup and come up with another plan."

"Keep fighting," Axon said.

Philune waved his sword wildly. "We can't last much longer."

She knew they were right. But this mess belonged to them, and they had to be the ones to fix it. Simple as that. They were not allowed to fail.

As she chopped across the midsection of another crayten, she thought of Zev. She could not get him out of her mind. Keeping him in the dark throughout his investigation had been more than wrong. In many ways, it was worse than if she had betrayed Pilot—and that was unthinkable.

Two more craytens scurried up to plug the hole she had carved out. Frustrating and exhausting, but she had managed to make a hole. "Keep fighting. We're getting somewhere."

Why did it bother her? She felt bad about King Robion, but it did not eat away at her. Zev on the other hand, she had to find a way to make things right. She had to hope winning this battle would be the first step—no, the first leap forward in that direction. But why?

Because he is the Frontier.

The thought planted into her mind, and she knew it to be true. The Frontier was a land of possibilities and freedom. A country in which anybody could rise in their life. A man from the wealthy East could become a farmer, if he had any talent for it, and when that failed, he could turn around and become a master solver. A woman born of privilege could choose to be a warrior. Even a Dacci witch could reinvent herself into—well, Axon did not know what Bellemont sought to be, but she knew that the Frontier was the most welcoming place the witch had to sort that out.

"For the Frontier," she bellowed as she sliced through another crayten.

Axon drove harder, chopping, chopping, chopping. She hacked through one crayten, then another, then another. Flesh and bone and blood burst off in all directions. She had become a madwoman butchering all in her path.

And that path had grown. She moved so quick and with such fury that the craytens could not keep up. After their previous battle, perhaps they lacked enough soldiers to replenish their ranks because the hole she created did not fill back fast enough.

She peered out at Thalia to encourage the witch forward. That's when everything collapsed.

It began when she saw Bellemont in the distance. The young witch stood in the tunnel with her hands raised above, her muscles taut, and blood draining down her neck. She had sacrificed a tooth—at least one—and now strained to keep the tunnel open.

Behind her, Axon saw two of the King's Guard fighting two Eastern soldiers. If they broke through, Bellemont would have to let the tunnel collapse, and hopefully, she would be able to sprint forward into the caves. If not, Axon did not know what would happen. She suspected it would not be good. If the tunnel collapsed on Bellemont, the witch would most likely be dead. Any other alternative would be horrifying.

As Axon watched, she realized she had given the craytens too much time. She whirled about and swung down at the nearest crayten. She had expected the hole to be mostly filled, but they had barely begun to repair the damage. Where had they gone?

The flanks.

As she pivoted toward Philune, a line of craytens rumbled into view. Three shot forward and slammed into Philune. One skewered itself on his sword but kept moving forward.

With snarling rage, they raced by her. Lifting Philune off the ground, his shouts lost amongst the thunder of their stampede, they bashed into Pilot's back and kept going.

Axon swung her Blade across the creatures' path, letting one crayten after another slice itself open upon her weapon. They continued onward, rushing around the fallen craytens until the whole line had passed through—many of them dying on their run.

When the last had circled around, they reformed the wall. Pilot and Philune lay in a heap to the side.

All thoughts of country vanished. All thoughts of betrayal vanished. All thoughts vanished but one—fight.

The world beyond disappeared. Axon only knew her body and her blade. They fused into one as she dived and dashed, swung and slashed her way through the enemy. She rolled forward, spiking to her feet, and punted aside several craytens. Following up with her Blade, she bisected one and decapitated another. Behind her, Pilot cursed in a nonstop, impressively fluent array of foul words as he batted and bludgeoned the craytens near him. He wrenched back his arm, bashing a crayten with the hilt of his sword, only to lunge forward in an attempt at piercing another.

Axon continued her dance. Her graceful moves spat death around her. It was ballet and blood, and for those few moments, she shined. She forgot all of what led to this moment and all of what might become. She lived in that present—at peace even amongst the violence.

With one final blow that sent a crayten off the ground and slammed it into the cave wall, the rest of the creatures broke off their attack. They scratched and clawed and skittered away on the floor until they had returned to the safety of their self-made wall. Breathing heavily, Axon watched as the hole she had hacked opened now filled in completely.

"Pilot?"

"Not doing that good. Can't use my left arm. And I think I've got a limp that won't be going away for the rest of my life."

"Philune?"

Nothing. Then, a soft gurgle.

Axon snapped her fingers at Pilot. She needed to keep her attention on their enemy, just in case. She could hear Pilot's uneven gait—he really did have a limp—and she waited for his report.

A moment later, Pilot said, "He's in bad shape. I need a hand to drag him to safety."

Backing up carefully, Axon reached down and scooped under Philune's arm. Always keeping her eyes on the crayten wall, she helped slide Philune back towards Thalia. He groaned. A good sign—the man was alive.

When they reached Thalia, Axon let go of Philune's arm and took on a fighting stance. She glowered at the crayten wall and waited. But nothing happened. The creatures did not advance. They didn't even break the wall formation.

"Is that it?" Pilot said.

"It's enough," Thalia said. "If I can't get to the Shield, this entire trip is pointless."

Axon eyed the battlefield. "They're hurting. We took out a huge number of them last time, and just now we took out a lot more. They've been slower to fix the gaps I made, and now they won't come after us. If they did, there wouldn't be enough of them left for their wall."

Pilot said, "Great. Doesn't really help us. I can't go back in there and be useful, and Philune's pretty worthless, now."

With a deep grunt, Philune set up. "Don't count me as dead, yet."

"Friend, you've lost so much blood, you don't even know what you're saying."

"I can get us in."

As Pilot laughed, Axon put her Water Blade away and crouched level with Philune. She checked his eyes. From the way he narrowed his focus on the wall, from the way he held his head steady, she didn't think he had become delusional. In fact, his face gained the coldest, most deadly seriousness.

"You have a plan?" she asked.

Nodding, he said, "Help me to my feet."

Pilot and Axon each took an arm and lifted the man. He yelped but managed to stay standing on his own. Then came that look again—narrowing on the wall, dark and filled with anger. Yet far away, too. The detached gaze of a man who had killed for the first time.

Axon snatched a glance back at the tunnel. Bellemont still held tight, her arms and legs shuddered and sweat stained the neck of her bloody dress. Behind her the guards continued to fight. They seemed to be holding well, but that did not guarantee for how long.

"If you've got a plan, if you can get Thalia to that Shield, let's hear it."

With each movement he winced, but he managed to snake his hand into his coat pocket. He pulled out a metal ball—rough and dull with a small nub at the top.

"What's that?" Axon asked.

"A little device that makes a big explosion. I'm going to blast half that wall away."

"That little thing can do that much damage?"

"I told you we make a lot more than just rifles."

Pilot said, "Hold on. If you throw that thing at the wall, won't it bounce off and maybe not even be near the wall when it explodes? Or worse, it might roll back at us."

Philune snickered, but the motion stabbed pain across his face. "You're really smart. I didn't even talk about the throwing part, but that's usually how these things work. Not this time. No. I'm going to walk it in."

"But then you'll—"

"Look at this wound." Blood flowed out his side and down his leg. "I'm not making it back, and I know what you all think of me. I'll even admit it—I have been a bit of a coward. But if I'm going to die, I might as well make it worthwhile."

Axon wanted to say something encouraging or comforting or anything, but the words stopped in her throat. Pilot and Thalia also appeared too choked to speak.

With a grim acknowledgment, Philune said, "Be ready. I don't want to have to come back and do this again." He chuckled as he made his way towards the wall. A dark path of blood painted the ground in his wake.

CHAPTER SEVEN

Zev

Darting around to the back of the Virgin Cart, Zev ducked next to Ashturov. He tried to hold still so that she could focus on his fast-moving face. Her furrowed brow and shocked eyes suggested she finally recognized him.

"We need your help," he said. "Thalia sent me to bring you to her. She's going to try to use the Shield."

Ashturov frowned and clasped her ears. Moving faster than his surroundings apparently sped up his voice as well. She probably only heard a high-pitched gibberish. When he stopped talking, she pointed to the Virgin Cart with one hand and to her wounded sister with the other.

"No," he said, trying to slow his words so that she might understand. "Thalia needs you."

With a slow turn, Ashturov put her back to Zev.

Not the answer he was looking for. He peeked over the top of the Virgin Cart, and his legs weakened. A group of Easterners had opened one of the coffins they had brought with them. Instead of pulling out a body, however, they pulled out a cylinder made of numerous hollow rods. Each one looked frighteningly like a rifle. Another Easterner had set up a mount, and though they moved slowly, it looked clear enough to Zev—the cylinder went on the mount and would be able to shoot numerous bullets at once.

But he could stop it. He could run over there and grab the weapon away from the Easterners. They would never be able to stop him.

Before he could move, however, the godwalkers' spell that slowed time finally failed. Even if everybody had not started moving at normal speed, Zev would have known—he felt the difference. The thick soup of air washed away, leaving behind the smooth and clear freshness of normality. As the men continued to set up this weapon, Zev crouched back down. He tapped Ashturov on the shoulder. "Can you understand me now?"

She whipped around. "Yes? What's going on?"

"The godwalkers—they cast a spell that slowed everybody, but I was given a counter spell. Thalia is trying to use the Shield, the real Shield, and we need—"

"I understood that part before. But Thalia does not need me. No, that's not why you were sent here."

"It was. They told me to get you."

"Thalia is the most skilled witch I've ever met and far more capable than me. She doesn't need me."

He paused. He saw it on her face. "They just sent me out of the way, didn't they?"

"When we left Taladoro, when we decided how we would handle the Shield, we agreed that we would never show anybody the cave. Too dangerous. Nobody should have all that power."

"And if I went with them, I might have figured out where it was or how to get back."

"That's why you were sent to me. So you'd understand. And maybe so you could help us out here."

Zev shook his head. "They've got a weapon. Unless you can cast a spell that will destroy them, it's going to do something awful."

"I'm a warrior. I cast spells, too, but I'm not very good at it." She lifted her head a little higher. "If all this is happening, and you know about the Shield, then who stole the fake?"

"Inx. Vost."

She opened her mouth to speak again, but an ear shattering roar rattled, shaking the air, breaking the world. The weapon.

Peering over the cart, Zev watched as several men operated the machine. Using a crank, the cylinder rolled, firing one rifle after another. They oscillated the cylinder on its base, spraying bullets across the ballroom. Every witch standing in the way fell. They barely had time to move. They cried out but no voice could be heard over the weapon's staccato howl.

No voice but the brutal cry of Red Veil. The hairy beast with spiked spine had lost all of its Dacci mind. Enraged, it thundered toward the machine, its jagged teeth anxious to rip into flesh, its strong bulk powerful enough to smash through that puny cylinder. But the rapid fire tore numerous holes into the creature's muscular chest until it tumbled forward, coming to rest in a bloody heap near the center.

The onslaught finally died down.

An unsettling quiet took over.

Every soul in that ballroom stilled, stunned by the violent power unleashed. With heavy footsteps, Lord Radugo paraded in front of his men. He pushed out his belly and lifted his rosy face toward the Dacci. "Surrender. Do so now and the last of you will not die." He turned toward the stage. "You, too, King Robion. I think we have shown quite clearly who will dominate any war between us all. The witches are done for. If we must, we will slaughter all of your court until you will also bend your knee to us."

In the next few seconds, as King Robion walked proudly toward the edge of the stage, time slowed for Zev. He had to look around, wondering if the godwalkers had found a second surge of energy. But no. It was his fire surging within, his wrath fuming up through his gut. After all he had been through, after all the sacrifices his friends had made, to have it end at the feet of this bloated blowhard—Zev could not stomach the idea.

He heard the soft whimpers of the witches still alive. He saw the beautiful ballroom floor slick with blood and cratered with bullets. He saw shock on some of the Easterners—but not all. No. There were many who smiled at the victory Lord Radugo brought their way.

Zev recognized the type. They would accept any leader, any law, any ideal or practicality as long as they benefited. If it hurt others, so be it. If it helped others but did not help them, they were against it. They were the worst kind of follower—loyal out of selfishness.

Well, Zev could be loyal, too.

Before he knew what he was doing, before Ashturov knew what he was doing, he climbed atop of the Virgin Cart. Hopefully, this part of the story they had told him would prove to be true. He opened the door.

Axon

When Philune detonated his portable bomb, Axon gaped in awe. That metal sphere, no bigger than a hand, created such a massive force that craytens blasted upward nearly halfway to the ceiling. The terrifying volume of the explosion shook the cave walls. Bright fire poured between the seams of the craytens, and Axon watched as those closest to Philune disintegrated in the billowing blaze.

As the echoes of violence faded, a horrific rain fell upon them— shell and flesh and stone dropped from above. Philune's sacrifice had cut a massive gap in the crayten wall, and the creatures did not attempt to repair it. They couldn't—not after the shock of destruction they had experienced. At least, not yet.

Axon guessed the craytens were dumbstruck. Much like herself. Which meant that whoever acted first would prevail.

She grabbed Thalia by the arm and yanked the woman to her feet. Pulling out the Water Blade, she stomped toward the Shield. Weaving through shredded craytens, Axon put all her focus into the goal—the Shield.

"You ready?" she called back to Thalia.

"As much as I ever can be."

"That's not very reassuring."

"At least I won't be short on dead material to cast with."

Two craytens rushed from the right, but Axon had no difficulty dispatching them. They were slow and reacted poorly. Those closest to the explosion that had survived staggered and lurched as if they had smoked too much tarkweed.

Axon led the way through the gap in the crayten wall and marched straight to the base holding up the Shield. Another crayten made a half-hearted attempt to block them, but she cut it down. Pointing to the corpse, she said, "Get started."

She gazed back at Pilot and Bellemont. Pilot had scooted against the cave wall. He was done for this battle. Further back, Bellemont continued to hold the tunnel open, but Axon swore the tunnel looked smaller.

Thalia pulled out her tooth extractor and dropped tooth after tooth onto the ground. She moved with fervor, growling like a rabid hound. Ripping away her mask, she pulled more teeth.

Axon looked away—partly to keep an eye on their enemies, partly to avoid watching this gruesome display. She wanted to ask something—anything—but the woman had taken all her teeth out. No more teeth meant no more spells. Whatever Thalia would become in her final years, she would not be a witch.

Finally, Axon found her voice. She had no idea why the words summoned from her body came out, but she did not stop them. "I promise that I will speak your praises. You and Philune both. Whether we succeed or fail, your sacrifices won't go unheard."

The craytens that still made up the wall disengaged from each other. Despite their lethargic movement, they were more coordinated than before. They had begun to shake off the concussive effects of Philune's bomb. Like a swarm of drunken insects, they gathered together in a smooth pile off to the side. Axon kept her Water Blade at the ready and inched in front of Thalia.

"Hurry up with that spell, please."

Thalia rose to her knees and placed her hands against the Shield base. Blood streamed from her mouth and cascaded upon the stone.

In the distance, Axon caught sight of the Easterners shooting the King's Guards. Three men stormed into the Gardens. They pulled up short of the tunnel, peering in, anxious to rush forward but fearing the spells.

The craytens congregated around the center of the cave, moving like one large snake yet crawling over each other like a hive. They passed close to Pilot and he clenched his sword, ready to fight until they overtook him. But they did not attack. They shifted, climbing on top of each other higher and higher, building themselves into a large block.

Axon readjusted her stance, held the Water Blade before her, and bared her teeth. "I'll give you all the time I can, but we are about done."

With a painful grit to her voice, Thalia spoke, but Axon only heard wet mumbling.

The Easterners took a tentative step into the tunnel. They held their rifles up and squinted as the torchlight of the Garden failed to reach beyond the edge of the tunnel.

The craytens started their run forward. Axon understood their intention—as long as Thalia cast the spell, Axon could not move. They planned to smash Axon and the witch against the stone of the Shield.

Thalia shouted. Over her shoulder, Axon said, "I can't understand you."

Bellemont spun to see the approaching Easterners. They seemed to comprehend that she held the tunnel open—possibly the only thing saving their lives.

Pilot tried to hack at the back of the crayten block, but they were out of reach. And they were moving, building momentum.

Once more, Thalia let loose an urgent cry. Axon did not want to take her eyes off the enemy, but she dared a quick glance at the witch.

And she saw the answer in the witch's eyes, in the glisten of tears, in the blood staining her chin, in the arch of her head that revealed the throbbing veins of her neck.

"Are you sure?" Axon said. She could hear the craytens reaching a fast trot. She needed to turn back and fight them off, break up that block, do something. But she stared at Thalia.

Thalia steepled her fingers against the rock and closed her eyes as she nodded. Though she lacked all her teeth, she tried one more time to speak. Just one word. At any other moment, Axon would never have understood the word, but whether by spell or situation, she knew exactly what Thalia had said—

Sacrifice.

Not waiting to debate in her mind, Axon let out a furious wail as she heaved the Water Blade up and overhead. She used every bit of training she possessed—relaxed her muscles and twisted her core so as to bring down that Blade as fast and as strong as possible. It sliced through Thalia's neck, gaining no resistance, until the Blade hit the stone floor.

A bright golden light emerged from the witch's neck. It shot into the stone base like a geyser of energy.

Axon stumbled back. Like the branches of a tree, this golden light grew up and into the Shield. Axon had no fear of the craytens now. She could hear their lack of movement. She knew they were as stunned as her.

The ground quaked. Thalia's body dropped—no more than an empty shell. Bits of stone crumbled off the edges of the Shield. More light burst out from these fissures.

Axon turned away. She bolted toward Pilot, holding her Water Blade at her side in case any craytens still wanted to fight. But they were scattering. They dove through cracking holes in the cave walls, escaping to darker, less volatile areas.

The ground trembled harder, and Axon stumbled to her knees. She put away the Water Blade, and crawled over to Pilot.

"I think you broke it," Pilot said as he placed his arm around her shoulder. Together, they clambered toward the tunnel.

The Easterners had the sense to back away, to seek safety in the Garden.

Axon could see the pain on Bellemont's face. Just a little longer. Hold on just a little longer.

As they reached the edge of the tunnel, the walls in front of her brightened as if the sun burst a new day inside the cave. She thought she heard thunder breaking directly behind her. She thought she felt a huge fist punch her in the back. She thought many things—but it all became a blur as this force from behind lifted her off the ground.

PART V
THE BEGINNING

CHAPTER ONE

When Zev awoke in the Ridnight Recovery, the best health facility in all the Frontier, a sense of peace overcame him. The crisp blue gowns of the staff, the gentle strums of the quartet down the hall, even the soft trickles of water from a small fountain in the corner—it all contributed as a calming reminder that decent people existed in the world. People worth fighting for.

Over the next several days, Zev bobbed into consciousness only to fall back under a short time later. At length, he managed to stay conscious more often than not. Eventually, his rattled head returned to normal. That was when he discovered Bellemont rested only two rooms over. The remainder of his recovery time, he spent at her bedside.

King Robion visited them once. That was the first time Zev and Bellemont learned what had actually happened.

"If I had not known about the Shield," King Robion said, "then I would surely have believed Qareck had convinced all the gods and goddesses to work together in stopping us. Walls of sunlight cut down from above and separated every Dacci witch from every Eastern rifleman from every member of the Frontier. The walls weaved through the crowd with such speed and purpose that I am still shocked nobody was hurt."

In the end, the Shield closed these walls around each group, a blinding flash covered the room, and they were gone. Zev and the rest of the Frontier were alone in the ballroom. The most recent reports suggested that all of the Dacci were returned to the Western border and all the Easterners were returned to their border. The dead included. But an additional report which King Robion felt it important to share only with Zev and Bellemont suggested that the Lost witch Ashturov and the Virgin Cart had yet to be located.

"This won't stop the war," Zev said.

"But it will postpone it. All sides are injured and willing to discuss matters. It's a frail moment, one I do not believe the Easterners will allow to last, but it is what we have for now."

A few nights later, Zev went to visit Bellemont and found Pilot sitting in the room. They were laughing and though she wore her Dacci veil, he could see the smiles crinkling the corners of her eyes.

"I understand you're to be congratulated," Zev said.

Pilot flashed a bright smile and folded his hands across his fit waist. "Thank you. I wasn't expecting the King to reinstate my old position, but as I hear it, Axon took all the blame. She told the King that I was only obeying her orders. I told the King that wasn't true. That I'm no blind fool. I wouldn't do what I thought was wrong. But he decided to keep me on anyway."

"I'm glad. Truly. We've got a lot of hard times ahead, and we could use men like you leading the way."

"Well now, I don't know how much it is that I'm going to be doing, but I'll try my best to make sure my men make it through alive."

One afternoon, as Zev picked over the last of his lunch, Lady Jos entered his room. No longer dressed for a gala, she looked stunning in a simple traveling suit with her hair flowerless and hanging down her back. Zev smiled.

"How are you here?" he asked.

"You don't really think I would let something as small as potential war get in the way of visiting an injured friend, do you? Granted, it took me a short time to pull myself together, but then I arranged travel back here while it was still possible."

"Then they haven't closed the borders, yet."

"My, you really are the genius. I assumed my mere presence would tell you that much. Yes, the borders are still open, but there's no guarantee for how long." She placed her gloved hand in his. "I'll have to return to the East almost at once. But I simply had to know if you were alive. I had to see." Blushing, she stepped back. "I've made a fool of myself."

"Not at all." He tried his best to offer a gentle, warm smile that did not convey too much encouragement but did not deny the possibilities between them either. Based on her confused frown, he guessed he failed. "A lot has happened. I need time to think it over."

Composing herself, Lady Jose straightened. "Of course. That's only sensible. I'll be heading back East. Please, if your deliberations suggest that you wish to spend more time in my presence, then I urge you not to dally. This war could make our... friendship...difficult."

She left. For a while, he thought he might have dreamed the entire encounter. But the lingering smell of Feral Moon flowers said otherwise.

Zev should have seen it coming. Over the final weeks of their rehabilitation, he found Pilot in Bellemont's room more and more. They held a warmth between them and shared jokes that only they would laugh at. More and more, Zev felt as if he intruded on them.

When Zev's physician finally cleared him to leave, he went in to share the good news with Bellemont. He would go back to Fernbund and get the office set up. Everything would be in order, and when she was cleared, she could join him on their next investigation.

That's when she told him.

"I'm happy for you. But I won't be coming back."

Zev stood in the doorway as if he had been clocked on the side of the head. Once he regained his senses, he brought his hands together and gave them a firm shake. "You've fallen in love with Pilot, haven't you?"

Bellemont reddened. "I don't know. It's possible, eventually, but not now. Besides, I wouldn't alter the course of my life just because I became attracted to a man."

"Then why are you staying here?"

Propping her pillows so she could sit up straighter, she said, "I've enjoyed the last couple years I've spent working with you. I've learned a lot watching how your mind works and seeing the way you care for the problems you solve. Those years have helped me immensely. They've helped me find my place and have led me here. I know now that I belong in the Frontier."

"Fernbund is in the Frontier, too."

"With everything that's happened and that's going to happen, I want to be a significant part of protecting places like Fernbund. But not just that one town. All the towns of the Frontier will need help."

"But if you work with me—"

"War is on the way, and the only spellcasters the King has are the godwalkers. They're good, better than I ever expected them to be, but I still have teeth in me. I'm not used up yet. So, if I'm going to cast any more spells in my life, I want them to be important, worthy—like Thalia's final spells. And fighting for the cause of the Frontier seems like a worthy fight."

Zev held her gaze and beamed with fatherly pride. He walked over and kissed the top of her head. "I hope to see you again someday."

Before she could respond, he turned and left. Some partings in life are best left in the warmth of love and friendship.

Z ev returned to Fernbund and attempted to keep his investigation business going. Two cases came his way. One involved a robbery that turned out to be over a love affair that fell apart. The scorned party snuck into the lover's house hoping to get back a family heirloom. The second involved stolen undergarments.

That did it.

Bellemont had been right. Zev could not go on with the small cases—not after the things he had experienced. But he didn't want another high-stakes case, either. Sitting at his desk, half-drunk and fully-angry, he came to the conclusion that he knew had been shadowing him for a long time.

The Mayor tried to get him to change his mind. Offered numerous concessions if only Zev would stay. After Zev removed his sign from the window, sold some furniture, and began packing up the office, several members of the town came by to chat. They implored him to put the sign back up. They wanted him to know how greatly they valued him, how much he meant to the community, how much they would miss him.

Though Zev enjoyed the praise, he knew better than to believe them. During his years in Fernbund, the townspeople made him as welcome as a Dacci witch. They wanted him to stay because he had achieved some fame. That brought people from all around to visit or to hire him—and that brought money.

With a manufactured grin, he offered his appreciation for their sentiments, but made it clear that he would not change his decision. The Mayor came one last time. He did not try to dissuade Zev. Rather, he gave Zev a painting of the town crest. Oval shaped, it fit in the palm of Zev's hand and had a silver frame.

The next day, as Zev boxed up the last of his desk, it did not surprise him when another knock came to his door. The voice he heard, however, that did surprise him—Axon.

"I heard you were quitting the solving business, but I didn't know if I should believe it," she said as she entered the building.

She looked good—strong, healthy, the only evidence of their ordeal was a light scar running from just under her ear down her neck. The result of one lucky hit by a crayten.

"What are you doing here?" Though his tone lacked any harshness, she flinched nonetheless.

"The King fired me."

"I heard."

"It's okay. I've given my life in service of the Frontier, and I will continue to do so. Kings come and go, but the Frontier is always here."

Zev stood still. He did not know what she wanted him to say, and he had nothing he wanted to add.

"I'm sorry." She took another step in. "I'd hoped that by now you would have thought over everything that happened, picked it over the way your brain does, and you would've finally understood why I did the things I did. But I can see on your face that you still hate me."

"I've never hated you."

"Well, whatever emotion you feel towards me, be prepared to fill up with more of it."

"What does that mean?"

With a braver face, Axon crossed the room and leaned against his desk. He wanted to put more distance between them, but he found it difficult to move as if his legs had decided they knew better than his brain.

"When I was young," she said, "my father once told me that he admired my tenacity. That even though my mother kept putting obstacle upon obstacle in front of me, even though I had been raised to become this one thing, I defied all of it. I fought against it even when I was in it. I would keep trying, no matter what happened, until I got where I wanted to go."

"Is this story going somewhere?"

"It's going wherever you go. This country needs you. It needs you and Pilot and Bellemont and even me. It doesn't matter what the King wants—it's what the country needs."

Zev picked up the tiny painting of the town crest. "The country needs you to be a warrior."

"The King has taken that from me. I put him in the position of having to choose between me and his duty—I accept that. But I'm still here. I'm not going to wither away in some corner of the world and forget about everybody."

"That's good. War is coming."

"War is upon us. We've stalled it twice now, but I doubt we can do it again. The Frontier is going to need a lot of talented people. That includes your brains. And you have the bad habit of getting yourself in dangerous situations. So, like it or not, I've decided that I'm going to be your bodyguard."

Zev fumbled the painting and it banged against the desk as it fell. "Excuse me?"

"You're closing down your business. You've made no indications that you've purchased a home or that you're moving to another town in the Frontier. You certainly aren't going to the Feral Lands. All of that says to me that you're doing what most people do when they feel a little lost—you're going home."

"Not bad. I would've expected Bellemont to figure that out, but she's been hanging around me a long time. You got it on your first try."

"I'm coming with you. You don't get a say in the matter. If you try and lose me, I'll find you. Don't think you can outsmart me. I'm better at tracking than you are."

Zev picked up the painting and put it in the box. "Don't you think tagging along with me would only put me in danger? I'm from the East. If I'm alone, I'll blend in. I'll visit my family."

"You won't blend in. Not after the last several years. You're one of the Frontier now, and even though everyone will give you the deference that comes with the name Asterling, you'll be in danger every moment that you are there. I'm going to make sure you return to the Frontier safely."

"And I don't get a choice?"

"You get to choose how easy or difficult you want to make this on both of us. I'm not asking you to forgive me, and I'm not asking you to be my friend. In fact, you're going to have to pay me to be your bodyguard. I don't have a lot of money since most of my previous life had been taken care of by the King. And my parents still disapprove of me. They'd give me money—well, my father would—but I refuse to put them in that position."

With his arms crossed and his mouth rolled in tight, Zev paced to the end of the room and back. He looked up and saw both stern determination and an open plea in her eyes. He broke out laughing.

"What?" she said. "I'm serious about all this."

Dabbing at his eyes as he continued laughing, he said, "I know. I know." Then he fell into more laughter.

"This is not funny. You're going on a trip fraught with peril."

The more she protested, the funnier the situation became. He simply could not stop laughing. He went well beyond the point of logical humor into laughter that doubled onto itself—making him laugh harder at nothing. It took him a few moments, but he eventually calmed enough to speak. Taking deep breaths, he said, "I appreciate what you're trying to do. And since I know you well, I know there's no point in fighting you on this."

"Good."

"I suppose I'll pay you, too. That makes you my employee which means you have to follow my rules—and there will be rules."

"That's fine."

"You haven't heard the rules yet. So, the choice becomes yours. You follow what I lay out or you make things hard by forcing me to have to ditch you as long as I can. Agreed?"

She stepped right up to him. "You still don't understand. This isn't about redemption for me. This is about saving the Frontier. I know how important you are, so I'm coming along to protect one of the Frontier's most valuable assets—your big old brain."

Zev stepped back and surveyed the empty office. "Okay, then. We're heading east to visit my father. Hopefully he won't be dead by the time I get there." He thought it best not to bring up Lady Jos at that moment. Instead, he gestured to the box. "You can start by carrying that."

She hesitated but finally stepped over and picked up the box. Zev's eyes drifted upward to the rifle mounted on the wall. He walked over and pulled it down. "You still have the Water Blade?"

"Of course. The King isn't stupid enough to try to take that away from me."

"Still, I think I should bring this along."

"Most definitely."

Resting the rifle on his shoulder, Zev led the way out of the office. Together, they packed up their horses. He chuckled. She was right— the moment they entered an Eastern town on horseback, everybody would know they were from the Frontier. He mounted up and looked off to the East. A sharp wind blew across his face—harsh and threatening.

Exactly, he thought as he set off down the road.

Read on for a sneak preview of Book Three of The Ridnight Mysteries - Waterfire!

ACKNOWLEDGEMENTS

Releasing the Ridnight books at a rate of one-per-month has been an exciting, fun, and crazy experience. There's no doubt that having Falstaff Books alongside throughout has made it far easier (and more fun). So, big thanks once again to John Hartness, Melissa McArthur, Tuppence Van de Vaarst, Joe Crowe, Natania Barron, and all at Falstaff Books who continue to help make this project a success. As always, thanks to my wife and son for putting up with hearing me talk about this bizarre and disgusting magic system. But I reserve my deepest thanks to you, my reader. Without you, I'm the crazy guy walking down the middle of the street talking about stolen shields and magic swords of water. For my sanity (and my career), thank you.

ABOUT THE AUTHOR

Stuart Jaffe is the madman behind *The Max Porter Paranormal Mysteries, The Malja Chronicles, The Bluesman, Founders, Real Magic,* and much more. He trained in martial arts for over a decade until a knee injury ended that practice. Now, he plays lead guitar in a local blues band, *The Bootleggers,* and enjoys life on a small farm in rural North Carolina. For those who continue to keep count, the animal list is as follows: one dog, two cats, three aquatic turtles, and seven chickens. As best as he's been able to manage, Stuart sees that the chickens do not live in the house.

ALSO BY STUART JAFFE

The Way of the Power

The Way of the Soul

Nathan K Thrillers

Immortal Killers

Killing Machine

The Cardinal

Yukon Massacre

The First Battle

Immortal Darkness

A Spy for Eternity

Prisoner

Desert Takedown

Lone Star Standoff

The Parallel Society

The Infinity Caverns

Book on the Isle

Rift Angel

Lost Time

Short Story Collections

The Marshall Drummond Case Files: Cabinet 1

The Marshall Drummond Case Files: Cabinet 2

*For more from Stuart Jaffe, visit him
on his website — www.stuartjaffe.com*

FRIENDS OF FALSTAFF

Thank You to All our Falstaff Books Patrons, who get extra digital content each month! To be featured here and see what other great rewards we offer, go to www.patreon.com/falstaffbooks.

PATRONS

Dino Hicks

John Hooks

John Kilgallon

Larissa Lichty

Travis & Casey Schilling

Staci-Leigh Santore

Sheryl R. Hayes

Scott Norris

Samuel Montgomery-Blinn

Junkle